Jack Vance

Son of the Tree

The Houses of Iszm

Jack Vance

Son of the Tree

The Houses of Iszm

Spatterlight Press Signature Series, Volume 8

Copyright © 1951, 1954, 2005 by Jack Vance

Published by Spatterlight Press

Cover art by Howard Kistler

ISBN 978-1-61947-131-3

Spatterlight Press LLC

Spatterlight
P R E S S
340 S. Lemon Ave #1916
Walnut, CA 91789

www.jackvance.com

CONTENTS

Son of the Tree

Chapter I

A BRIGHT PENETRATING CHIME struck into two hundred minds, broke two hundred bubbles of trance.

Joe Smith awoke without drowsiness. He was constricted, shrouded like a cocoon. He tensed, he struggled, then the spasm of alarm died. He relaxed, peered intently through the darkness.

The air was musky and humid with warm flesh — flesh of many men, above, below, to right and left, twisting, straining, fighting the elastic mesh.

Joe lay back. His mind resumed a sequence of thought left off three weeks ago. Ballenkarch? No — not yet. Ballenkarch would be further on, further out in the fringes. This would be Kyril, the world of the Druids.

A thin ripping sound. The hammock split along a magnetic seam. Joe eased himself out onto the catwalk. His legs were limp as sausages and tender. There was little tone in his muscles after three weeks under hypnosis.

He walked the catwalk to the ladder, descended to the main deck, stepped out the port. At a desk sat a dark-skinned youth of sixteen, wide-eyed and smart, wearing a jumper of tan and blue pliophane. "Name, please?"

"Joe Smith."

The youth made a check on a list, nodded down the passage. "First door for sanitation."

Joe slid back the door, entered a small room thick with steam and antiseptic vapor. "Clothes off," bawled a brassy-voiced woman in tight trunks. She was wolf-lean — her blue-brown skin streamed with perspiration. She yanked off the loose garment issued him by ship's stores — then, standing back, she touched a button. "Eyes shut."

Jets of cleansing solutions beat at his body. Various pressures, various temperatures, and his muscles began to waken. A blast of warm air dried him and the woman, with a careless slap, directed him to an adjoining chamber, where he shaved off his stubbly beard, trimmed his hair and finally donned the smock and sandals which appeared in a hopper.

As he left the room a steward halted him, placed a nozzle against his thigh, blew under his skin an assortment of vaccines, anti-toxins, muscle toners and stimulants. So fortified, Joe left the ship, walked out on a stage, down a ramp to the soil of Kyril.

He took a deep breath of fresh planetary air and looked about him. A sky overhung with a pearly overcast. A long gently-heaving landscape checked with tiny farms rolled away to the horizon — and there, rising like a tremendous plume of smoke, stood the Tree. The outlines were hazed by distance and the upper foliage blended with the overcast but it was unmistakable. The Tree of Life.

He waited an hour while his passport and various papers of identification were checked and countersigned at a small glass-sided office under the embarkation stage. Then he was cleared and directed across the field to the terminal. This was a rococo structure of heavy white stone, ornately carved and beaded with intricate intaglios.

At the turnstile through the glass wall stood a Druid, idly watching the disembarkation. He was tall, nervously thin, with a pale fine ivory skin. His face was controlled, aristocratic — his hair jet-black, his eyes black and stern. He wore a glistening cuirass of enameled metal, a sumptuous robe falling in elaborate folds almost to the floor, edged with orphreys embroidered in gold thread. On his head sat an elaborate morion, built of cleverly fitted cusps and planes of various metals.

Joe surrendered his passage voucher to the clerk at the turnstile desk.

"Name please."

"It's on the voucher."

The clerk frowned, scribbled. "Business on Kyril?"

"Temporary visitor," said Joe shortly. He had discussed himself, his antecedents, his business, at length with the clerk in the disembarkation office. This new questioning seemed a needless annoyance. The Druid turned his head, looked him up and down. "Spies, nothing but spies!" He made a hissing sound under his breath, turned away.

Something in Joe's appearance aroused him. He turned back. "You there —" in a tone of petulant irritation.

Joe turned. "Yes?"

"Who's your sponsor? Whom do you serve?"

"No one. I'm here on my own business."

"Do not dissemble. Everyone spies. Why pretend otherwise? You arouse me to anger. Now — whom, then, do you serve?"

"The fact of the matter is that I am not a spy," said Joe, holding an even courtesy in his voice. Pride was the first luxury a vagrant must forego.

The Druid smiled with exaggerated thin-lipped cynicism. "Why else would you come to Kyril?"

"Personal reasons."

"You look to be a Thuban. What is your home world then?"

"Earth."

The Druid cocked his head, looked at him sidewise, started to speak, halted, narrowed his eyes, spoke again. "Do you mock me with the child's myth then — a fool's paradise?"

Joe shrugged. "You asked me a question. I answered you."

"With an insolent disregard for my dignity and rank."

A short plump man with a lemon-yellow skin approached with a strutting cocksure gait. He had wide innocent eyes, a pair of well-developed jowls and he wore a loose cloak of heavy blue velvet.

"An Earthman *here*?" He looked at Joe. "You, sir?"

"That's right."

"Then Earth is an actuality."

"Certainly it is."

The yellow-skinned man turned to the Druid. "This is the second Earthman I've seen, Worship. Evidently —"

"Second?" asked Joe. "Who was the other?"

The yellow-skinned man rolled his eyes up. "I forget his name. Parry — Larry — Barry…"

"Harry? Harry Creath?"

"That's it — I'm sure of it. I had a few words with him out at Junction a year or two ago. Very pleasant fellow."

The Druid swung on his heel, strode away. The plump man watched him go with an impassive face, then turned to Joe. "You seem to be a stranger here."

"I just arrived."

"Let me advise you as to these Druids. They are an emotional race, quick to anger, reckless, given to excess. And they are completely provincial, completely assured of Kyril's place as the center of all space, all time. It is wise to speak softly in their presence. May I inquire from curiosity why you are here?"

"I couldn't afford to buy passage farther."

"And so?"

Joe shrugged. "I'll go to work, raise some money."

The plump man frowned thoughtfully. "Just what talents or abilities will you use to this end?"

"I'm a good mechanic, machinist, dynamist, electrician. I can survey, work out stresses, do various odd jobs. Call myself an engineer."

His acquaintance seemed to be considering. At last he said doubtfully, "There is a plentiful supply of cheap labor among the Laity."

Joe swung a glance around the terminal. "From the look of that truss I'd say they were pretty shaky on the slide-rule."

The other pursed his lips in dubious agreement. "And of course the Druids are xenophobic to a high degree. A new face represents a spy."

Joe nodded, grinned. "I've noticed that. The first Druid I see raked me over the coals. Called me a Mang spy, whatever that is."

The plump man nodded. "It is what I am."

"A Mang — or a spy?"

"Both. There is small attempt at stealth. It is admitted. Every Mang on Kyril is a spy. Likewise with the Druids on Mangtse. The two worlds are striving for dominance, economic at the moment, and there is a great deal of rancor between us." He rubbed his chin further. "You want a position then, with remuneration?"

"Correct," said Joe. "But no spying. I'm not mixing in politics. That's out. Life's too short as it is."

The Mang made a reassuring gesture. "Of course. Now as I mentioned the Druids are an emotional race. Devious. Perhaps we can play on these qualities. Suppose you come with me to Divinal. I have an appointment with the District Thearch and if I boast to him about the efficient technician I have taken into my service…" He left the rest of the sentence floating, nodded owlishly at Joe. "This way then."

Joe followed him through the terminal, along an arcade lined with shops to a parking area. Joe glanced down the line of air-cars. Antique design, he thought — slipshod construction.

The Mang motioned him into the largest of these cars. "To Divinal," he told the waiting driver.

The car arose, slanted up across the gray-green landscape. For all the apparent productivity of the land the country affected Joe unpleasantly. The villages were small, cramped and the streets and alleys glistened with stagnant water. In the fields he could see teams of men — six, ten, twenty — dragging cultivators. A dreary uninspiring landscape.

"Five billion peasants," said the Mang. "The Laity. Two million Druids. And one Tree."

Joe made a noncommittal sound. The Mang lapsed into silence. Farms below — interminable blocks, checks, rectangles, each a different tone of green, brown or gray. A myriad conical huts leaking smoke huddled in the corners of the fields. And ahead the Tree bulked taller, blacker, more massive.

Presently ornate white stone palaces appeared, huddled among the buttressed roots, and the car slanted down over the heavy roofs. Joe glimpsed a forest of looping balustrades, intricate panels, mullioned skylights, gargoyles, columns, embellished piers.

Then the car set down on a plat in front of a long high block of a structure, reminding Joe vaguely of the Palace at Versailles. To either side were carefully tended gardens, tessellated walks, fountains, statuary. And behind rose the Tree with its foliage hanging miles overhead.

The Mang alighted, turned to Joe. "If you'll remove the side panel to the generator space of this car and act as if you are making a minor repair I believe you will shortly be offered a lucrative post."

Joe said uncomfortably, "You're going to a great deal of effort for a stranger. Are you a — philanthropist?"

The Mang said cheerfully, "Oh no. No, *no!* I act as the whim moves me but I am not completely selfless in my acts. Let me express it this way — if I were sent to do an unspecified repair job I would take with me as wide a variety of tools as I was able.

"So, in my own — ah — mission I find that many persons have special talents or knowledges which turn out to be invaluable. Therefore I cultivate as wide and amicable an acquaintanceship as possible."

Joe smiled thinly. "Does it pay off?"

"Oh indeed. And then," said the plump man blandly, "courtesy is a reward in itself. There is an incalculable satisfaction in helpful conduct. Please don't consider yourself under obligation of any sort."

Joe thought, without expressing himself aloud, "I won't."

The plump man departed, crossed the plat to a great door of carved bronze.

Joe hesitated a moment. Then, perceiving nothing to be lost by following instructions, he unclamped the side panel. A band of lead held it in place like a seal. Joe hesitated another instant, then snapped the band, lifted the panel off.

He now looked into a most amazing mechanism. It had been patched together out of spare parts, bolted with lag screws into wooden blocks, bound to the frame with bits of rope. Wires lay exposed without insulation. The force-field adjustment had been made with a wooden wedge. Joe shook his head, marveling. Then recollecting the flight from the terminal, he sweated in retrospect.

The plump yellow-skinned man had instructed him to act as if he were repairing the motor. Joe saw that pretense would be unnecessary. The power-box was linked to the metadyne by a helter-skelter tubing. Joe reached in, pulled the mess loose, re-oriented the poles, connected the units with a short straight link.

Across the plat another car landed and a girl of eighteen or nineteen jumped out. Joe caught the flash of eyes in a narrow vital face as she looked toward him. Then she had left the plat.

Joe stood looking after the sapling-slender form. He relaxed, turned back to the motor. Very nice — girls were nice things. He compressed his lips, thinking of Margaret. An entirely different kind of girl was Margaret. Blonde in the first place — easy-going, flexible, but inwardly — Joe paused in his work. What was she, in her heart of hearts, where he had never penetrated?

When he had told her of his plans she had laughed, told him he was born thousands of years too late. Two years now — was Margaret still waiting? Three months was all he had thought to be gone — and then he had been led on and on, from planet to planet, out of Earth space, out across the Unicorn Gulf, out along a thin swirl of stars, beating his way from world to world.

On Jamivetta he had farmed moss on a bleak tundra and even the third-class passage to Kyril had looked good. *Margaret,* thought Joe, *I hope you're worth all this travail.* He looked at where the dark-haired Druid girl had run into the palace.

A harsh voice said, "What's this you're doing — tearing apart the air-car? You'll be killed for such an act."

It was the driver of the car the girl had landed in. He was a coarse-faced thick-bodied man with a swinish nose and jaw. Joe, from long and bitter experience on the outer worlds, held his tongue, turned back to investigate the machine further. He leaned forward in disbelief. Three condensers, hooked together in series, dangled and swung on their connectors. He reached in, yanked off the extraneous pair, wedged the remaining condenser into a notch, hooked it up again.

"Here, here, *here!*" bellowed the driver. "You be leaving your destructive hands off a delicate bit of mechanism!"

It was too much. Joe raised his head. "Delicate bit of machinery! It's a wonder this pitiful tangle of junk can fly at all."

The driver's face twisted in fury. He took a quick heavy step forward, then halted as a Druid came sweeping out on the plat — a big man with a flat red face and impressive eyebrows. He had a small hawk's-beak of a nose protruding like an afterthought between his cheeks, a mouth bracketed by ridges of stubborn muscle.

He wore a long vermilion robe with a cowl of rich black fur, an edging of fur along the robe to match. Over the cowl he wore a morion of black and green metal with a sunburst in red-and-yellow enamel cocked over one temple.

"Borandino!"

The driver cringed. "Worship."

"Go. Put away the Kelt."

"Yes, Worship."

The Druid halted before Joe. He saw the pile of discarded junk, his face became congested. "What are you doing to my finest car?"

"Removing a few encumbrances."

"The best mechanic on Kyril services that machinery!"

Joe shrugged. "He's got a lot to learn. I'll put that stuff back if you want me to. It's not my car."

The Druid stared fixedly at him. "Do you mean to say that the car will run after you've pulled all that metal out of it?"

"It should run better."

The Druid looked Joe over from head to foot. Joe decided that this must be the District Thearch. The Druid, with the faintest suggestion of furtiveness in his manner, looked back over his shoulder toward the palace, then back to Joe.

"I understand you're in the service of Hableyat."

"The Mang? Why — yes."

"You're not a Mang. What are you?"

Joe recalled the incident with the Druid at the terminal. "I'm a Thuban."

"Ah! How much does Hableyat pay you?"

Joe wished he knew something of the local currency and its value. "Quite a bit," he said.

"Thirty stiples a week? Forty?"

"Fifty," said Joe.

"I'll pay you eighty," said the Thearch. "You'll be my chief mechanic."

Joe nodded. "Very well."

"You'll come with me right now. I'll inform Hableyat of the change. You'll have no further contact with that Mang assassin. You are now a servant to the Thearch of the District."

Joe said, "At your service, Worship."

Chapter II

THE BUZZER SOUNDED. JOE flicked down the key, said "Garage."

A girl's voice issued from the plate, the peremptory self-willed voice of Priestess Elfane, the Thearch's third daughter, ringing now with an overtone Joe could not identify.

"Driver, listen very closely. Do exactly as I bid."

"Yes, Worship."

"Take out the black Kelt, rise to the third level, then drop back to my apartment. Be discreet and you'll profit. Do you understand?"

"Yes, Worship," said Joe in a leaden voice.

"Hurry."

Joe pulled on his livery. Haste — discretion — stealth? A lover for Elfane? She was young but not too young. He had already performed somewhat similar errands for her sisters, Esane and Phedran. Joe shrugged. He could hope to profit. A hundred stiples, perhaps more.

He grinned ruefully as he backed the black Kelt from under the canopy. A tip from a girl of eighteen — and glad to get it. Sometime, somewhere — when he returned to Earth and Margaret — he'd dust off his pretensions to pride and dignity. They were useless to him now, a handicap.

Money was money. Money had brought him across the galaxy and Ballenkarch was at last at hand. At night when the temple searchlights left the sky he could see the sun Ballen, a bright star in the constellation the Druids called the "Porphyrite". The cheapest passage, hypnotized and shipped like a corpse, cost two thousand stiples.

From a salary of eighty stiples a week he was able to save seventy-five. Three weeks had passed — twenty-four more would buy him passage to Ballenkarch. Too long, with Margaret, blonde, gay, lovely, waiting on Earth. Money was money. Tips would be accepted with thanks.

Joe took the car up the palace free-rise, wafting up alongside the Tree, up toward the third level. The Tree hung over him as if he had never left the ground and Joe felt the awe and wonder which three weeks in the very shadow of the trunk had done nothing to diminish.

A vast breathing sappy mass, a trunk five miles in diameter, twelve miles from the great kneed roots to the ultimate bud — the "Vital Exprescience" in the cant of the Druids. The foliage spread out and fell away on limber boughs, each as thick through as the Thearch's palace, hung like the thatch on an old-fashioned hayrick.

The leaves were roughly triangular, three feet long — bright yellow in the upper air, darkening through lime, green, rose, scarlet, blue-black, toward the ground. The Tree ruled the horizons, shouldered aside the clouds, wore thunder and lightning like a wreath of tinsel. It was the soul of life, raw life, trampling and vanquishing the inert, and Joe understood well how it had come to be worshipped by the first marveling settlers on Kyril.

The third level. Down again, down in the black Kelt to the plat beside Priestess Elfane's apartments. Joe landed the car, jumped out, stepped across the gold-and-ivory inlay. Elfane herself slid aside the door — a vivid creature with a rather narrow face, dark, vital as a bird. She wore a simple gown of sheer white cloth without ornament and she was barefoot. Joe, who had seen her only in her official vestments, blinked, looked again with interest.

She motioned. "This way. Hurry." She held back the panel and Joe entered a tall chamber, elegant but of little warmth. Bands of white marble and dark blue dumortierite surfaced two walls, bands inset with copper palettes carved with exotic birds. The third wall was hung with a tapestry depicting a group of young girls running down a grassy slope and along this wall ran a low cushioned settee.

Here sat a young man in the vesture of a Sub-Thearch — a blue robe embroidered with the red and gray orphreys of his rank. A morion inlaid with gold leaf-patterns lay beside him on the settee and a baton lathed from the Sacred Wood — an honor given only to those of Ecclesiarch degree — hung at his belt. He had lean flanks, wide spare shoulders and the most striking face of Joe's experience.

It was a narrow passionate face, wide across high cheekbones, with flat cheeks slanting down to a prow of a chin. The nose was long and straight, the forehead broad. The eyes were flat black disks in narrow expressionless sockets, the brows ink-black, the hair an ink-black mop of ringlets, artfully disarranged. It was a clever, cruel face, full of fascination, overrich, overripe, without humor or sympathy — the face of a feral animal only coincidentally human.

Joe paused in mid-stride, stared into this face with instant aversion, then looked down to the corpse at the Ecclesiarch's feet — a sprawled grotesquely-rigid form oozing bright yellow blood into a crimson cloak.

Elfane said to Joe, "This is the body of a Mangtse ambassador. A spy but nevertheless an ambassador of high rank. Someone either killed him here or brought his body here. It must not be discovered. There must be no outcry. I trust you for a loyal servant. Some very delicate negotiations with the Mang Rule are underway. An incident like this might bring disaster. Do you follow me?"

Palace intrigue was none of Joe's affair. He said, "Any orders you may give, Worship, I will follow, subject to the permission of the Thearch."

She said impatiently, "The Thearch is too busy to be consulted. Ecclesiarch Manaolo will assist you in conveying the corpse into the Kelt. Then you will drive us out over the ocean and we'll dispose of it."

Joe said woodenly, "I'll bring the car as close as possible."

Manaolo rose to his feet, followed him to the door. Joe heard him mutter over his shoulder, "We'll be crowded in that little cabin."

Elfane answered impatiently, "It's the only one I can drive."

Joe took his time arranging the car against the door, frowning in deep thought. The only car she could drive…He looked across fifty feet of space to the next plat along the side of the palace. A short man in a blue cloak, with hands clasped behind his back stood watching Joe benignly.

Joe re-entered the room. "There's a Mang on the next balcony."

"*Hableyat!*" exclaimed Manaolo. He strode to the door, looked out without disclosing himself. "He above all must not discover!"

"Hableyat knows everything," said Elfane gloomily. "Sometimes I think he has mastered second-sight."

Joe knelt beside the corpse. The mouth hung open, showing a rusty orange tongue. A well-filled pouch hung at his side, half-concealed by the cloak. Joe opened it. From behind came an angry word. Elfane said, "No, let him satisfy himself."

Her tone, her contemptuous condescension, stung Joe. But money was money. Ears burning, he reached into the pouch, pulled out a sheaf of currency. Hundred-stiple notes, a dozen at least. He returned to the pouch and found a small hand-weapon of a make he did not recognize. He tucked it into his blouse. Then he wrapped the corpse in the scarlet robe, and rising, caught hold under the armpits.

Manaolo took the ankles. Elfane went to the door. "He's gone. Hurry!"

Five seconds saw the corpse stowed in the back. Elfane said to Joe, "Come with me."

Wary of turning his back on Manaolo, Joe followed. She led him into a dressing room, pointed to a pair of cases. "Take them, load them in the back of the Kelt."

Luggage, thought Joe. He obeyed. From the corner of his eye he saw that Hableyat had once more come out on the balcony and was smiling blandly in his direction. Joe returned inside.

Elfane was wearing sandals and a dark blue robe like a girl of the Laity. It accentuated her sprite-like appearance, the tang, the spice, which seemed an essential part of her. Joe wrenched his eyes away. Margaret would not have dealt so casually with a corpse.

He said, "The Kelt is ready to go, Worship."

"You will drive," said Elfane. "Our route will be up to the fifth level, south over Divinal, across the bay and out to sea."

Joe shook his head. "I'm not driving. In fact I'm not going."

The sense of his words failed to penetrate at once. Then Elfane and Manaolo together turned their heads. Elfane was surprised with a lack of comprehension on her face rather than anger. Manaolo stood expressionless, his eyes dull, opaque.

Elfane said in a sharper voice, as if Joe had not understood her, "Go on out — you will drive."

Joe casually slid his hand inside his blouse, where the little weapon rested. Manaolo's eyes flickered, the only movement of his face, but Joe knew his mind was agile and reckless.

"I don't intend driving you," said Joe. "You can easily ditch that corpse without me. I don't know where you're going or why. I know I'm not going with you."

"I order you!" exclaimed Elfane. This was fantastic, insane — contrary to the axioms of her existence.

Joe shook his head, watching warily. "Sorry."

Elfane dismissed the paradox from her mind. She turned to Manaolo. "Kill him here then. *His* corpse, at least, will provoke no speculation."

Manaolo grinned regretfully. "I'm afraid the clobberclaw is aiming a gun at us. He will refuse to let me kill him."

Elfane tightened her lips. "This is ridiculous." She whirled. Joe brought out the gun. Elfane halted stock-still, words failing in her mouth.

"Very well," she said in a subdued voice. "I'll give you money to be silent. Will that satisfy you?"

"Very much," said Joe, smiling crookedly. Pride? What was pride? If it weren't for Margaret he'd enjoy... But no, she was plainly running off with this brilliant and dangerous Manaolo. Who would want a woman after his handling of her?

"How much?" asked Manaolo idly.

Joe calculated rapidly. He had four hundred stiples in his room, about a thousand he had taken from the corpse. He dismissed his calculations. Make it big. "Five thousand stiples and I've forgotten everything I've seen today."

The figure apparently did not seem exorbitant to either of them. Manaolo felt in one pocket, then another, found a money-flap, riffled out a number of notes, tossed them to the floor.

"There's your money."

Without a backward glance Elfane ran out on the plat, jumped into the Kelt. Manaolo strolled after her.

The Kelt jerked up, swung off into the clean air of Kyril. Joe was alone in the tall chamber.

He picked up the notes. Five thousand stiples! He went to the window, watched the air-car dwindle to a dot.

There was a small throb in his throat, a pang. Elfane was a wonderful creature. On Earth, had it not been for Margaret, he would have been entranced. But this was Kyril, where Earth was a fable. And Margaret, supple, soft, blonde as a field full of jonquils, was waiting for him to return. Or at least knew that *he* was expecting her to wait. With Margaret, Joe thought ruefully, the idea might not mean the same thing. Damn Harry Creath!

He became uneasily aware of his surroundings. Any one of a dozen persons might enter and find him. There would be difficulty explaining his presence. Somehow he had to return to his own quarters. He froze in his tracks. The sound of a door sliding brought an instant quickening of the pulse, a flush of sweat. He backed against the tapestry. Steps, slow, unhurried, came down the passageway.

The door scraped back. A man entered the room — a short yellow-skinned man in a blue velvet cloak — Hableyat.

Chapter III

HABLEYAT GLANCED BRIEFLY around the room, shook his head dolefully. "A bad business. Risky for all concerned."

Joe, standing stiffly at the wall, found ready assent. Hableyat took a couple steps forward, peered at the floor. "Careless. Still much blood."

He looked up, became conscious of Joe's stance. "But by all means be at your ease. Indeed be at your ease." For a moment he inspected Joe impersonally. "No doubt your mouth has been crammed with money. A marvel you still live."

Joe said dryly, "I was summoned here by the Priestess Elfane, who drove off in the Kelt. Otherwise I disassociate myself from the entire affair."

Hableyat shook his head wistfully. "If you are found here with the blood on the floor you will be questioned. And since every effort will be made to hush up Empoing's assassination you will undoubtedly be killed to ensure your silence."

Joe licked his lips. "But isn't it you from whom they want to hide the killing?"

Hableyat nodded. "No doubt. I represent the Power and Reach of the Mangtse Dail — that is, the Bluewater Faction. Empoing was born to the Red-streams, who follow a different school of thought. They believe in a swift succession of events."

A strange idea formed in Joe's mind and would not be dismissed. Hableyat noticed the shift of his features. His mouth, a short fleshy crevice between the two yellow jowls, drew in at the corners.

"Yes indeed. I killed him. It was necessary, believe me. Otherwise he would have slaughtered Manaolo, who is engaged on a very important mission. If Manaolo were deterred it would be — from one view-point — a tragedy."

The ideas were coming too fast — they fled by Joe's mind like a school of fish past a dip-net. It was as if Hableyat were displaying a tray full of bright wares, waiting to see which Joe would select.

Joe said warily, "Why are you telling me all this?"

Hableyat shrugged his meaty shoulders. "Whoever you are you are no simple chauffeur."

"Ah — but I *am!*"

"Who or what you are has not yet been established. These are complex times, when many people and many worlds want irreconcilable things and every man's origin and intentions must be closely analyzed. My information traces you to Thuban Nine, where you served as an instructor of civil engineering at the Technical Institute. From Thuban you came to Ardemizian, then to Panapol, then to Rosalinda, then to Jamivetta, finally to Kyril.

"On each planet you remained only long enough to earn transportation to the next. There is a pattern here and where there is a pattern there is a plan. Where there is a plan there is an intent and where there is an intent there are ends to be gained. And when ends are gained someone is the loser. But I see you are uneasy. Evidently you fear discovery. Am I right?"

"I do not care to be killed."

"I suggest that we repair to my apartment, which is nearby, and then perhaps we will have a chat. I am always eager to learn and possibly in gratitude for a safe exit from this apartment —"

A chime cut him short. He started, moved rapidly to the window, looked up, down. From the window he ran to the door, listened. He motioned to Joe. "Stand aside."

The chime sounded again — a heavy knuckle rapped at the door. Hableyat hissed under his breath. A scratch, a scrape. The door slid aside.

A tall man with a wide red face and a little beak of a nose strode into the room. He wore a flowing white robe with a cowl and a black-green-and-gold morion atop the cowl. Hableyat slid behind him, executed a complex gesture involving a kick at the back of the man's legs, a clip of the forearm, a wrench at the wrist — and the Druid fell face down on the floor.

Joe gasped, "It's the Thearch himself! We'll be flayed..."

"Come," said Hableyat, once more a benevolent man of business. They stepped swiftly down the hall. Hableyat slid back his door. *"In."*

Hableyat's suite was larger than the chambers of the Priestess Elfane. The sitting room was dominated by a long rectangular table, the top cut from a single slab of polished dark wood inlaid with arabesque copper leaves.

Two Mang warriors sat stiffly on each side of the door — short stocky men, craggy of feature, lemon-yellow of skin — sitting as if neither had moved in hours. Hableyat paid them no heed, passed them as if they were inanimate. Noting Joe's inquiring glance, he appeared to observe them for the first time.

"Hypnotized," he said off-handedly. "So long as I'm in the room or the room is empty they won't move."

Joe gingerly moved past him into the room, reflecting that he was as open to suspicion here as he was in the Priestess' apartment.

Hableyat seated himself with a grunt, motioned Joe to a chair. Rather than trust himself to a maze of unknown corridors Joe obeyed. Hableyat lay his plump palms flat on the table, fixed Joe with candid eyes.

"You appear to be caught up in an unpleasant situation, Joe Smith."

"Not necessarily," said Joe with a forlorn attempt at spirit. "I could go to the Thearch, tell my story and that would be an end to it."

Hableyat's face quivered as he chortled, opening his mouth like a squirrel. "And then?"

Joe said nothing.

Hableyat slapped the table heartily. "My boy, you are not yet familiar with the Druid psychology. To them killing is the response to almost any circumstance — a casual act like turning out the light on leaving a room. So when you had told your story you would be killed. For no particular reason other than that it is easier to kill than not to kill." Hableyat idly traced the pattern of a tendril with his yellow fingernail, spoke as if musing aloud.

"Sometimes the strangest organisms are the most efficient. Kyril operates in a manner remarkable for its utter simplicity. Five billion lives devoted to feeding and pampering two million Druids and one Tree. But the system works, it perpetuates itself—which is the test for viability.

"Kyril is a grotesque ultimate of religious dedication. Laity, Druids, Tree. Laity works, Druids conduct the rites, Tree is—is immanent. Amazing! Humanity creates from the same protoplasm the clods of the Laity, the highly-tempered Druids."

Joe stirred restlessly. "What is all this to me?"

"I merely indicate," said Hableyat gently, "that your life is not worth the moist spot where I spit to anyone but yourself. What is life to a Druid? See this workmanship? The lives of ten men have been spent on this table. The slabs of marble on the wall—they were ground to fit by hand. Cost? Druids have no awareness of the concept. Labor is free, manpower unlimited.

"Even the electricity which powers and lights the palace is generated by hand in the cellars—in the name of the Tree of Life, where the poor blind souls ultimately hope to reside, serene in the sunlight and wind. The Druids thereby justify the system to their consciences, to the other worlds.

"The Laity knows nothing better. An ounce of meal, a fish, a pot of greens—so they survive. They know no marriage rites, no family, no tradition, not even folklore. They are cattle on a range. They breed with neither passion nor grace.

"Controversies? The Druid formula is simple. Kill both parties and so the controversy is dead. Unassailable—and the Tree of Life looms across the planet, the mightiest promise of life eternal the galaxy has ever known. Pure massive vitality!"

Joe hitched himself forward in his seat, looked to his right at the immobile Mang warriors. To his left, across the deep orange rug, out the window. Hableyat followed his gaze with a quizzical purse to his lips.

Joe said in a tight voice, "Why are you keeping me here? What are you waiting for?"

Hableyat blinked rapidly, reproachfully. "I am conscious of no intent to detain you. You are free to leave any time you wish."

"Why bring me here in the first place?" demanded Joe.

Hableyat shrugged. "Sheer altruism possibly. If you returned to your quarters now you are as good as dead. Especially after the regrettable intrusion of the Thearch."

Joe relaxed into the chair. "That's not — necessarily true."

Hableyat nodded vigorously. "I'm afraid it is. Consider — it is known or will be known, that you took up the black Kelt, which subsequently was driven away by Priestess Elfane and Ecclesiarch Manaolo. The Thearch, coming to his daughter's apartments, perhaps to investigate, perhaps in response to a summons, is attacked. Shortly afterwards the chauffeur returns to his quarters." He paused, opened plump hands out significantly.

Joe said, "All right then. What's on your mind?"

Hableyat tapped the table with his fingernail. "These are complex times, complex times. You see," he added confidentially, "Kyril is becoming overpopulated with Druids."

Joe frowned. "Overpopulated? With two million Druids?"

Hableyat laughed. "Five billion Laity are unable to provide a dignified existence for more. You must understand that these poor wretches have no interest in producing. Their single aspiration is to pass through life as expeditiously as possible so as to take their place as a leaf on the Tree.

"The Druids are caught in a dilemma. To increase production they must either educate and industrialize — thus admitting to the Laity that life offers pleasures other than rapt contemplation — or they must find other sources of wealth and production. To this end the Druids have decided to operate a bank of industries on Ballenkarch. So we Mangs and our highly industrialized world become involved. We see in the Druid plan a threat to our own well-being."

Joe asked with an air of tired patience, "How does this involve *me?*"

"My job as emissary-at-large," said Hableyat, "is to promote the interests of my world. To this end I require a great deal of information. When you arrived here a month ago you were investigated. You were traced back as far as a planet of the distant sun Thuban. Before that, your trail eludes us."

Joe said with incredulous anger, "But you *know* my home world! I told you the first time I saw you. Earth. And you said that you had spoken to another Earthman, Harry Creath."

Hableyat nodded briskly. "Exactly. But it has occurred to me that 'Earth' as a place of origin offers a handy anonymity." He peered at Joe slyly. "Both for you and Harry Creath."

Joe took a deep breath. "You know more of Harry Creath than you let me believe."

Hableyat appeared surprised that Joe should consider this fact exceptional. "Of course. It is necessary for me to know many things. Now this 'Earth' you speak of — is its identity actually more than verbal?" And he eyed Joe inquisitively.

"I assure you it is," said Joe, heavily sarcastic. "You people are so far out along this little wisp of stars that you've forgotten the rest of the universe."

Hableyat nodded, drummed his fingers on the table. "Interesting, interesting. This brings a rather new emphasis to light."

Joe said impatiently, "I'm not aware of any emphasis, either old or new. My business, such as it is, is personal. I have no interest in your enterprises and least of all do I want to become involved."

There was a harsh pounding at the door. Hableyat rose to his feet with a grunt of satisfaction. This was what he had been waiting for, Joe thought.

"I repeat," said Hableyat, "that you have no choice. You are involved in spite of any wish to the contrary. Do you want to live?"

"Of course I want to live." Joe half-rose to his feet as the pounding was resumed.

"Then agree to whatever I say — no matter how far-fetched it may seem to you. Do you understand?"

"Yes," said Joe with resignation.

Hableyat spoke a sharp word. The two warriors bounded to their feet like mechanical men: "Open the door."

The door slid back. The Thearch stood in the opening, his face wrathful. Behind him stood a half dozen Druids in robes of different colors — Ecclesiarchs, Sub-Thearchs, Presbytes, Hierophants.

Hableyat was transformed. His overt characteristics became intensified. His benignity softened to obsequiousness; his bland ease of manner became a polished unction. He trotted forward as if the Thearch's visit afforded him tremendous pride and delight.

The Thearch towered in the doorway, glaring up and down the room. His eyes passed over the two warriors, came to rest on Joe.

He raised a hand, pointed portentously. "There's the man! A murderous blackguard! Lay hold, we'll see the end of him before the hour's out."

The Druids swept forward in a swift rustle of robes. Joe reached for his weapon. But the two Mang warriors, moving so deftly and easily that they seemed not to have moved at all, blocked the doorway. A hot-eyed Druid in a brown-and-green robe reached to thrust them aside.

There was a twinkle of blue light, a crackle, a startled exclamation and the Druid leapt back, trembling in indignation. "He's charged with static!"

Hableyat bustled forward, all dismay and alarm. "Your Worship, what is happening?"

The Thearch's expression was vastly contemptuous. "Stand aside, Mang, call off your electrified go-devils. I'll have that man."

Cried Hableyat, "But Worship, Worship — you dismay me. Can it be that I've taken a criminal into my service?"

"*Your* service?"

"Surely your Worship is aware that in order to pursue a realistic policy my government employs a number of unofficial observers?"

"Cutthroat spies!" roared the Thearch.

Hableyat rubbed his chin. "If such is the case, your Worship, I am disillusioned, since the Druid spies on Mangtse are uniformly self-effacing. Just what is my servant accused of?"

The Thearch thrust his head forward, said with soft fervor, "I'll tell you what he's done — he's killed one of your own men — a Mang! There's yellow blood all over the floor of my daughter's chamber. Where there's blood, there's death."

"Your Worship!" exclaimed Hableyat. "This is serious news! Who is it that is dead?"

"How do I know? Enough that there's a man killed and that this —"

"But your Worship! This man has been in my company all day. Your news is alarming. It means that a representative of my government has been attacked. I fear that there will be tumult in the Lathbon. Where did you notice this blood? In the chamber of your daughter, the Priestess? Where is she? Perhaps she can shed some light on the matter."

— 21 —

"I don't know where she is." He turned, pointed a finger. "Alamaina — find the Priestess Elfane. I wish to speak to her." Then to Hableyat, "Do I understand that you are taking this blackguard spy under your protection?"

Hableyat said courteously, "Our security officers have been solicitous in guarding the safety of the Druids representing your Worship on Mangtse."

The Thearch turned on his heel, strode off through the hooded forms of his Druids.

Joe said, "So now I'm a Mang spy."

"What would you have?" inquired Hableyat.

Joe returned to his seat. "For some reason I can't imagine you are determined to attach me to your staff."

Hableyat made a gesture of deprecation.

Joe stared at him a moment. "You murder your own men, you strike down the Thearch in his daughter's sitting-room — and somehow I find myself held to account for it. It's not possible that you planned it that way?"

"Now, now, now," murmured Hableyat.

Joe asked politely, "May I presume upon your courtesy further?"

"Certainly. By all means." Hableyat waited attentively.

Joe said boldly, without any real expectation of Hableyat's assent, "Take me to the Terminal. Put me on the packet to Ballenkarch which leaves today."

Hableyat, raising his eyebrows sagely, nodded. "A very reasonable request — and one which I would be unkind to deny. Are you ready to leave at once?"

"Yes," said Joe dryly, "I am."

"And you have sufficient funds?"

"I have five thousand stiples given me by the Priestess Elfane and Manaolo."

"Hah! I see. They were anxious then to be on their way?"

"I received that impression."

Hableyat looked up sharply. "There is suppressed emotion in your voice."

"The Druid Manaolo arouses a great deal of aversion in me."

"Hah!" said Hableyat with a sly wink. "And the Priestess arouses a great deal of the opposite? Oh, you youngsters! If only I had my youth back how I would enjoy myself!"

Joe said in precise tones, "My future plans involve neither Manaolo nor Elfane."

"Only the future can tell," intoned Hableyat. "Now then — to the Terminal."

Chapter IV

THERE WAS NO SIGNAL which Joe could perceive but in three minutes, during which Hableyat sat silently hunched in a chair, a heavy well-appointed air-car swung alongside the plat. Joe went cautiously to the window, looked along the side of the Palace. The sun was low. Shadows from the various balconies, landing stages, carved work, ran obliquely along the stone, creating a confusion of shape in which almost anything might be hidden.

Below were the garage and his cubicle. Nothing there of value — the few hundred stiples he had saved from his salary as chauffeur he dismissed. Beyond rose the Tree, a monstrous mass his eye could not encompass at one glance. To see edge to edge he had to turn his head from right to left. The shape was uncertain from this close distance of a mile or so. A number of slow-swinging members laden with foliage overhung the Palace.

Hableyat joined him at the window. "It grows and grows. Some day it will grow beyond its strength or the strength of the ground. It will buckle and fall in the most terrible sound yet heard on the planet. And the crash will be the crack of doom for the Druids."

He glanced carefully up and down the face of the Palace. "Now walk swiftly. Once you are in the car you are safe from any hidden marksmen."

Again Joe searched the shadows. Then gingerly he stepped out on the plat. It seemed very wide, very empty. He crossed to the car with a naked tingling under his skin. He stepped through the door and the car swayed under him. Hableyat bounced in beside him.

"Very well, Juliam," said Hableyat to the driver, a very old Mang, sad-eyed, wrinkled of face, his hair gone brindle-brown with age.

"We'll be off—to the Terminal. Stage Four, I believe. The *Belsaurion* for Junction and Ballenkarch."

Juliam trod on the elevator pedal. The car swung up and away. The Palace dwindled below and they rose beside the dun trunk of the Tree, up under the first umbrella of fronds.

The air of Kyril was usually filled with a smoky haze but today the slanting sun shone crisply through a perfectly clear atmosphere. The city Divinal, such as it was—a heterogeneity of palaces, administrative offices, temples, a few low warehouses—huddled among the roots of the Tree and quickly gave way to a gently rolling plain thronged with farms and villages.

Roads converged in all directions toward the Tree and along these roads walked the drab men and women of the Laity—making their pilgrimage to the Tree. Joe had watched them once or twice as they entered the Ordinal Cleft, a gap between two great arched roots. Tiny figures like ants, they paused, turned to stare out across the gray land before continuing on into the Tree. Every day brought thousands from all corners of Kyril, old and young. Wan dark-eyed men, women, children—dusty, hungry, thirsty—their souls aflame for the peace of the Tree.

They crossed a flat plain covered with small black capsules. To one side a mass of naked men performed calisthenics—jumping, twisting in perfect time.

Hableyat said, "There you see the Druid space-navy."

Joe looked sharply to see if he were indulging in sarcasm but the pudgy face was immobile.

"They are well suited to the defense of Kyril, which is to say, the Tree. Naturally anyone wishing to defeat the Druids by violence would think to destroy the Tree, thus demolishing the morale of the natives. But in order to destroy the Tree a flotilla must approach relatively close to Kyril, say within a hundred thousand miles, for any accuracy of bombardment.

"The Druids maintain a screen of these little boats a million miles out. They're crude but very fast and agile. Each is equipped with a warhead—in fact they are suicide boats and to date they are admitted to be an effective defense for the Tree."

Joe sat a moment in silence. Then, "Are these boats made here? On Kyril?"

"They are quite simple," said Hableyat with veiled contempt. "A shell, a drive, an oxygen tank. The Lay soldiers are not expected to demand or appreciate comfort. There's a vast number of these little boats. Why not? Labor is free. The idea of cost has no meaning for the Druids. I believe the control equipment is imported from Belan and likewise the firing release. Otherwise the boats are hand-made here on Kyril."

The field full of beetle-boats slanted, faded astern. Ahead appeared the thirty-foot wall surrounding the Terminal. The long glass station stretched along one side of the rectangle. Along another was a line of palatial mansions — the consular offices of off-planets.

Across the field, in the fourth of five bays, a medium-sized combination freight-passenger vessel rested and Joe saw that it was ready to take off. The cargo hatch had been battened, the loading trams swung back and only a gangplank connected the ship with the ground.

Juliam set the car down in a parking area to the side of the station. Hableyat put a restraining hand on Joe's arm.

"Perhaps — for your own safety — it might be wise if I arranged your passage. The Thearch might have planned some sort of trouble. One never knows where these unpredictable Druids are concerned." He hopped out of the car. "If you'll remain here then — out of sight — I'll return very shortly."

"But the money for the passage —"

"A trifle, a trifle," said Hableyat. "My government has more money than it knows how to spend. Allow me to invest two thousand stiples toward a fund of good will with our legendary Mother Earth."

Joe relaxed dubiously into the seat. Two thousand stiples was two thousand stiples and it would help him on his way back to Earth. If Hableyat thought to hold him under obligation Hableyat was mistaken. He stirred in his seat. Better get out while the getting was good. Things like this did not happen without some unpleasant *quid pro quo*. He raised a hand toward the door and met Juliam's eye. Juliam shook his head.

"No, no, sir. Lord Hableyat will be back at once and his wishes were that you remain out of sight."

In a spasm of defiance, Joe said, "Hableyat can wait."

He jumped from the car and, ignoring Juliam's querulous voice, strode off toward the station. His anger cooled as he walked and in his green-white-and-black livery he felt conspicuous. Hableyat had a rude habit of being consistently right.

A sign across the walk read, *Costumes of all worlds. Change here. Arrive at your destination in a fitting garb.*

Joe stepped in. Through the glass window he would be able to see Hableyat if he left the station, returning to the car. The proprietor stood quietly at his command, a tall bony man of nameless race with a wide waxy face, wide guileless eyes of pale blue.

"My Lord wishes?" he inquired in even tones which ignored the servant's livery which Joe was stripping off.

"Get rid of these. Give me something suitable for Ballenkarch."

The shop-keeper bowed. He ran a grave eye over Joe's form, turned to a rack, brought forward a set of garments which made Joe blink — red pantaloons, a tight blue sleeveless jacket, a voluminous white blouse. Joe said doubtfully, "That's not quite — it's not subdued, is it?"

"It is a typical Ballenkarch costume, my Lord — typical, that is to say, among the more civilized clans. The savages wear skins and sacks." He twisted the garments to display front and back. "As it is, it denotes no particular rank. A vavasour hangs a sword at his left side. A grandee of the Vail Alan Court wears a chap-band of black in addition. The Ballenkarch costumes, Lord, are marked by a rather barbaric flamboyance."

Joe said, "Give me a plain gray traveling suit. I'll change to Ballenkarch style when I arrive."

"As you wish, Lord."

The traveling suit was more to his liking. With deep satisfaction Joe zipped close the seams, snugged the ankles and wrists, belted the waist.

"And what style morion, Lord?"

Joe grimaced. Morions were *comme il faut* among the rank of Kyril. Laymen, louts, menials, were denied the affectation of a glistening complex morion. He pointed to a low shell of bright metal with a sweeping rakehell brim. "That one if it will fit."

The shopkeeper bent his form almost into an inverted U. "Yes, your Worship."

Joe glanced at him sharply, then considered the morion he had selected — a glistening beautiful helmet, useful for nothing other than decorative head-dress. It was rather like the one Ecclesiarch Manaolo had worn. He shrugged, jammed it on his head, transferred the contents of his pockets. Gun, money, wallet with identification papers. "How much do I owe you?"

"Two hundred stiples, your Worship."

Joe gave him a pair of notes, stepped out on the arcade. As he walked it occurred to him that his step was firmer, that in fact he was swaggering. The change from livery into the gray suit and swashbuckling morion had altered the color of his psychology. Morale, confidence, will-to-win — they were completely intangible, yet so ultimately definite. Now to find Hableyat.

There was Hableyat ahead of him, walking arm in arm with a Mang in green-blue-and-yellow uniform, speaking very earnestly, very expressively. Joe wished he were able to read lips. The two stopped at the ramp down to the field. The Mang officer bowed curtly, turned, marched back along the arcade. Hableyat ambled down the ramp, started across the field.

It occurred to Joe that he would like to hear what Juliam said to Hableyat and Hableyat's comments on his absence. If he ran to the end of the arcade, jumped the wall, ran around behind the parking lot, he would be able to approach the car from the rear, probably unseen.

Suiting action to thought he turned, raced the length of the terrace, heedless of startled glances. Lowering himself to the blue-green turf he dodged close to the wall, kept as many of the parked cars as possible between himself and the leisurely Hableyat. He reached the car, flung himself to his hands and knees unseen by Juliam, who had his eyes on Hableyat.

Juliam slid back the door. Hableyat said cheerfully, "Now then, my friend, everything is —" He stopped. Then sharply to Juliam, "Where is he? Where has he gone?"

"He left," said Juliam, "a little after you did."

Hableyat muttered a pungent syllable. "The confounded unpredictability of the man! I gave him strict instructions to remain here."

Juliam said, "I reminded him of your instructions. He ignored me."

"That's the difficulty," said Hableyat, "in dealing with men of limited intellect. They cannot be trusted for logical performance. A thousand times would I prefer to wrestle with a genius. His methods, at least, would be understandable... If Erru Kametin sees him all my plans will be defeated. Oh," he groaned, "the bull-headed fool!"

Juliam sniffed but held his tongue. Hableyat spoke incisively. "You go — look along the arcade. If you see him send him back quickly. I'll wait here. Then telephone Erru Kametin — he'll be at the Consulate. Identify yourself as Aglom Fourteen. He will inquire further and you will reveal that you were an agent for Empoing, who is now dead — that you have important information for his ears.

"He will wish you to appear but you will profess fear of Druid counteraction. You will tell him that you have definitely identified the courier, that he will be traveling with the article in question on the *Belsaurion*. You will give a quick description of this man and then return here."

"Yes, Lord."

Joe heard the shuffle of Juliam's feet. He slid back, ducked behind a long blue carryall, rose to his feet. He saw Juliam cross the field, then by a roundabout route he returned to the car, entered.

Hableyat's eyes were glittering but he said in a careless tone, "So there you are, young man. Where have you been?... Ah, new garments, I see. Very wise, very wise, though of course it was rash to appear along the arcade."

He reached into his pouch, came out with an envelope. "Here is your ticket, Ballenkarch via Junction."

"Junction? What or where is Junction?"

Hableyat put the tips of his fingers together, said in a tone of exaggerated precision, "Kyril, Mangtse and Ballenkarch, as you may be aware, form a triangle approximately equilateral. Junction is an artificial satellite at its center. It is also situated along the Mangtse–Thombol–Belan traffic lane and, at a perpendicular, along the Frums–Outer System passage and so makes a very convenient way station or transfer point.

"It is an interesting place from many aspects. The unique method of construction, the extremities of the efforts made to entertain visitors, the famous Junction Gardens, the cosmopolitan nature of the people encountered there. I'm sure you will find it an interesting voyage."

"I imagine I shall," said Joe.

Hableyat glanced at him sharply. "But also a word of caution. The Druids," he chose his words carefully, "with their anachronistic thought-processes, are fanatic on the subject of vengeance. And they stop at nothing.

"There will be spies aboard — everywhere, indeed, there are spies. One cannot move his foot without kicking a spy. Their instructions in regard to you may or may not include violence. I counsel the utmost vigilance — though, as is well known, a skillful assassin cannot be denied opportunity."

Joe said with grim good-humor, "I've got a gun."

Hableyat met his eyes with limpid innocence. "Good — excellent. Now the ship leaves almost any minute. You had better get aboard. I won't go with you but wish you good luck from here."

Joe jumped to the ground. "Thanks for your efforts," he said evenly.

Hableyat raised a monitory hand. "No thanks, please. I'm glad that I'm able to assist a fellow-man when he's in trouble. Although there is a slight service I'd like you to render me. I've promised my friend, the Prince of Ballenkarch, a sample of the lovely Kyril heather and perhaps you will convey him this little pot with my regards."

Hableyat displayed a plant growing in an earthenware pot. "I'll put it in this bag. Please be careful with it. Water it once a week if you will."

Joe accepted the potted plant. A hoot from the ship's horn rang across the field. "Hurry then," said Hableyat. "Perhaps we'll meet again some day."

"Goodby," said Joe. He turned, walked toward the ship, anxious now to embark.

Last-minute passengers were crossing the field from the station. Joe stared at a couple not fifty feet distant — a tall broad-shouldered young man with the face of a malicious satyr, a slender dark-haired girl — Manaolo and the Priestess Elfane.

Chapter V

THE SKELETON-WORK of the embarkation stage made a black web on the overcast sky. Joe climbed the worn plank stairs to the top deck. No one was behind. No one observed him. He reached under an L-beam, set the potted plant on the flange out of sight. Whatever it was, it was dangerous. He wanted nothing to do with it. Hableyat's *quid pro quos* might come high.

Joe smiled sourly. 'Limited intellect' and 'bull-headed fool' — there was an ancient aphorism, to the effect that eavesdroppers hear no good of themselves. It seemed to apply in his own case.

Joe thought, *I've been called worse things. And once I get to Ballenkarch it won't make any difference...*

Ahead of him Manaolo and Elfane crossed the stage, looking neither to right or left but straight ahead with that fixed and conscious will characteristic of the Druids. They climbed the gangplank, turned into the ship. Joe grimaced. Elfane's slim legs twinkling up the stairs had sent sweet-sour chills along his nerves. And the proud back of Manaolo — it was like taking two drugs with precisely opposite effects.

Joe cursed old Hableyat. Did he imagine that Joe would be so obsessed with infatuation for the Priestess Elfane as to challenge Manaolo? Joe snorted. *Over-ripe old hypocrite!* In the first place he had no slightest intimation that Elfane would consider him as a lover. And after Manaolo's handling of her — his stomach muscles twisted. Even, he amended dutifully, if his loyalty to Margaret would permit his interest. He had enough problems of his own without inviting others.

At the gangplank stood a steward in a red skin-tight uniform. Rows of trefoil gold frogs decorated his legs, a radio was clamped to his ear with a mike pressed to his throat. He was a member of a race strange to Joe — white-haired, loose-jointed, with eyes as green as emeralds.

Joe felt the tenseness rising up in himself, if the Thearch suspected that he were on his way off-planet, now he would be stopped.

The steward took his ticket, nodded courteously, motioned him within. Joe crossed the gangplank to the convex black hulk, entered the shadowed double port. At a temporary desk sat the purser, another man of the white-haired race. Like the steward he wore a scarlet suit which seemed like a second skin. In addition he wore glass epaulets and a small scarlet skullcap.

He extended a book to Joe. "Your name and thumb-print, please. They waive responsibility for accidents incurred en route."

Joe signed, pressed his thumb on the indicated square while the purser examined his ticket. "First class passage, Cabin Fourteen. Luggage, Worship?"

"I have none," said Joe. "I imagine there's a ship's store where I can buy linen."

"Yes, your Worship, yes indeed. Now, if you'll kindly step to your cabin, a steward will secure you for take-off."

Joe glanced down at the book he had signed. Immediately before his signature he read in a tall angular hand, *Druid Manaolo kia Benlodieth*, and then in a round backhand script, *Alnietho kia Benlodieth*. Signed as his wife — Joe chewed at his lip. Manaolo was assigned to Cabin Twelve, Elfane to 13.

Not strange in itself. These freighter-passenger ships, unlike the great passenger packets flashing out from Earth in every direction, offered little accommodation for passengers. Cabins, so-called, were closets with hammocks, drawers, tiny collapsible bathroom facilities.

A steward in the skin-tight garment, this time a firefly blue, said, "This way, Lord Smith."

Joe thought — to excite reverence all a man needed was a tin hat.

He followed the steward past the hold, where the steerage passengers already lay entranced and bundled into their hammocks, then through a combination saloon-dining room. The far wall was faced with two tiers of doors, with a web-balcony running under the second tier. No. 14 was the last door on the top row.

As the steward led Joe past No. 13 the door was thrust aside and Manaolo came bursting out. His face was pale, his eyes widened to curious elliptical shape, showing the full disk of the dead black retinas. He was plainly in a blind fury. He shouldered Joe aside, opened the door to No. 12, passed within.

Joe slowly pulled himself back from the rail. For an instant all sense, all reason, had left him. It was a curious sensation — one unknown to him before. An unlimited elemental aversion which even Harry Creath had never aroused. He turned slowly back along the catwalk.

Elfane stood in the door of her cabin. She had removed the blue cloak and stood in her soft white dress — a dark-haired girl with a narrow face, mobile and alive, now clenched in anger. Her eyes met Joe's. For an instant they stared eye to eye, faces two feet apart.

The hate in Joe's heart moved over for another emotion, a wonderful lift into clean air, a delight, a ferment. Her eyebrows contracted in puzzlement, she half-opened her mouth to speak. Joe wondered with a queer sinking feeling, if she recognized him? Their previous contacts had been so careless, so impersonal. He was a new man in his new clothes.

She turned, shut the door. Joe continued to No. 14, where the steward webbed him into his hammock for the take-off.

Joe awoke from the take-off trance. He said, "Whatever you're looking for, I haven't got it. Hableyat gave you a bum steer."

The man across the cabin froze into stillness, back turned toward Joe.

Joe said, "Don't move, I've got my gun on you."

He jerked up from the hammock but the webbing held him. At the sound of his efforts the intruder stole a glance over his shoulder, ducked, slid from the cabin like a ghost.

Joe called out harshly but there was no sound. Throwing off the web he ran to the door, looked out into the saloon. It was empty.

Joe turned back, shut the door. Waking from the trance he had no clear picture of his visitor. A man short and stocky, moving on joints set at curious splayed angles. There had been a flashing glimpse of the man's face but all Joe could recall was a sallow yellow tinge as if the underlying blood ran bright yellow. A Mang.

Joe thought, *Now it's starting. Damn Hableyat, setting me up as his stalking horse!* He considered reporting to the captain, who, neither Druid nor Mang, might be unsympathetic to lawlessness aboard his ship. He decided against the action. He had nothing to report — merely a prowler in his cabin. The captain would hardly put the entire passenger list through a psycho-reading merely to apprehend a prowler.

Joe rubbed his face, yawned. Out in space once more, on the last leg of his trip. Unless, of course, Harry had moved on again.

He raised the stop-ray shield in front of the port, looked out into space. Ahead, in the direction of flight, a buffer-screen absorbed what radiation the ship either overtook or met. Otherwise the energy, increased in frequency and hardness by the Doppler action due to the ship's velocity, would have crisped him instantly.

Light impinging from abeam showed him stars more or less with their normal magnitudes, the perspectives shifting and roiling as he watched — and the stars floating, eddying, drifting like motes in a beam of light. To the stern was utter darkness — no light could overtake the vessel. Joe dropped the shutter. The scene was familiar enough to him. Now for a bath, his clothes, food...

Looking at his face in the mirror he noticed a stubble of beard. The shaver lay on a glass shelf over the collapsible sink. Joe reached — yanked his hand to a halt, an inch from the shaver. When first he had entered the cabin it had hung from a clasp on the bulkhead.

Joe eased himself away from the wall, his nerves tingling. Certainly his visitor had not been shaving? He looked down to the deck — saw a mat of coiled woven brass. Bending, he noticed a length of copper wire joining the mat to the drain pipe.

Gingerly he scooped the shaver into his shoe, carried it to his bunk. A metal band circled the handle with a tit entering the case near the unit which scooped power from the ship's general field.

In the long run, thought Joe, he had Hableyat to thank — Hableyat who had so kindly rescued him from the Thearch and put him aboard the *Belsaurion* with a potted plant.

Joe rang for the steward. A young woman came, white-haired like the other members of the crew. She wore a parti-colored short-skirted garment of orange and blue that fitted her like a coat of paint. Joe dumped the shaver into a pillow-case. He said, "Take this to the electrician. It's very dangerous — got a short in it. Don't touch it. Don't let anyone touch it. And — will you please bring me another shaver?"

"Yes, sir." She departed.

Finally bathed, shaved and as well-dressed as his limited wardrobe permitted, he sauntered out into the saloon, stepping high in the ship's half-gravity. Four or five men and women sat along the lounges to the side, engaging in guarded conversation.

Joe stood watching a moment. Peculiar, artificial creatures, he thought, these human beings of the Space Age — brittle and so completely formal that conversation was no more than an exchange of polished mannerisms. So sophisticated that nothing could shock them as much as naive honesty.

Three Mangs sat in the group — two men, one old, the other young, both wearing the rich uniforms of the Mangtse Red-Branch. A young Mang woman with a certain heavy beauty, evidently the wife of the young officer. The other couple, like the race which operated the ship, were human deviants unfamiliar to Joe. They were like pictures he had seen in a childhood fairy-book — wispy fragile creatures, big-eyed, thin-skinned, dressed in loose sheer gowns.

Joe descended the stairs to the main deck and a ship's officer, the head steward presumably, appeared. Gesturing politely to Joe he spoke to the entire group. "I present Lord Joe Smith of the planet —" he hesitated "— the planet Earth."

He turned to the others in the group. "Erru Kametin —" this was the older of the two Mang officers "— Erru Ex Amma and Erritu Thi Amma, of Mangtse." He turned to the fairy-like creatures. "Prater Luli Hassimassa and his lady Hermina of Cil."

Joe bowed politely, seated himself at the end of the lounge. The young Mang officer, Erru Ex Amma, asked curiously, "Did I understand that you claim *Earth* for your home planet?"

"Yes," said Joe half-truculently. "I was born on the continent known as North America, where the first ship ever to leave Earth was built."

"Strange," muttered the Mang, eyeing Joe with an expression just short of disbelief. "I've always considered talk of Earth one of the superstitions of space, like the Moons of Paradise and the Star Dragon."

"I can assure you that Earth is no legend," said Joe. "Somehow in the outward migrations, among the wars and the planetary programs of propaganda, the real existence of Earth has been called to question. And we travel very rarely into this outer swirl of the galaxy."

The fairy-woman spoke in a piping voice which suited her moth-frail appearance. "And you maintain that all of us — you, the Mangs, we Cils, the Belands who operate the ship, the Druids, the Frumsans, the Thablites — they are *all* ultimately derived from Earth stock?"

"Such is the fact."

A metallic voice said, "That is not entirely true. The Druids were the first fruit of the Tree of Life. That is the well-established doctrine, and any other allegation is false."

Joe said in a careful voice, "You are entitled to your belief."

The steward came forward. "Ecclesiarch Manaolo kia Benlodieth of Kyril."

There was a moment of silence after the introductions. Then Manaolo said, "Not only am I entitled to my belief, but I must protest the propagation of incorrect statements."

"That also is your privilege," said Joe. "Protest all you like."

He met Manaolo's dead black eyes and there seemed no human understanding behind them, no thought — only emotion and obstinate will.

There was movement behind; it was Priestess Elfane. She was presented to the company and without words she settled beside Hermina of Cil. The atmosphere now had changed and even though she but murmured pleasantries with Hermina her presence brought a piquancy, a sparkle, a spice…

Joe counted. Eight with himself — fourteen cabins — six passengers yet unaccounted for. One of the thirteen had tried to kill him — a Mang.

A pair of Druids issued from cabins two and three, and were introduced — elderly sheep-faced men en route to a mission on Ballenkarch. They carried with them a portable altar, which they immediately set up in a corner of the saloon, and began a series of silent rites before a small representation of the Tree. Manaolo watched them without interest a moment or two, then turned away.

Four unaccounted for, thought Joe.

The steward announced the first meal of the day, and at this moment another couple appeared from their cabins, two Mangs in non-military attire — loose wrappings of colored silk, light loose cloaks, jewelled corselets. They bowed formally to the company and, since the steward was arranging the collapsible table, they took their places without introduction. Five Mangs, thought Joe. Two soldiers, two civilians, a woman. Two cabins still concealed their occupants.

Cabin No. 10 opened, and an aged woman of extreme height stepped slowly out on the balcony. She was bald as an egg and her head was flat on top. She had a great bony nose, black bulging eyes. She wore a black cape and on each finger of both hands was a tremendous jewel.

One more to go. The door to cabin No. 6 remained closed.

The meal was served from a menu surprisingly varied, to serve the palates of many races. Joe, in his planet-to-planet journey across the galaxy, perforce had dismissed all queasiness. He had eaten organic matter of every conceivable color, consistency, odor and flavor.

Familiar items he could put a name to — ferns, fruits, fungus, roots, reptiles, insects, fish, molluscs, slugs, eggs, spore-sacs, animals and birds — and at least as many objects he could neither define nor recognize and whose sole claim to his appetite lay in the example of others.

His place at the table was directly opposite Manaolo and Elfane. He noticed that they did not speak and several times he felt her eyes on him, puzzled, appraising, half-furtive. *She's sure she's seen me,* thought Joe, *but she can't remember where.*

After the meal the passengers separated. Manaolo retired to the gymnasium behind the saloon. The five Mangs sat down to a game played with small rods of different colors. The Cils went up to the promenade along the back rib of the ship. The tall demon-woman sat in a chair, gazing blankly into nothingness.

Joe would likewise have taken exercise in the gymnasium but the presence of Manaolo deterred him. He selected a film from the ship's library, prepared to return to his room.

Priestess Elfane said in a low voice, "Lord Smith, I wish to speak to you."

"Certainly."

"Will you come to my room?"

Joe looked over his shoulder. "Won't your husband be annoyed?"

"Husband?" She managed to inject an enormous weight of contempt and angry disgust into her voice. "The relationship is purely nominal." She stopped, looked away, apparently regretting her words. Then she continued in a cool voice, "I wish to speak to you." She turned away, marched for her cabin.

Joe chuckled quietly. The vixen knew no other world than that in her own brain, had no conception that wills could exist in opposition to hers. Amusing now — but what a devil when she grew older! It occurred to Joe that it would be a pleasant experience to be lost with her on an uninhabited planet — taming her wilfulness, opening up her consciousness.

He leisurely followed to her cabin. She sat on the bunk. He took a seat on the bench. "Well?"

"You say your home is the planet Earth — the mythical Earth. Is that true?"

"Yes, it's true."

"Where is Earth?"

"In toward the Center, perhaps a thousand light-years."

"What is Earth like?" She leaned forward, elbow on her knee, chin on her hand, watching him with interested eyes.

Joe, suddenly flustered, shrugged. "You ask a question I can't answer in a word. Earth is a world of great age. Everywhere are ancient buildings, ancient cities, traditions. In Egypt stand the Great Pyramids, built by the first civilized men. In England a circle of chipped stones, Stonehenge, are relics of a race almost as old. In the caves of France and Spain, far underground, are drawings of animals, scratched by men hardly removed from the beasts they hunted."

She drew a deep breath. "But your cities, your civilization — are they different from ours?"

Joe put on a judicious expression. "Naturally they are different. No two planets are alike. Ours is an old stable culture — mellowed, kindly. Our races have merged — I am the result of their mingling. In these outer regions men have been blocked off and separated and have specialized once again. You Druids, who are very close to us physically, correspond to the ancient Caucasian race of the Mediterranean branch."

"But do you have no Great God — no Tree of Life?"

"At present," said Joe, "there is no organized religion on Earth. We are free to express our joy at being alive in any way which pleases us. Some revere a cosmic creator — others merely acknowledge the physical laws controlling the universe to almost the same result. The worship of fetishes, anthropoid, animal or vegetable — like your Tree — has long been extinct."

She sat up sharply. "You — you deride our sacred institution."

"Sorry."

She rose to her feet, then sat down, swallowing her wrath. "You interest me in many ways," she said sullenly, as if justifying her forbearance to herself. "I have the peculiar feeling that you are known to me."

Joe, on a half-sadistic impulse, said, "I was your father's chauffeur. Yesterday you and your — husband were planning to kill me."

She froze into unblinking rigidity, staring, mouth half-open. Then she relaxed, shuddered, shrank back. "*You* — are you —"

But Joe had caught sight of something behind her on a night-shelf over her bunk — a potted plant, almost identical with the one he had left on Kyril.

She saw the direction of his gaze. Her mouth came shut. She gasped, "You know then!" It was almost a whisper. "Kill me, destroy me, I am tired of life!"

She rose to her feet, arms out defenselessly. Joe arose, moved a step toward her. It was like a dream, a time past the edge of reason, without logic, cause, effect. Her eyes widened, not in fear now. He put his hands on her shoulders. She was warm and slender, pulsing like a bird.

She pulled away, sat back on her bed. "I don't understand," she said in a husky voice. "I understand nothing."

"Tell me," said Joe in a voice almost as husky. "What is this Manaolo to you? Is he your lover?"

She said nothing; then at last gave her head a little shake. "No, he is nothing. He has been sent to Ballenkarch on a mission. I decided I wanted release from the rituals. I wanted adventure, and cared nothing for consequence. But Manaolo frightens me. He came to me yesterday — but I was afraid."

Joe felt a wonderful yeastiness around his heart. The image of Margaret appeared, mouth puckered accusingly. Joe sighed regretfully. The mood changed. Elfane's face was once more that of a young Druid Priestess.

"What is your business, Smith?" she asked coolly. "Are you a spy?"

"No, I'm not a spy."

"Then why do you go to Ballenkarch? Only spies and agents go to Ballenkarch. Druids and Mangs or their hirelings."

"It is business of a personal nature." Looking at her he reflected that this vivid Priestess Elfane had gaily suggested killing him only yesterday.

She noticed his scrutiny, tilted her head in a whimsical harlequin grimace — the trick of a girl aware of her appeal, a flirtatious trick. Joe laughed — stopped, listened. There had been a scraping sound against the wall. Elfane followed his gaze.

"That's my cabin!" Joe rose to his feet, opened the door, bounded down the balcony, threw open the door to his cabin. Erru Ex Amma, the young Mang officer, stood facing him, a wide mirthless grin on his face, showing pointed yellow teeth. He held a gun which was directed at Joe's middle.

"Back up!" he ordered. *"Back!"*

Joe slowly retreated out on the balcony. He looked over into the saloon. The four Mangs were at their game. One of the civilians glanced up, muttered to the others and they all turned their heads, looked up. Joe caught the flash of four citron-yellow faces. Then they were back to their game.

"Into the she-Druid's cabin," said Ex Amma. *"Quick!"* He moved his gun, still smiling the wide smile that was like a fox showing its fangs.

Joe slowly backed into Elfane's cabin, eyes flicking back and forth between the gun and the Mang's face.

Elfane gasped, sighed in terror. The Mang saw the pot with the bit of plant sprouting from it. "Ahhhh!"

He turned to Joe. "Back against the wall." He gave his gun a little forward motion, grimaced with anticipation and Joe knew he was about to die.

The door behind slid open; there was a hiss. The Mang stiffened, bent backward in an agonized arc, threw up his head, his jaw strained in a soundless scream. He fell to the deck.

Hableyat stood in the doorway, smiling primly. "I'm very sorry that there should have been this disturbance."

Chapter VI

HABLEYAT'S EYES WENT TO the plant on the shelf. He shook his head, clicked his tongue, turned a reproachful gaze on Joe. "My dear fellow, you have been instrumental in ruining a very careful plan."

"If you had asked me," said Joe, "if I wanted to donate my life to the success of your schemes I could have saved you a lot of grief."

Hableyat bleated his laugh without moving a muscle of his face. "You are charming. I am happy that you are still with us. But now I fear there is to be a quarrel."

The three Mangs were marching in belligerent single-file along the balcony, the old officer, Erru Kametin, in the lead, followed by the two civilians. Erru Kametin came to a stiff halt, bristling like an angry cur. "Lord Hableyat, this is sheer outrage. You have interfered with an officer of the Reach in his duty."

"'Interfered'?" protested Hableyat. "I have killed him. As to his 'duty' — since when has a rakehelly Redbranch tag-at-heels been ranked with a member of the Ampianu General?"

"We have our orders direct from Magnerru Ippolito. You have no slightest supercession —"

"Magnerru Ippolito, if you recall," said Hableyat smoothly, "is responsible to the Lathbon, who sits with the Bluewater on the General."

"A pack of white-blooded cravens!" shouted the officer. "You and the rest of the Bluewaters!"

The Mang woman on the main deck, who had been straining to glimpse the events on the balcony, screamed. Then came Manaolo's metallic voice. "Miserable dingy dogs!"

He bounded up to the balcony, lithe and strong, tremendous in his fury. With one hand he seized the shoulder of one civilian, hurled him to the catwalk, did the same for the other. He lifted Erru Kametin, tossed him bodily over the balcony. Dropping slowly in the half-gravity Erru Kametin landed with a grunt. Manaolo turned to Hableyat, who held out a protesting hand.

"A moment, Ecclesiarch, please use no force on my poor corpulence."

The wild face showed no flicker of emotion. The crouch of his body was answer to Hableyat's words.

Joe drew in his breath, stepped forward, threw a left jab, a hard right and Manaolo sprawled to the deck, where he lay looking at Joe with dead-black eyes.

"Sorry," lied Joe. "But Hableyat just saved my life and Elfane's. Give him time to talk anyway."

Manaolo jumped to his feet, without a word entered Elfane's cabin, shut and locked the door. Hableyat turned, stared quizzically at Joe. "We have returned each other compliments."

Joe said, "I'd like to know what's going on. No, I don't either — I want to mind my own business. I have my own troubles. I wish you'd keep yours to yourself."

Hableyat shook his head slowly as if in puzzled admiration. "For one of your professed intent you hurl yourself into the thick of things. But if you'll come to my cabin I have an excellent aquavit which will form the basis of a pleasant relaxation."

"Poison?" inquired Joe.

Hableyat shook his head gravely. "Merely excellent brandy."

The captain of the vessel called a meeting of the passengers. He was a large heavy man with dead-white hair, a flat-white face, liquid-green eyes, a thin pink mouth. He wore the Beland skin-tight garment of dark-green with glass epaulets and a scarlet ruff above each elbow.

The passengers sat in the deep couches — the two civilian Mangs; the woman, red-eyed from crying, Erru Kametin, Hableyat, serene and easy in a loose robe of a dull white stuff with Joe next to him. Beside Joe sat the gaunt bald woman in the black gown and she had a sickly-sweet odor about her that was neither floral nor animal. Then came the Cils, then the two Druids, placid and secure, then Elfane and last, Manaolo.

He wore a striking garment of light-green sateen with gold striping along the legs. A light flat morion perched jauntily on his dark curls.

The captain spoke ponderously. "I am aware that a tension exists between the worlds of Kyril and Mangtse. But this ship is the property of Belan, and we are resolved to remain dispassionate and neutral.

"There was a killing this morning. So far as I have been able to gather Erru Ex Amma was discovered searching the cabin of Lord Smith and, when apprehended, forced Smith into the cabin of the Priestess Alnietho —" using the name Elfane had signed to the passenger list "— where he threatened to kill them both. Lord Hableyat, in a praiseworthy effort to avoid an interplanetary incident, appeared and killed his countryman Erru Ex Amma.

"The other Mangs, protesting, were engaged violently by Ecclesiarch Manaolo, who also began to attack Lord Hableyat. Lord Smith, anxious lest Manaolo, in his ignorance of the true state of affairs, injure Lord Hableyat, struck Manaolo with his fist. I believe, in essence, that is the gist of the affair."

He paused. No one spoke. Hableyat sat twiddling his forefingers around each other with his plump lower lips hanging loose. Joe was aware of Elfane sitting stiff and silent and he felt a slow look from Manaolo drift over him — his face, shoulders, legs.

The captain continued. "To the best of my belief, the culprit in this case, Erru Ex Amma, has been punished by death. The rest of you are guilty of nothing more than hot tempers. But I do not propose to countenance further incidents. On any such occasion the participants will be hypnotized and webbed into their hammocks for the duration of the voyage.

"It is Beland tradition that our ships are neutral ground and our livelihood stems from this reputation. I will not see it challenged. Quarrels, personal or interplanetary, must wait till you are away from my authority." He bowed heavily. "Thank you for your attention."

The Mangs immediately arose, the woman departing for her cabin to weep, the three men to their game with the colored bars, Hableyat to the promenade. The gaunt woman sat without movement, staring at the spot where the captain had stood. The Cils wandered to the ship's library. The Druid missionaries converged on Manaolo.

Elfane arose, stretched her slim young arms, looked quickly toward Joe, then to Manaolo's broad back. She made up her mind, crossed the room to Joe, settled on the couch beside him. "Tell me, Lord Smith — what did Hableyat talk to you about when he took you to his room?"

Joe moved uneasily in his seat. "Priestess — I can't be a tale-bearer between Druids and Mangs. In this particular case we spoke of nothing very important. He asked me about my life on Earth, he was interested in the man I've come out here seeking. I described a number of the planets I've stopped at. We drank a good deal of brandy, and that was about all there was to it."

Elfane bit her lip impatiently. "I cannot understand why Hableyat protected us from the young Mang…What does he gain? He is as completely Mang as the other. He would die rather than allow the Druids to take sovereignty over Ballenkarch."

Joe said, "You and Manaolo are certainly not en route to take over sovereignty of Ballenkarch?"

She gave him a wide-eyed stare, then drummed her fingers on her leg. Joe smiled to himself. In anyone else the assumptions of unlimited authority would be a matter of serious irritation. In Elfane — Joe, charmed and bewitched, dismissed it as an intriguing mannerism. He laughed.

"Why do you laugh?" she asked suspiciously.

"You remind me of a kitten dressed up in doll's clothes — very proud of itself."

She flushed, her eyes sparkled. "So — you laugh at me!"

After an instant of contemplation Joe asked, "Don't you ever laugh at yourself?"

"No. Of course not."

"Try it some time." He arose to his feet, went to the gymnasium.

Chapter VII

JOE WORKED UP A SWEAT in an obstacle treadmill, jumped out, sat panting on the bench. Manaolo came slowly into the gymnasium, looked up and down the floor, then slowly back to Joe. Joe thought, *Here comes trouble.*

Manaolo glanced back over his shoulder, then turned, crossed the room in three strides. He stood looking down at Joe. His face was not a man's face but a glimpse into a fantasy of the underworld.

He said, "You touched me with your hands."

"Touched you, hell!" said Joe. "I knocked you A over T."

Manaolo's mouth, tender enough to be a woman's but also hard and muscular, sunk at the corners. He writhed his shoulders, leaned forward, kicked. Joe bent double in silent agony, clasping his lower abdomen. Manaolo stepped lightly back, kicked under Joe's jaw.

Joe slid slowly, laxly to the deck. Manaolo bent swiftly, a little metal device glittering in his hands. Joe raised his arm feebly — Manaolo kicked it aside. He hooked the metal instrument in Joe's nostrils, jerked. Two little hooked knives sliced the cartilage. A cloud of powder seared the flesh.

Manaolo jumped back, the corners of his mouth pushed in deeper. He turned on his heel, swung jauntily out of the room.

The ship's doctor said, "There — it's not too bad. You'll have the two scars for a while but they shouldn't be too noticeable."

Joe examined his reflection in the mirror — his bruised chin, the plastered nose. "Well — I've still got a nose."

"You've still got a nose," the doctor agreed woodenly. "Lucky I got you in time. I've had some experience with that powder. It's a hormone promoting the growth of skin. If it hadn't been removed, the splits would be permanent and you'd have three flaps on your face."

"You understand," said Joe, "this was an accident. I wouldn't want to trouble the captain with any report and I hope you won't."

The doctor shrugged, turned, put away his equipment. "Strange accident."

Joe returned to the saloon. The Cils were learning the game with the colored bars, chatting gaily with the Mangs. The Druid missionaries, heads together, were performing some intricate ritual at their portable altar. Hableyat was spread comfortably on a couch, examining his fingernails with every evidence of satisfaction. The door from Elfane's cabin opened, Manaolo stepped out, swung easily along the balcony, down the steps. He gave Joe an expressionless glance, turned up toward the promenade.

Joe settled beside Hableyat, felt his nose tenderly. "It's still there."

Hableyat nodded composedly. "It will be as good as new in a week or two. These Beland medics are apt, very apt. Now on Kyril, where doctors are nonexistent, the man of the Laity would apply a poultice of some vile material and the wound would never heal.

"You will notice a large number of the Laity with tri-cleft noses. Next to killing it is a favorite Druid punishment." He surveyed Joe from under half-closed lids. "You seem to be rather less exercised than would be permissible under the circumstances."

"I'm not pleased."

"Let me cite you a facet of Druid psychology," said Hableyat. "In Manaolo's mind the infliction of the wound terminated the matter. It was the final decisive act in the quarrel between you two. On Kyril the Druids act without fear of retaliation in the name of the Tree. It gives them a peculiar sense of infallibility. Now, I mention this merely to point out that Manaolo will be surprised and outraged if you pursue the matter farther."

Joe shrugged.

Hableyat said in a querulous voice, "You say nothing, you make no threats, you voice no anger."

Joe smiled a rather thin smile. "I haven't had time for much but amazement. Give me time."

Hableyat nodded.

"Ah, I see. You were shocked by the attack."

"Very much so."

Hableyat nodded again, a series of wise little jerks that set his dewlaps quivering. "Let us change the subject then. Now your description of the European pre-Christian Druids interests me."

"Tell me something," said Joe. "What is that pot that all the fuss is about? Some kind of message or formula or military secret?"

Hableyat's eyes widened. "Message? Military secret? What *are* these? No, my dear fellow, to the best of my knowledge the pot is merely an honest pot and the plant an honest plant."

"Why the excitement then? And why try to stick me with a ringer?"

Hableyat said musingly, "Sometimes in affairs of planetary scope it becomes necessary to sacrifice the convenience of one person for the eventual benefit of many. You were to carry the plant to decoy my pistol-flourishing compatriots from that conveyed by the Druids."

"I don't get it," said Joe. "Aren't you both working for the same government?"

"Oh indeed," said Hableyat. "Our aims are identical — the glorification and prosperity of our beloved planet. No one is more dedicated than myself. But there is a rather odd cleavage in the Mang system, separating the Redbranch Militars from the Bluewater Commercials. They exist like two souls in one body, two husbands married to the same wife.

"Both love Mangtse. Both use their peculiar means for displaying this love. To some extent they cooperate but only as is expedient. They are ultimately responsible only to the Lathbon and, a step lower, to the Ampianu General, in which body both seat members. In many ways the arrangement works well — sometimes two approaches to a problem are valuable.

"In general the Redbranch is direct and forceful. They believe that the best way to end our difficulties with the Druids is to seize the planet in a military operation. We Bluewaters point out that many men would be killed, much material destroyed and, if by some miracle we finally overcame the religion-crazed hordes of the Laity, we would have destroyed whatever usefulness Kyril might have for us.

"You see," he nodded wisely at Joe, "with a productive peasantry Kyril can produce the raw materials and hand-crafts for our Mang industries. We form a natural couple but the current Druid policy is a disturbing factor. An industrialized Ballenkarch ruled by the Druids would upset the balance. Now the Redbranches want to destroy the Druids. We Bluewaters hope to influence a gradual metamorphosis toward an economy on Kyril channeled into production instead of into the Tree."

"And how do you propose to work that out?"

Hableyat wagged a solemn finger. "In the strictest confidence, my dear fellow — by letting the Druids proceed undisturbed with their intrigues."

Joe frowned, touched his nose absently. "But — this flowerpot — how does it enter the picture?"

"That," said Hableyat, "is what the poor single-minded Druids conceive to be the most cogent instrument of their plan. I hope it will be one of the instruments of their defeat. So I mean to see that the pot reaches Ballenkarch if I must kill twenty of my fellow Mangs in the process."

"If you're telling the truth, which I doubt —"

"But my dear fellow, why should I lie to you?"

"— I commence to understand some of this madhouse."

Junction — a many-sided polyhedron one mile in diameter, swimming in a diffused luminescence. A dozen space-ships suckled up close like leeches and nearby space was thick with firefly flecks of light — men and women in air-suits, drifting through the void, venturing off ten, twenty, thirty miles, feeling the majesty of deep space.

There seemed to be no formalities connected with landing — a matter which surprised Joe, who had become accustomed to elaborate checking and rechecking, indexes, reserve numbers, inspections, quarantine, passes, visas, reviews, signatures and countersignatures. The *Belsaurion* nosed up to a vacant port, clamped itself to the seal with mesonic glue-fields and so came to rest.

The hypnots in the hold lay undisturbed.

The Beland captain once again called a meeting of the passengers.

"We are now at Junction, and will remain thirty-two hours while we take on mail and freight. Now some of you have been here before. I need not caution you to discretion.

"For those who visit Junction for the first time I will state that it lies in no planet's jurisdiction, that its law is at the whim of the owner and his comptroller, that their main interest is in extracting money from your pockets through pleasures and pastimes of various natures.

"Thus I urge you, beware of the gambling cages. I say to you women — do not enter the Perfume Park alone for that is a signal that you wish a paid escort. The men who patronize Tier Three will find it expensive and perhaps dangerous. There have been cases of murder for robbery reported. A man engrossed with a girl is an easy target for a knife. Again films have been made of persons engaged in questionable acts, and these have been used for blackmail.

"Lastly let no desire for excitement or thrill take you down to the Arena — because you may easily be forced into the ring and set to fighting an expert warrior. Once you pay admission you put yourself at the choice of whoever is victor at the moment. It is astonishing how many casual visitors, whether under the influence of drugs, alcohol, lust for excitement or sheer bravado, dare the Arena. A good number of them are killed or seriously injured.

"Enough for the warnings. I do not wish to alarm you. There are a number of legitimate pleasures you may indulge in. The Nineteen Gardens are the talk of the Universe. In the Celestium you may dine on food of your planet, hear your native music. The shops along the Esplanade sell anything you may desire at very reasonable prices.

"So with this warning I put you on your own. Thirty-two hours from now we leave for Ballenkarch."

He withdrew. There was a general shuffling of feet. Joe noticed that Manaolo followed Elfane to her cabin. The two Druid missionaries returned to their portable altar, apparently with no intention of going ashore. The Mang officer, Erru Kametin, marched off with the young widow at his heels and after them went the two Mangs in civilian dress.

The gaunt bald old woman moved not an inch from her chair but sat staring across the floor. The Cils, giggling, stepping high, rushed from the ship. Hableyat stopped before Joe, plump arms clasped behind his back. "Well, my friend, are you going ashore?"

"Yes," said Joe. "I think I probably will. I'm waiting to see what the Priestess and Manaolo will do."

Hableyat teetered on his heels. "Steer clear of that chap is my best advice. He's a vicious example of megalomania — conditioned, I may add, to its most exquisite pitch by his environment. Manaolo considers himself divine and ordained — actually, literally — to a degree neither of us can imagine. Manaolo knows no right or wrong. He knows pro and con Manaolo."

The door to cabin 13 opened. Manaolo and Elfane stepped out on the balcony. Manaolo, in the lead, carried a small parcel. He wore a chased cuirass of gold and bright metal and a long green cloak, embroidered with yellow leaves, was flung back from his shoulders. Looking to neither right nor left he strode down the stairs, across the cabin, out the port.

Elfane halted on reaching the saloon deck, looked after him, shook her head — a motion eloquent of annoyance. She turned, crossed the saloon to Joe and Hableyat.

Hableyat made a respectful inclination of the head, which Elfane acknowledged coolly. She said to Joe, "I want you to conduct me ashore."

"Is that an invitation or an order?"

Elfane raised her eyebrows quizzically. "It means I want you to take me ashore."

"Very well," said Joe, rising to his feet. "I'll be glad to."

Hableyat sighed. "If only I were young and handsome —"

Joe snorted. "Handsome?"

"— no lovely young lady would need to ask me twice."

Elfane said in a tight voice, "I think it's only fair to mention that Manaolo promised to kill you if he finds you talking to me."

There was silence. Then Joe said in a voice that sounded strange in his own ears, "So the very first thing, you come over and ask me to take you ashore."

"Are you frightened?"

"I'm not brave."

She turned sharply, started for the port. Hableyat said curiously, "Why did you do that?"

Joe snorted angrily. "She's a trouble-maker. She has a ridiculous notion that I'll risk some crazy Druid shooting me down like a dog merely for the privilege of walking her around." He watched her leave the ship, slim as a birch in her dark blue cape. "She's right," said Joe. "I *am* just that kind of damn fool."

He started off after her on the run. Hableyat watched them go off together, smiled sadly, rubbed his hands together. Then unbuckling the robe from around his paunch, he sat back on the couch once again, dreamily followed the devotions of the two Druids at their altar.

Chapter VIII

THEY WERE WALKING DOWN a corridor lined with small shops. "Look," said Joe, "are you a Druid Priestess, about as likely to lop the life out of a commoner as not — or are you a nice kid out on a date?"

Elfane tossed her head, tried to look dignified and worldly. "I am a very important person and one day I will be the Suppliant for the entire Shire of Kelminester. A small shire, true, but the guidance of three million souls to the Tree will be in my hands."

Joe gave her a disgusted look. "Won't they do just as well without you?"

She laughed, relaxed for an instant to become a gay dark-haired girl. "Oh — probably. But I'm forced to keep up appearances."

"The trouble is that after a while you'll start believing all that stuff."

She said nothing for a moment. Then, mischievously, "Why are you looking about so attentively? Is this corridor so interesting then?"

"I'm watching for that devil Manaolo," said Joe. "It would be just like him to be lurking in one of these shadows and step out and stab me."

Elfane shook her head. "Manaolo has gone down to Tier Three. He has tried to make me his lover every night of the voyage but I have no desire for him. This morning he threatened that unless I yielded he would debauch himself along the Tier. I told him by all means to do so and then perhaps his virility would not be so ardently directed against me. He left in a huff."

"Manaolo always seems to be in a state of offended dignity."

"He is a man with a very exalted rank," said Elfane. "Now let us go down here. I wish to —"

Joe took her arm, swung her around, gazed into her startled eyes, her nose an inch from his.

"Look here, young lady. I'm not trying to assert my virility but I'm not trotting here and there after you, carrying your bundles like a chauffeur."

He knew it was the wrong word.

"Chauffeur, *ha!* Then —"

"If you don't like my company," said Joe, "now's the time to leave."

After a moment she said, "What's your name beside Smith?"

"Call me Joe."

"Joe — you're a very remarkable man. Very strange. You puzzle me, Joe."

"If you want to come with me — a chauffeur, a mechanic, a civil engineer, a moss-planter, a bar-tender, a tennis instructor, a freight docker, a dozen other things — we're going down to the Nineteen Gardens and see if they sell Earth-style beer."

The Nineteen Gardens occupied a slice through the middle of the construction — nineteen wedge-shaped sections surrounding a central platform which served as a restaurant.

They found a vacant table and, to Joe's surprise, beer in frosted quart beakers was set before them without comment.

"If it pleases your Divinity," said Elfane meekly.

Joe grinned sheepishly. "You don't need to carry it that far. It must be a Druid trait, an avalanche one way, another way, all the way. Well, what did you want?"

"Nothing." She turned in her seat, looked out across the gardens. At this point Joe realized that willy-nilly, for good or bad, he was wildly enamored. Margaret? He sighed. She was far away, a thousand light-years.

He looked across the gardens, nineteen of them, flora of nineteen different planets, each with its distinctive color timbres — black, gray and white of Kelce — oranges, yellows, hot lime green of Zarjus — the soft pastel pink, green, blue and yellow blossoms which grew on the quiet little planets of Jonapah — green in a hundred rich tones, gay red, sky blue — Joe started, half-rose to his feet.

"What's the matter?" asked Elfane.

"That garden there — those are Earth plants or I'm a ring-tailed monkey." He jumped up, went to the rail and she followed. "Geraniums, honeysuckle, petunias, zinnia, roses, Italian cypress, poplars, weeping willows. And a lawn. And hibiscus..." He looked at the descriptive plaque. "Planet Gea. Location uncertain."

They returned to the table. "You act as if you're homesick," said Elfane in an injured voice.

Joe smiled. "I am — very homesick. Tell me something about Ballenkarch."

She tasted the beer, looked at it in surprise, screwed up her face.

"Nobody likes beer when they first drink it," said Joe.

"Well — I don't know too much about Ballenkarch. Up to a few years ago it was completely savage. No ships stopped there because the autochthones were cannibals. Then the present prince united all of the smaller continent into a nation. It happened overnight. Many people were killed.

"But now there is no more murder and ships can land in comparative safety. The Prince has decided to industrialize and he's imported much machinery from Belan, Mangtse, and Grabo across the stream. Little by little he's extending his rule over the main continent — winning over the chiefs, hypnotizing them or killing them.

"Now you must understand the Ballenkarts have no religion whatever and we Druids hope to tie their new industrial power to us through the medium of a common faith. Then we will no longer depend on Mangtse for manufactured goods. The Mangs naturally don't care for the idea and so they are..." Her eyes widened. She reached across, grasped his arm. "Manaolo! Oh Joe, I hope he doesn't see us."

Joe's mantle of caution ripped. Humility is impossible when the object of your love is fearing for your safety.

He sat back in his seat, watched Manaolo come striding onto the terrace like a Demonland hero. A beige-skinned woman, wearing orange pantaloons, pointed slippers of blue cloth and a blue cloth cap, hung on his arm. In his other arm he carried the parcel he had taken off the ship. In the flicker of his dead eyes he saw Elfane and Joe, changed his course without expression, sauntered across the floor, casually drawing a stiletto from his belt.

"This is it," muttered Joe. "This is it!" He rose to his feet.

Diners, drinkers, scattered. Manaolo stopped a yard distant, the ghost of a smile on his dark face. He set the parcel on the table, then easily stepped forward, thrust. It was done with an almost naive simplicity as if he expected Joe to stand still to be stabbed. Joe threw the beer into his face, hit his wrist with the beaker and the stiletto tinkled to the ground.

"Now," said Joe, "I'm going to beat you within an inch of your life."

Manaolo lay on the ground. Joe, panting, straddled him. The bandage across his nose had broken. Blood flowed down his face, down his chin. Manaolo's hand fell on the stiletto. With a subdued grunt he swung. Joe gripped the arm, guided it past him into Manaolo's shoulder.

Manaolo grunted once more, plucked the blade loose. Joe seized it away, stuck it through Manaolo's ear into the wooden floor, pounded it deep with blows of his fist, jumped to his feet, stood looking down.

Manaolo flopped like a fish, lay still, exhausted. An impassive litter crew came through the crowd, removed the stiletto, loaded him on the litter, bore him away. The beige-skinned woman ran along beside him. Manaolo spoke to her. She turned, ran to the table, took the parcel, ran back to where the attendants were loading Manaolo into a wheeled vehicle, placed the parcel on his chest.

Joe sank back into his chair, took Elfane's beer, drank deeply.

"Joe," she whispered. "Are you — hurt?"

"I'm black and blue all over," said Joe. "Manaolo's a rough boy. If you hadn't been here I would have ducked him. But," he said with a blood-smeared grin, "I couldn't let you see me ducking my rival."

"Rival?" she looked puzzled. "Rival?"

"For you."

"Oh!" in a colorless tone.

"Now don't say 'I'm the Royal Druid God-almighty Priestess'!"

She looked up startled. "I wasn't thinking of that. I was thinking that Manaolo never was — your rival."

Joe said, "I've got to clean up and get some new clothes. Would you like to come with me or —"

"No," said Elfane, still in the colorless voice. "I'll stay here awhile. I want to — to think."

※

Thirty-one hours. The *Belsaurion* was due to take off. The passengers trickled back on board to be checked in by the purser.

Thirty-one and a half hours. "Where's Manaolo?" Elfane asked the purser. "Has he come aboard?"

"No, Worship."

Elfane chewed her lip, clenched her hands. "I'd better check at the hospital. You won't go off without me?"

"No, Worship, certainly not."

Joe followed her to a telephone. "Hospital," she said to the mechanical voice. Then, "I want to inquire about Ecclesiarch Manaolo, who was brought in yesterday. Has he been discharged?…Very well but hurry. His ship is waiting to take off…" She turned a side comment to Joe. "They've gone to check at his room."

A moment passed; then she bent to the ear-phone. "*What!* No!"

"What's the trouble?"

"He's dead. He's been murdered."

The captain agreed to hold the ship until Elfane returned from the hospital. She ran to the elevator with Joe at her heels. In the hospital she was led to a lank Beland nurse with white hair wound into a severe bun.

"Are you his wife?" asked the nurse. "If so will you please make the arrangements for the body."

"I'm not his wife. I don't care what you do with the body. Tell me, what became of the parcel he brought in here with him?"

"There's no parcel in his room. I remember he brought one in with him — but it's not there now."

Joe asked, "What visitors did he have?"

"I'm not sure. I could find out, I suppose."

Manaolo's last visitors were three Mangs, who had signed unfamiliar names to the register. The corridor attendant had noticed that one of them, an elderly man with a rigid military posture, had emerged from the room carrying a parcel.

Elfane leaned against Joe's shoulder. "That was the pot with the plant in it." He put his arms around her, patted her dark head. "And now the Mangs have it," she said hopelessly.

"Excuse me if I'm excessively curious," said Joe. "But what is there in that pot which makes it so important?"

She looked at him tearfully, finally said, "The second most important living thing in the universe. The only living shoot from the Tree of Life."

They slowly returned along the blue-tiled corridor toward the ship. Joe said, "I'm not only curious but I'm stupid as well. Why bother to carry a shoot from the Tree of Life all over creation? Unless, of course —"

She nodded. "As I told you we wished to form a bond with the Ballenkarts — a religious bond. This shoot, the Son of the Tree, would be the vital symbol."

"Then," said Joe, "the Druids would gradually infiltrate, gradually dominate, until Ballenkarch was another Kyril. Five billion miserable serfs, a million or two high-living Druids, one Tree." He examined her critically. "Aren't there any on Kyril who consider the system — well, unbalanced?"

She burnt him with an indignant look. "You're a complete Materialist. On Kyril Materialism is an offense punishable by death."

" 'Materialism' meaning 'distribution of the profits'," suggested Joe, "Or maybe 'incitement to rebellion'."

"Life is a threshold to glory," said Elfane. "Life is the effort which determines one's place on the Tree. The industrious workers become leaves high in the Scintillance. The sluggard must grope forever through dark slime as a rootlet."

"If Materialism is the sin you seem to believe it is — why do the Druids eat so high off the hog? Which means, live in such pampered luxury? Doesn't it seem strange to you that those who stand to lose the most by 'Materialism' are those most opposed to it?"

"Who are you to criticize?" she cried angrily. "A barbarian as savage as the Ballenkarts! If you were on Kyril your wild talk would quickly be shut off!"

"Still the tin goddess, aren't you?" said Joe contemptuously.

In outraged silence she stalked ahead. Joe grinned to himself, followed her back to the ship.

The lock into the ship opened. Elfane stopped short. "The Son is lost — probably destroyed." She looked sidewise at Joe. "There is no reason why I should continue to Ballenkarch. My duty is to return home, report to the College of Thearchs."

Joe rubbed his chin ruefully. He had been hoping that this aspect to the matter would not occur to her. He said tentatively, not quite sure how much anger she felt toward him, "But you left Kyril with Manaolo to escape the life of the palace. The Thearchs will learn every detail of Manaolo's death through their spies."

She inspected him with an expression unreadable to his Earthly perceptions. "You want me to continue with you?"

"Yes, I do."

"Why?"

"I'm afraid," said Joe with a sad droop to his mouth, "that you affect me very intensely, very pleasantly. This in spite of your warped philosophy."

"That was the right answer," announced Elfane. "Very well, I will continue. Perhaps," she said importantly, "perhaps I'll be able to persuade the Ballenkarts to worship the Tree on Kyril."

Joe held his breath for fear of laughing and so offending her once more. She looked at him somberly. "I realize you find me amusing."

Hableyat stood by the purser's desk. "Ah—back, I see. And Manaolo's assassins have escaped with the Son of the Tree?"

Elfane froze in her tracks. "How did you know?"

"My dear Priestess," said Hableyat, "the smallest pebble dropped in the pond sends its ripple to the far shore. Indeed, I see that I am perhaps even closer to the true state of affairs than you are."

"What do you mean by that?"

The port clanged, the steward politely said, "We take off in ten minutes. Priestess, my Lords, may I web you into your berths against the climb into speed?"

Chapter IX

JOE AWOKE FROM HIS TRANCE. Remembering the last awakening he jerked up in his web, searched the cabin. But he was alone and the door was locked, bolted, barred as he had arranged it before taking the pill and turning hypnotic patterns on the screen.

Joe jumped out of the hammock, bathed, shaved, climbed into the new suit of blue gabardine he had bought at Junction. Stepping out on the balcony, he found the saloon almost dark. Evidently he had awakened early.

He stopped by the door to Cabin 13, thought of Elfane lying warm and limp within, her dark hair tumbled on the pillow, her face, smoothed of doubts and prideful mannerisms. He put his hand to the door. It was as if something dragged it there. By an effort of will he pulled the arm back, turned, moved along the balcony. He stopped short. Someone sat in the big lounge by the observation port. Joe leaned forward, squinted into the gloom. Hableyat.

Joe continued along the balcony, down the steps. Hableyat made a courtly gesture of greeting. "Sit down, my friend, and join me in my pre-prandial contemplations."

Joe took a seat. "You awoke early."

"To the contrary," said Hableyat. "I did not submit to slumber. I have been sitting here in this lounge six hours and you are the first person I have seen."

"Whom were you expecting?"

Hableyat allowed a wise expression to form on his yellow face. "I expected no one *in particular*. But from a few adroit questions and interviews at the Junction I find that people are not all they seem. I was curious to observe any activity in the light of this new knowledge."

Joe said with a sigh, "After all, it's none of *my* business."

Hableyat waggled his plump forefinger. "No no, my friend. You are modest. You dissemble. I fear that you have become very much engrossed in the fortunes of the lovely young Priestess and so cannot be considered dispassionate."

"Put it this way. I don't care whether or not the Druids get their plant life to Ballenkarch. And I don't quite understand why you are so cooperative toward their efforts." He glanced at Hableyat appraisingly. "If I were the Druids I'd reconsider the whole idea."

"Ah, my dear fellow," beamed Hableyat, "you compliment me. But I work in the dark. I grope. There are subtleties I have not yet fathomed. It would surprise you to learn the duplicity of some of our acquaintances."

"Well, I'm willing to be surprised."

"For instance — that bald old woman in the black dress, who sits and stares into space like one already dead, what do you think of her?"

"Oh — harmless unprepossessing old buzzard."

"She is four hundred and twelve years old. Her husband, according to my informant, evolved an elixir of life when she was fourteen. She murdered him and only twenty years ago did she lose the freshness of her youth. During this time she has had lovers numbered by the thousands, of all shapes, sizes, sexes, races, bloods and colors. For the last hundred years her diet has consisted almost entirely of human blood."

Joe sank into the seat, rubbed his face. "Go on."

"I learn that one of my countrymen is a great deal higher in rank and authority than I had assumed, and that I must tread warily indeed. I find that the Prince of Ballenkarch has an agent aboard the ship."

"Continue," said Joe.

"I learned also — as perhaps I hinted before the take-off from Junction — that Manaolo's death and the loss of his flowerpot was perhaps not an unrelieved tragedy from the Druid standpoint."

"How so?"

Hableyat looked thoughtfully up along the balcony. "Has it ever occurred to you," he asked slowly, "that Manaolo was an odd choice for courier on a mission of such importance?"

Joe frowned. "I rather imagined that he fell into the commission

— 61 —

through his rank — which, according to Elfane, is — was — rather exalted. An Ecclesiarch, right under a Thearch."

"But the Druids are not completely inflexible and stupid," said Hableyat patiently. "They have managed to control five billion men and women with nothing more than a monstrous tree for almost a thousand years. They are not dolts.

"The College of Thearchs no doubt knew Manaolo for what he was — a swaggering egocentric. They decided that he would make the ideal stalking-horse. I, not understanding the intricacy of the plan, decided that Manaolo in turn needed a decoy to divert attention from him. For this purpose I selected you.

"But the Druids had foreseen the difficulty in the mission, and had made arrangements. Manaolo was sent out with a spurious seedling with exactly the right degree of ostentatious stealth. The real Son of the Tree was conveyed in another manner."

"And this other manner?"

Hableyat shrugged. "I can only theorize. Perhaps the Priestess has it cunningly concealed about her person. Perhaps the shoot has been entrusted to the baggage car — though this I doubt through fear of our spies. I imagine the shoot is in the custody of some representative of Kyril... Perhaps on this ship, perhaps on another."

"And so?"

"And so I sit here and watch to see if anyone shares my suspicion. So far you are the first to appear."

Joe smiled faintly. "And what conclusions do you draw?"

"None."

The white-haired steward appeared, his legs and arms thin and peculiarly graceful in the skin-tight cloth. Cloth? Joe, for the first time, looked closely. The steward asked, "Will you gentlemen take breakfast?"

Hableyat nodded. "I will."

Joe said, "I'll have some fruit." Then emboldened by his discovery of beer at Junction, "I don't suppose you have coffee."

"I think we can find some, Lord Smith."

Joe turned to Hableyat. "They don't wear many clothes. That's *paint* on them!"

Hableyat appeared to be amused. "Of course. Haven't you always known that the Belands wore more paint than clothes?"

"No," said Joe. "Clothes I've always taken for granted."

"That's a grave mistake," said Hableyat pompously. "When you're dealing with any creature or manifestation or personality on a strange planet — *never take anything for granted!* When I was young I visited the world Xenchoy on the Kim and there I made the mistake of seducing one of the native girls. A delicious creature with vines plaited into her hair. I remember that she submitted readily but without enthusiasm.

"In my most helpless moment she attempted to stab me with a long knife. I protested and she was dumbfounded. Subsequently I found that on Xenchoy only a person intending suicide will possess a girl out of wedlock and since there is no onus either on suicide or impudicity he so achieves humanity's dream, of dying in ecstasy."

"And the moral?"

"It is certainly clear. Things are not always what they seem."

Joe relaxed into the couch, musing, while Hableyat hummed a four-toned Mang fugue under his breath, accompanying himself on six tablets hanging around his neck like a pendant, each of which vibrated to a different note when touched.

Joe thought, *It's evident he either knows or suspects something which is plain as my face and I can't see it. Hableyat once said I have a limited intellect, maybe he's right. He's certainly given me enough hints. Elfane? Hableyat himself? No, he was talking about the Son of the Tree. A tremendous lot of excitement for a vegetable. Hableyat thinks it's still aboard, that's clear. Well, I haven't got it. He doesn't have it or he wouldn't talk so much. Elfane is in the dark. The Cils? The horrible old woman? The Mangs? The two Druid missionaries?*

Hableyat was observing him closely. As Joe sat up with a jerk Hableyat smiled. "Now do you understand?"

Joe said, "It seems reasonable."

The rating of passengers once more sat in the saloon but there was a different atmosphere now. The first leg of the voyage had suffered from tenseness but it had been a loose unpleasantness, a matter of personal likes and dislikes, dominated perhaps by the personality of Manaolo.

Now the individual relationships seemed submerged in more sweeping racial hatreds. Erru Kametin, the two Mang civilians — proctors of the Redbranch policy committee, so Joe learned from Hableyat — and the young Mang widow sat by the hour, playing their game with the colored bars, darting hot glances across the room at the imperturbable Hableyat.

The two Druid missionaries huddled over their altar in a dark corner of the saloon, busy with interminable rites before the representation of the Tree. The Cils, injured by the lack of response to their silken gambolings, kept to the promenade. The black-gowned woman sat still as death, her eyes moving an eighth of an inch from time to time. Perhaps once an hour she lifted a transparent hand up to her glass-bald pate.

Joe found himself buffeted by psychological cross-currents, like a pond thrashed by winds from every direction at once. First there was his own mission to Ballenkarch. Strange, thought Joe — only days, hours, to Ballenkarch and now his errand seemed drained of all urgency. He had only a given limited amount of emotion, of will, of power, and he seemed to have invested a large part of it in Elfane. Invested? It had been torn out of him, squeezed, wrenched.

Joe thought of Kyril, of the Tree. The palaces at Divinal clustered around the sub-planetary bulk of the trunk, the endless reaches of meager farms and ill-smelling villages, the slack-shouldered dead-eyed pilgrimage into the trunk, with the last triumphant gesture, the backward look off over the flat gray landscape.

He thought of Druid discipline — death. Though death was nothing to be feared on Kyril. Death was as common as eating. The Druid solution to any quandary — the avalanche — the all-the-way approach to existence. Moderation was a word with little meaning to men and women with no curb to any whim, indulgence or excess.

He considered what he knew of Mangtse — a small world of lakes and landscaped islands, a people with a love of intricate convolution, with an architecture of fanciful curves, looping wooden bridges over the streams and canals, charming picturesque vistas in the antique yellow light of the dim little sun.

Then the factories — neat, efficient, systematic, on the industrial islands. And the Mangs — a people as ornate, involute and subtle as their carved bridges. There was Hableyat, into whose soul Joe had seen for never an instant. There were the fire-breathing Redbranches bent on imperialism. In Earth terms — medievalists.

And Ballenkarch? Nothing except that it was a barbaric world with a prince intent on bringing an industrial complex into existence over-night. And somewhere on the planet, among the savages of the south or the barbarians of the north, was Harry Creath.

Harry had captured Margaret's imagination and taken light-hearted leave, leaving behind an emotional turmoil which could not be settled till Harry returned. Two years ago Harry had been only hours away on Mars. But when Joe arrived to bring him back to Earth for a showdown, Harry had left. Fuming at the delay, but tenacious and full of his obses-sion, Joe had persisted.

On Thuban he had lost the trail when a drunk's cutlass sent him to the hospital for three months. Then further months of agonized search and inquiry and at last the name of an obscure planet came to the surface — Ballenkarch. Then further months of working his way across the intervening galaxy. Now Ballenkarch lay ahead and somewhere on the planet was Harry Creath.

And Joe thought, *To hell with Harry!* Because Margaret was no longer at the focus of his mind. Now it was an unprincipled minx of a Priestess. Joe pictured himself and Elfane exploring Earth's ancient playgrounds — Paris, Vienna, San Francisco, the Vale of Kashmir, the Black Forest, the Sahara Sea.

Then he asked himself, would Elfane *fit?* There were no dazed drudges on Earth to be killed or beaten or pampered like animals. Maybe there was Hableyat's meaning — *Things are not always what they seem.* Elfane appeared — fundamentally — a creature of his own gen-eral pattern. Perhaps he had never quite understood the profundity of Druid egotism. Very well then, he'd find out.

Hableyat looked up blandly as Joe got to his feet. "If I were you, my friend, I think I would wait. At least another day. I doubt if as yet she has completely appreciated her own loneliness. I think that your appearance now, especially with that belligerent scowl on your face, would merely arouse her antagonism and she would class you with the rest of her enemies. Let her stew a day or so longer and then let her come upon you in the promenade — or the gymnasium, where I observe she spends an hour every day."

Joe sank back on the couch. He said, "Hableyat, you mystify me."

Hableyat shook his head sadly. "Ah, but I am transparent."

"First, on Kyril, you save my life. Then you try to get me killed."

"Only as a disagreeable necessity."

"At times I think you're friendly, sympathetic —"

"But of course!"

"— just as now you read my mind and give me fatherly advice. But — I'm never quite sure just what you're saving me for. Just as the goose being fattened for *pâté de foie gras* never understands the unstinting generosity of his master. Things aren't always what they seem." He laughed shortly. "I don't suppose you'll tell me what slaughter you're fattening me for?"

Hableyat performed a gesture of polite confusion. "Actually I am not at all devious. I make no pretenses, screen myself with nothing but honesty. My regard for you is genuine — but, I agree, that regard does not prevent me from sacrificing you for a greater end. There is no contradiction. I separate my personal tastes and aversions from my work. And so you know all about me."

"How do I know when you're working and when you're not?"

Hableyat threw out his hands. "It is a question not even I can answer."

But Joe was not entirely dissatisfied. He sat back in the couch and Hableyat relaxed the band around his plump midriff.

"Life is very difficult at times," said Hableyat, "and very improbable, very taxing."

"Hableyat," said Joe, "why don't you come back with me to Earth?"

Hableyat smiled. "I may well heed your suggestion — if the Redbranches defeat the Bluewaters in the Ampianu."

Chapter X

FOUR DAYS OUT from Junction, three days to Ballenkarch. Joe, leaning at the rail in the belly of the ship's promenade, heard a slow step along the composition. It was Elfane. Her face was pale and haunted, her eyes were large and bright. She stopped hesitantly beside Joe as if she were only pausing in her walk.

Joe said, "Hello," and looked back to the stars.

By some subtlety of pose Elfane gave him to understand that she had definitely stopped, that she had joined him. She said, "You've been avoiding me — when I need someone to talk to the most."

Joe said searchingly, "Elfane — have you ever been in love?"

Her face was puzzled. "I don't understand."

Joe grunted. "Just an Earth abstraction. Whom do you mate with on Kyril?"

"Oh — persons who interest us, whom we like to be with, who make us conscious of our bodies."

Joe turned back to the stars. "The subject is a little deep."

Her voice was amused and soft. "I understand very well, Joe."

He turned his head. She was smiling. Rich ripe lips, the passionate face, dark eyes holding an eagerness. He kissed her like a thirsty man drinking.

"Elfane...?"

"Yes?"

"On Ballenkarch — we'll turn around, head back for Earth. No more worry, no more plotting, no more death. There's so many places I want to show you — old places, old Earth, that's still so fresh and sweet."

She moved in his arms. "There's my own world, Joe — and my responsibility."

Tensely Joe said, "On Earth you'll see it as it is — a vile muck, as degrading to the Druids as it is miserable to the slaves."

"Slaves? They serve the Tree of Life. We all serve the Tree of Life in our different ways."

"The Tree of Death!"

Elfane disengaged herself without heat. "Joe — it's something which I can't explain to you. We're bound to the Tree. We are its children. You don't understand the great truth. There is one universe, with the Tree at the hub, and the Druids and the Laity serve the Tree, at bay to pagan space.

"Someday it will be different. All men will serve the Tree. We'll be born from the soil, we'll serve and work and finally give our lives into the Tree and become a leaf in the eternal light, each to his place. Kyril will be the goal, the holy place of the galaxy."

Joe protested, "But you give this vegetable — an enormous vegetable but still a vegetable — you give this vegetable a higher place in your mind than you do humanity. On Earth we'd chop the thing up for stove wood. No, that's not true. We'd run a spiral runway around the thing, send excursion trips up and sell hot dogs and soda pop on the top. We'd use the thing, not let it hypnotize us by its bulk."

She had not heard him. "Joe — you can be my lover. And we'll live our life on Kyril and serve the Tree and kill its enemies..." She stopped short, stunned by Joe's expression.

"That's no good — for either of us. I'll go back to Earth. You stay out here, find another lover to kill your enemies for you. And we'll each be doing what we want. But the other won't be included."

She turned away, leaned on the rail, stared dismally out at the midship stars. Presently, "Were you ever in love with any other woman?"

"Nothing serious," lied Joe. And, after a moment, "And you — have you had other lovers?"

"Nothing serious..."

Joe looked at her sharply but there was no trace of humor on her face. He sighed. Earth was not Kyril.

She said, "After we land on Ballenkarch what will you do?"

"I don't know — I haven't made up my mind. Certainly nothing to do with Druids and Mangs, I know that much. Trees and empires can all explode together so far as I'm concerned. I have problems of my own…" His voice dwindled, died.

He saw himself meeting Harry Creath. On Mars, with his mind full of Margaret — on Io, Pluto, Altair, Vega, Giansar, Polaris, Thuban, even as recently as Jamivetta and Kyril — he had been conscious of nothing quixotic, nothing ridiculous in his voyaging.

Now Margaret's image had begun to blur — but blurred as it was he heard the tinkling chime of her laugh. With a sudden flush of embarrassment he knew that she would find a great deal of amusement in the tale of his venturings — as well as astonishment, incredulity and perhaps the faintest hint of scorn.

Elfane was regarding him curiously. He came back to the present. Strange, how solid and real she seemed in contrast to his thought-waifs. Elfane would find nothing amusing in a man roaming the universe for love of her. On the contrary she would be indignant if such were not the case.

"What will you do on Ballenkarch then?" she asked.

Joe rubbed his chin, stared out at the shifting stars. "I guess I'll look up Harry Creath."

"And where will you look for him?"

"I don't know. I'll try the civilized continent first."

"None of Ballenkarch is civilized."

"The least barbarian continent, then!" said Joe patiently. "If I know Harry, he'll be in the thick of things."

"And if he's dead?"

"Then I'll turn around and go home with my conscience clear."

Margaret would say, "Harry dead?" And he saw the pert lift of her round chin. "In that case he loses by default. Take me, my chivalrous lover, sweep me away in your white spaceboat."

He stole a glance at Elfane, became aware of a tart flowering incense she was wearing. Elfane was galvanic with life and thought and wonder. She took life and emotion seriously. Of course Margaret had a lighter touch, an easier laugh, was not intent on killing enemies of her religion. Religion? Joe laughed shortly. Margaret barely recognized the word.

"Why do you laugh?" Elfane asked suspiciously.

"I was thinking of an old friend," said Joe.

※

Ballenkarch! A world of fierce gray storms and bright sunlight. A world of blazing color and violent landscape — of rock palisades like walls across the sky — of forests, dim, tall, sequestered — of savannahs ankle-deep in the greenest of grass, coursed by slow mighty rivers. In the low latitudes jungles crowded and jostled, trod under the weaker growths, built up mile after mile of humus until at last the elevation so created acted as a brake on their vitality.

And among the mountain passes, through the forests, wandering across the plains, rolled the Ballenkart clans in caravans of brightly-painted wains. They were great bull-voiced men in armor of steel and leather, wasting their blood in vendetta and duel.

They lived in an atmosphere of epic — of raids, massacres, fights with tall black jungle bipeds, fearsome and semi-intelligent. For weapons they used swords, lances, a portable arbalest which flung fist-size stones. Their language, divorced from the current of galactic civilization a thousand years, was a barely understandable pidgin and they wrote in pictographs.

The *Belsaurion* set down on a green plain drenched in sunlight. In the distance rain hung in veils from a black welter of clouds and a gorgeous rainbow arched over a forest of tall blue-green trees.

A rude pavilion of logs and corrugated metal served as depot and waiting room and when the *Belsaurion* finally shuddered to rest a little wagon with eight creaking wheels came chugging out across the grass, stopped alongside the ship.

Joe asked Hableyat, "Where is the city?"

Hableyat chuckled. "The Prince won't allow a ship any closer to his main settlements for fear of slavers. These burly Ballenkarts are much in demand on Frums and Perkins for bodyguards."

The port was opened to the outdoors. Fresh air, smelling of damp earth, swept into the ship. The steward announced to the saloon, "Passengers wishing to alight may do so. You are cautioned not to leave the vicinity of the ship until transportation has been arranged to Vail-Alan."

Joe looked around for Elfane. She was speaking vehemently to the two Druid missionaries and they listened with expressions of mulish obstinacy. Elfane became enraged, jerked away, marched white-faced to the port and outside. The Druids followed, muttering to each other.

Elfane approached the driver of the eight-wheeled vehicle. "I wish to be conveyed to Vail-Alan at once."

He looked at her without expression. Hableyat touched her elbow. "Priestess, an air-car shortly will arrive to convey us a great deal faster than this vehicle."

She turned, walked swiftly away. Hableyat leaned close to the driver, who whispered a few sentences. Hableyat's face changed in the slightest degree — a twitch of a muscle, a deepening of his jowl-crease. He saw Joe watching, instantly became businesslike and the driver was once more blank-faced.

Hableyat moved off by himself in a preoccupied manner. Joe joined him. "Well —" sardonically "— what's the news?"

Hableyat said, "Very bad — very bad indeed —"

"How so?"

Hableyat hesitated an instant, then blurted in as frank an exhibition of emotion as Joe had seen him express, "My opponents at home are much stronger with the Lathbon than I knew. Magnerru Ippolito himself is at Vail-Alan. He has reached the Prince and evidently has uttered some unsavory truths regarding the Druids. So now I learn that plans for a Druid cathedral and monastery have been abandoned and that Wanbrion, a Sub-Thearch, is guarded closely."

In exasperation Joe surveyed the portly Hableyat. "Well, isn't that what you want? Certainly a Druid advising the Prince wouldn't help the Mangs."

Hableyat shook his head sadly. "My friend, you are as easily gulled as my militant countrymen."

"I suppose I'm dense."

Hableyat held his hands out from his sides as if revealing all to Joe by the gesture. "It's so obvious."

"Sorry."

"In this manner — the Druids plan to assimilate Ballenkarch to themselves. My opponents on Mangtse, learning of this intent, rush forward to oppose it tooth and nail. They will not consider implications, probable eventualities. No, since it is a Druid scheme it must be countered. And with a program which, in my opinion, will seriously embarrass Mangtse."

"I see what you're driving at," said Joe, "but not how it works."

Hableyat faced him with an amused expression. "My dear fellow, human reverence is by no means infinite. I would say that the Kyril Laity lavish the maximum on their Tree. So — what will be the reaction to news of another divine Tree?"

Joe grinned. "It will cut their reverence toward the first tree in half."

"Naturally I am unable to estimate the diminution but in any event it will be considerable. Doubt, heresy, will find ears and the Druids will notice that the Laity is no longer unquestioning and innocent. They identify themselves now with the Tree. It is theirs, unique of its kind, solitary in the universe.

"Then — suddenly another Tree exists on Ballenkarch — planted by the Druids and there are rumors that its presence is politically motivated." He raised his eyebrows expressively.

"But the Druids, by controlling Ballenkarch and these new industries, can still wind up on the credit side."

Hableyat shook his head. "My friend, Mangtse is potentially the weakest world of the three. That's the crux of the entire matter. Kyril has its manpower, Ballenkarch has the mineral and agricultural wealth, an aggressive population, a warlike tradition. In any association of worlds Ballenkarch eventually will be the cannibal mate devouring his spouse.

"Think of the Druids — the epicures, the sophisticated masters of five billion slaves. Picture them trying to dominate Ballenkarch. It is laughable. In fifty years the Ballenkarts would be whipping the Thearchs from the gates of Divinal and burning the Tree for a victory bonfire.

"Consider the alternative — Ballenkarch tied to Mangtse. A period of tribulation, profit for none. And now the Druids will have no choice — they will have to buckle down and *work*. With the Ballenkart industries denied them they will of necessity bring new ways to Kyril — factories, industries, education. The old ways will go.

"The Druids might or might not lose the reins of power — but Kyril would remain an integrated industrial unit and there would go the natural market for Mang products. So you see, with the Kyril and Ballenkarch markets both removed our own Mang economy would dwindle, suffer. We would be forced to recover our markets by military action and we might lose."

"I understand all this," said Joe slowly, "but it gets nowhere. Just what do you want?"

"Ballenkarch is self-sufficient. At the moment neither Mangtse nor Kyril can exist alone. We form a natural couple. But as you see the Druids are dissatisfied with the influx of wealth. They demand more and they think to acquire it by controlling the Ballenkarch industries.

"I want to prevent this — and I also want to prevent a Mangtse–Ballenkarch understanding, which would be *prima facie* unnatural. I wish to see a new regime on Kyril, a government committed to improving the productive and purchasing power of the Laity, a government committed to the natural alliance with Mangtse."

"Too bad the three worlds can't form a common council."

Hableyat sighed. "That idea, while felicitous, flies in the face of three realities. First, the current policy of the Druids — second, the ascendancy of the Redbranch on Mangtse — and third, the ambitions of the Prince of Ballenkarch. Change all three of these realities and such a union might be consummated. I for one would approve it — why not?" he mused as if to himself and behind the bland yellow mask Joe glimpsed the face of a very tired man.

"What will happen to you now?"

Hableyat pursed his lips dolefully. "If my authority actually has been superseded I will be expected to kill myself. Don't look bewildered — it is a Mang custom, a method of underscoring disapproval. I fear I am not long for the world."

"Why not return to Mangtse and repair your political fences?"

Hableyat shook his head. "That is not our custom. You may smile but you forget that societies exist through general agreement as to certain symbols, necessities which must be obeyed."

"Here comes the air-car," said Joe. "If I were you, instead of committing suicide, I'd try to work out some kind of scheme to get the Prince on your side. He seems to be the key. They're both after him, Druids and Mangs."

Hableyat shook his head. "Not the Prince. He's a queer man, a mixture of bandit, jester and visionary. He seems to regard this new Ballenkarch as an interesting game, a sportive recreation."

Chapter XI

THE AIR-CAR LANDED, a big-bellied transport in need of paint. Two large men in red knee-length breeches, loose blue jackets, black caps, swaggered from the air-car, wearing the placidly arrogant expressions of a military élite.

"Lord Prince sends his greetings," said the first to the Beland officer. "He understands that there are foreign agents among the passengers, so he will have all who land conveyed before him at once."

There was no further conversation. Into the car trooped Elfane and Hableyat, the two Druids clutching their portable altar, the Mangs, glaring yellow-eyed at Hableyat, and Joe. These were all for Ballenkarch — the Cils and the aged woman in the black gown would continue their journey to Castelgran, Cil or Belan and none were discharged from the hold.

Joe crossed the fuselage, dropped into a seat beside Elfane. She turned her head, showed him a face which seemed drained of its youth. "What do you want with me?"

"Nothing. Are you angry with me?"

"You're a Mang spy."

Joe laughed uneasily. "Oh — because I'm thick with Hableyat?"

"What did he send you to tell me now?"

The question took Joe aback. It opened up a vista for speculation. Could it be possible that Hableyat was using him as a means to convey ideas of Hableyat's choosing to the Druids through Elfane?

He said, "I don't know whether or not he wanted this to reach you. But he explained to me why he's been helping you bring your tree here and it sounds convincing to me."

"In the first place," said Elfane scathingly. "We have no more tree.

It was stolen from us at Junction." Her eyes widened and she looked at him with a sudden suspicion. "Was that your doing too? Is it possible that…"

Joe sighed. "You're determined to think the worst of me. Very well. If you weren't so damned beautiful and appealing I wouldn't think twice about you. But you're planning to bust in on the Prince with your two milk-faced Druids and you think you can wind him around your finger. Maybe you can. I know very well you'd stop at nothing. And now I'll get off my chest what Hableyat said and you can do what you like with the information."

He glared at her, challenging her to speak, but she tossed her head and stared hard out the window.

"He believes that if you succeed in this mission, then you and your Druids will wind up playing second fiddle to these tough Ballenkarts. If you don't succeed — well, the Mangs will probably figure out something unpleasant for you personally but the Druids — according to Hableyat — eventually will come out ahead."

"Go away," she said in a choked voice. "All you do is scare me. Go away."

"Elfane — forget all this Druid-Mang-Tree-of-Life stuff and I'll take you back to Earth. That is if I get off the planet alive."

She showed him the back of her head. The car buzzed, vibrated, rose into the air. The landscape dished out below them. Massive mountains shot and marbled with snow and ice, luxuriant meadowland with grass glowing the sharp bright color of prismatic green, spread below. They crossed the range. The car jerked, jolted in bumpy air, slanted down toward an inland sea.

A settlement, obviously raw and new, had grown up on the shore of this sea. Three heavy docks, a dozen large rectangular buildings — glass-sided, roofed with bright metal — formed the heart of the town. A mile beyond a promontory covered with trees overlooked the sea and in the shadow of this promontory the car grounded.

The door opened. One of the Ballenkarts motioned brusquely. "This way."

Joe followed Elfane to the ground and saw ahead a long low building with a glass front looking across the vista of sea and plain. The

Ballenkart corporal made another peremptory motion. "To the Residence," he said curtly.

Resentfully Joe started for the building, thinking that these soldiers made poor emissaries of good will. His nerves tautened as he walked. The atmosphere was hardly one of welcome. The tension, he noticed, gripped everyone. Elfane moved as if her legs were rigid. Erru Kametin's jaw shone bright yellow along the bone line.

At the rear Joe noticed Hableyat speaking urgently with the two Druid missionaries. They seemed reluctant. Hableyat raised his voice. Joe heard him say, "What's the difference? This way you at least have a chance, whether you distrust my motives or not." The Druids at last appeared to acquiesce. Hableyat marched briskly ahead and said in a loud voice, "Halt! This impudence must not go on!"

The two Ballenkarts swung around in amazement. With a stern face Hableyat said, "Go, get your master. We will suffer this indignity no longer."

The Ballenkarts blinked, slightly crestfallen to find their authority questioned. Erru Kametin, eyes snapping, said, "What are you saying, Hableyat? Are you trying to compromise us in the eyes of the Prince?"

Hableyat said, "He must learn that we Mangs prize our dignities. We will not stir from this ground until he advances to greet us in the manner of a courteous host."

Erru Kametin laughed scornfully. "Stay then." He flung his scarlet cloak about him, turned, proceeded toward the Residence. The Ballenkarts conferred and one accompanied the Mangs. The other eyed Hableyat with truculent eyes. "Wait until the Prince hears of this!"

The rest had rounded a corner. Hableyat leisurely drew his hand from his cloak, discharged a tube at the guard. The guard's eyes became milky, he tumbled to the ground.

"He's merely stunned," said Hableyat to Joe, who had turned protestingly. To the Druids, "Hurry."

Lifting their robes they ran to a nearby bank of soft dirt. One dug a hole with a stick, the other opened the altar, tenderly lifted out the miniature Tree. A small pot surrounded its roots.

Joe heard Elfane gasp. "You two —"

"Silence," rapped Hableyat. "Attend your own concerns if you are wise. These are Arch-Thearchs, both of them."

"Manaolo — a dupe!"

Into the hole went the roots. Soil was patted firm. The Druids closed the altar, dusted off their hands, and once more became empty-faced monks. And the Son of the Tree stood firm in the ground of Ballenkarch, bathing in the hot yellow light. Unless one looked closely, it was merely another young shrub.

"Now," said Hableyat placidly, "we continue to the Residence."

Elfane glared at Hableyat and the Druids, her eyes flaming with rage and humiliation. "All this time you've been laughing at me!"

"No, no, Priestess," said Hableyat. "Calmness, I implore you. You'll need all your wits when you face the Prince. Believe me, you served a very useful function."

Elfane turned blindly as if to run off toward the sea but Joe caught hold of her. For a moment she stared into his eyes, her muscles like wire. Then she relaxed, grew limp. "Very well, I'll go in."

They continued, meeting halfway a squad of six soldiers evidently sent out to escort them in. No one heeded the numb form of the guard.

At the portal they were subjected to a search, quick but so detailed and thorough as to evoke angry protests from the Druids and an outraged yelp from Elfane. The arsenal so discovered was surprising — hand-conics from each of the Druids, Hableyat's stun-tube and a collapsible dagger, Joe's gun, a little polished tube Elfane carried in her sleeve.

The corporal stood back, gestured. "You are permitted to enter the Residence. See that you observe the accepted forms of respect."

Passing through an antechamber painted with grotesque half-demoniac animals they entered a large hall. The ceiling beams were great timbers, hand-hewn and notched into a formalized pattern, the walls were surfaced with woven rattan. At either side banks of green and red plants lined the wall and the floor was covered by a soft rug of fiber woven and dyed in a striking pattern of scarlet, black and green.

Opposite the entrance was a dais, flanked by two heavy balustrades of rust-red wood, and a wide throne-like seat of the same russet wood. At the moment the throne was empty.

Twenty or thirty men stood about the room — large, suntanned, some with bristling mustaches — awkward and ill at ease as if unused to a roof over their heads. All wore red knee-length breeches. Some wore blouses of various colors while others were bare-chested with capes of black fur slung back from their shoulders. All bore short heavy sabers in their belts and all eyed the newcomers without friendliness.

Joe looked from face to face. Harry Creath would not be far from Vail-Alan, the center of activity. But he was not in the hall.

Beside the dais in a group stood the Redbranch Mangs. Erru Kametin spoke in a harsh staccato to the woman. The two proctors listened silently, half-turned away.

A house-marshal with a long brass clarion stepped into the room, blew a brilliant fanfare. Joe smiled faintly. Like a musical comedy — warriors in bright uniforms, pageantry, pomp, punctilio...

The fanfare again — *tantara-tantivy* — shrill, exciting.

"The Prince of Vail-Alan! Ruler Preemptor across the face of Ballenkarch!"

A blond man, slight beside the Ballenkarts, stepped briskly up on the dais, seated himself on the throne. He had a round bony face with lines of humor around his mouth, nervous twitching hands, an air of gay intelligence, reckless impatience. From the crowd came a hoarse *"Aaaaah"* of reverence.

Joe nodded slowly without surprise. Who else?

Harry Creath flicked his eyes around the room. They rested on Joe, passed, swung back. For a minute he stared in amazement.

"Joe Smith! What in Heaven's name are you doing out here?"

This was the moment he had come a thousand light years for. And now Joe's mind refused to function correctly. He stuttered the words he had rehearsed for two years, through toil, danger, boredom — the words which expressed the two-year obsession — "I came out to get you."

He had said them, he was vindicated. The compulsion which was almost auto-suggestion had been allayed. But the words had been spoken and Harry's mobile face expressed astonishment. "Out here? All the way — to get me?"

"That's right."

"Get me to do what?" Harry leaned back and his wide mouth broke into a grin.

"Well — you left some unfinished business on Earth."

"None that I know of. You'd have to talk long and fast to get me in motion." He turned to a tall guard with a face like a rock. "Have these people been searched for weapons?"

"Yes, Prince."

Harry turned back to Joe with a grimace of jocular apology. "There's too many people interested in me. I can't ignore the obvious risks. Now, you were saying — you want me to go back to Earth. Why?"

Why? Joe asked himself the question. *Why?* Because Margaret thought herself in love with Harry and Joe thought she was in love with a dream. Because Joe thought that if Margaret could know Harry for a month, rather than for two days, if she could see him in day-to-day living, if she could recognize that love was not a series of lifts and thrills like a roller-coaster ride — that marriage was not a breathless round of escapades.

In short, if Margaret's pretty frivolous head could be rattled loose from its nonsense — then there would be room in it for Joe. Was that it? It had seemed easy, flying out to Mars for Harry only to find Harry had departed for Io. And from Io to Pluto, the Jumping-off Place. And then the compulsion began to take hold, the doggedness. Out from Pluto, on and on and on. Then Kyril, then Junction, now Ballenkarch.

Joe blushed, intensely aware of Elfane at his back, watching him with bright-eyed speculation. He opened his mouth to speak, closed it again. *Why?*

Eyes were on him, eyes from all over the room. Curious eyes, cold uninterested eyes, hostile eyes, searching eyes — Hableyat's placid, Elfane's probing, Harry Creath's mocking eyes. And into Joe's confused mind one hard fact emerged — he would be displaying himself as the most consummate ass in the history of the universe if he told the truth.

"Something to do with Margaret?" asked Harry mercilessly. "She send you out here?"

Joe saw Margaret as if in a vision, inspecting the two of them derisively. His eyes swung to Elfane. A hellion, obstinate, intolerant, too intense and full of life for her own good. But sincere and decent.

"Margaret?" Joe laughed. "No. Nothing to do with Margaret. In fact I've changed my mind. Keep to hell away from Earth."

Harry relaxed slightly. "If it had to do with Margaret — why, you're rather outdated." He craned his neck. "Where the devil is she? *Margaret!*"

"Margaret?" muttered Joe.

She stepped up on the dais beside Harry. "Hello, Joe —" as if she'd taken leave of him yesterday afternoon "— what a nice surprise."

She was laughing inside, very quietly. Joe grinned also, grimly. Very well, he'd take his medicine. He met their eyes, said, "Congratulations." It occurred to him that Margaret was in sheer fact living the life she claimed she wanted to lead — excitement, intrigue, adventure. And it seemed to agree with her.

Chapter XII

HARRY HAD BEEN SPEAKING to him. Joe suddenly became aware of his voice. "— You see, Joe, this is a wonderful thing we're doing out here, a wonderful world. It's busting open with high-grade ore, timber, organic produce, manpower. I've got a picture in my mind, Joe — Utopia.

"There's a good bunch of lads behind me, and we're working together. They're a little rough yet but they see this world the way I see it and they're willing to take a chance on me. To begin with, of course, I had to knock a few heads together but they know who's boss now and we're getting on fine." Harry looked fondly over the crowd of Ballenkarts, any one of whom could have strangled him with one hand.

"In another twenty years," said Harry, "you won't believe your eyes. What we're going to do to the planet! It's marvelous, I tell you, Joe. Excuse me now, for a few minutes. There's affairs of state." He settled himself into his chair, looked from Mangs to Druids.

"We might as well talk it over now. I see it's all fresh and ripe in your minds. There's my old friend Hableyat." He winked at Joe. "Foxy Grandpa. What's the occasion, Hableyat?"

Hableyat strutted forward. "Your Excellency, I find myself in a peculiar position. I have not communicated with my home government and I am not sure as to the extent of my authority."

Harry said to a guard. "Find the Magnerru." To Hableyat, "Magnerru Ippolito is fresh from Mangtse and he claims to speak with the voice of your Ampianu General."

From an archway to the side a Mang approached — a sturdy square-faced Mang with the brightest of black eyes, a lemon-yellow skin, bright orange lips. He wore a scarlet robe embroidered with a border of purple and green squares, a cubical black hat.

Erru Kametin and the other Mangs of his party bowed deeply, saluting with outflung arms. Hableyat nodded respectfully, a fixed smile on his plump lips.

"Magnerru," said Prince Harry, "Hableyat wants to know the extent of his freedom to make policy."

"None," rasped the Magnerru. "None whatever. Hableyat and the Bluewaters have been discredited in the Ampianu, the Lathbon sits with the Redbranch. Hableyat speaks with no voice but his own and it will soon be stilled."

Harry nodded. "Then it will be wise to hear, before his demise, what his views are."

"My Lord," said Hableyat, his face still frozen in its jovial mask, "my words are trivial. I prefer to hear the enunciations of the Magnerru and of the two Arch-Thearchs we have with us. My Lord, I may state that the highest of Kyril face you — Arch-Thearchs Oporeto Implan and Gameanza. They will ably present their views."

"My modest residence is thick with celebrities," said Harry.

Gameanza stepped forward with a glittering glance for the Magnerru. "Prince Harry, I consider the present atmosphere unsuited to discussion of policy. Whenever the Prince desires — the sooner the better — I will communicate to him the trend of Druid policy together with my views in regard to the political and ethical situation."

The Magnerru said, "Talk to the dry-mouthed slug. Listen to his efforts to fix the slave system on Ballenkarch. Then send him back to his fetid gray world in the hold of a cattle ship."

Gameanza stiffened. His skin seemed to become brittle. He said to Harry in a sharp brassy voice, "I am at your pleasure."

Harry rose to his feet. "Very well, we'll retire for half an hour and discuss your proposals." He raised a hand to the Magnerru. "You'll have the same privilege, so be patient. Talk over old times with Hableyat. I understand he formerly occupied your position."

Arch-Thearch Gameanza followed him as he jumped from the dais and left the hall and after moved the Arch-Thearch Oporeto Implan. Margaret waved a casual hand to Joe. "See you later." She slipped away through another door.

Joe found a bench to the side of the room, wearily seated himself.

Before him like a posed tableau stood the rigid Mangs, the exquisite wisp of flesh that was Elfane, Hableyat — suddenly gone vague and helpless — the Ballenkarts in their gorgeous costumes, troubled, confused, unused to the bickering of sharp wits, glancing uneasily at each other over heavy shoulders, muttering.

Elfane turned her head, gazed around the room. She saw Joe, hesitated, then crossed the floor, seated herself beside him. After a moment she said haughtily, "You're laughing at me — mocking me."

"I wasn't aware of it."

"You've found the man you were seeking," she said with eyebrows arched. "Why don't you do something?"

Joe shrugged. "I've changed my mind."

"Because that yellow-haired woman — Margaret — is here?"

"Partly."

"You never mentioned her to me."

"I had no idea you'd be interested."

Elfane looked stonily across the audience hall. Joe said, "Do you know why I changed my mind?"

She shook her head. "No. I don't."

"It's because of you."

Elfane turned back with glowing eyes. "So it *was* the blonde woman who brought you out here."

Joe sighed. "Every man can be a damn fool once in his life. At *least* once..."

She was not appeased. "Now, I suppose, if I sent you to look for someone you wouldn't go? That she meant more to you than I do?"

Joe groaned. "Oh Lord! In the first place you've never given me any reason to think that you — oh, hell!"

"I offered to let you be my lover."

Joe eyed her with exasperation. "I'd like to..." He recalled that Kyril was not Earth, that Elfane was a Priestess, not a college girl.

Elfane laughed. "I understand you very well, Joe. On Earth men are accustomed to having their own way and the women are auxiliary inhabitants. And don't forget, Joe, you've never told *me* anything — that you loved me."

Joe growled, "I've been afraid to."

"Try me."

Joe tried and the happy knowledge came to him that, in spite of a thousand light-years and two extremes of culture, girls were girls. Priestesses or co-eds.

Harry and the Arch-Druid Gameanza returned to the room and a set expression hung like a frame on the Druid's white face. Harry said to the Magnerru, "Perhaps you will be good enough to exchange a few words with me?"

The Magnerru clapped his hands in repressed anger against his robe, followed Harry into the inner chambers. Evidently the informal approach found no responsive chord in him.

Hableyat settled beside Joe. Elfane looked stonily to one side. Hableyat wore a worried expression. His yellow jowls hung flaccid, the eyelids drooped over his eyes.

Joe said, "Cheer up, Hableyat, you're not dead yet."

Hableyat shook his head. "The schemes of my entire life are toppling into fragments."

Joe looked at him sharply. Was the gloom exaggerated, the sighs over-doleful? He said guardedly, "I have yet to learn your positive program."

Hableyat shrugged. "I am a patriot. I wish to see my planet prosperous, waxing in wealth. I am a man imbued with the culture of my world; I can conceive of no better way of life, and I wish to see this culture expand, enriching itself with the cultures of other worlds, adapting the good, overcoming the bad."

"In other words," said Joe. "You're as strenuous an imperialist as your military friends. Only your methods are different."

"I'm afraid you have defined me," sighed Hableyat. "Furthermore I fear that in this era military imperialism is almost impossible — that cultural imperialism is the only practicable form. A planet cannot be successfully subjugated and occupied from another planet. It may be devastated, laid waste, but the logistics of conquest are practically insuperable. I fear that the adventures proposed by the Redbranch will exhaust Mang, ruin Ballenkarch and make the way easy for a Druid religious imperialism."

Joe felt Elfane stiffen. "Why is that worse than Mang cultural imperialism?"

"My dear Priestess," said Hableyat, "I could never argue cogently enough to convince you. I will say one word — that the Druids produce very little with a vast potentiality — that they live on the backs of a groaning mass — and that I hope the system is never extended to include me among the Laity."

"Me either," said Joe.

Elfane jumped to her feet. "You're both vile!"

Joe surprised himself by reaching, pulling her back beside him with a thud. She struggled a moment, then subsided.

"Lesson number one in Earth culture," said Joe cheerfully. "It's bad manners to argue religion."

A soldier burst into the chamber, panting, his face twisted in terror. "Horrible — out along the road...Where's the Prince? Get the Prince — a terrible growth!"

Hableyat jumped to his feet, his face sharp, alert. He ran nimbly out the door and after a second Joe said, "I'm going too."

Elfane, without a word, followed.

Joe had a flash impression of complete confusion. A milling mob of men circled an object he could not identify — a squat green-and-brown thing which seemed to writhe and heave.

Hableyat burst through the circle, with Joe at his side and Elfane pressing at Joe's back. Joe looked in wonder. The Son of the Tree?

It had grown, become complicated. No longer did it resemble the Kyril Tree. The Son had adapted itself to a new purpose — protection, growth, flexibility.

It reminded Joe of a tremendous dandelion. A white fuzzy ball held itself twenty feet above the ground on a slender swaying stalk, surrounded by an inverted cone of flat green fronds. At the base of each frond a green tendril, streaked and speckled with black, thrust itself out. Clasped in these tendrils were the bodies of three men.

Hableyat squawked, "The thing's a devil," and clapped his hand to his pouch. But his weapon had been impounded by the Residence guards.

A Ballenkarch chieftain, his face pale and distorted, charged the Son, hacking with his saber. The fuzzy ball swayed toward him a trifle, the tendrils jerked back like the legs of an insect, then snapped in from all sides, wrapped the man close, pierced his flesh. He bawled, fell silent, stiffened. The tendrils flushed red, pulsed, and the Son grew taller.

Four more Ballenkarts, acting in grim concert, charged the Son, six others followed. The tendrils thrust, snapped and ten bodies lay stiff and white on the ground. The Son expanded as if it were being magnified.

Prince Harry's light assured voice said, "Step aside... Now then, step aside."

Harry stood looking at the plant — twenty feet to the top of the fronds while the fuzzy white ball reared another ten above them.

The Son pounced, with a cunning quasi-intelligence. Tendrils unfurled, trapped a dozen roaring men, dragged them close. And now the crowd went wild, swayed back and forth in alternate spasms of rage and fear, at last charged in a screeching mêlée.

Sabres glittered, swung, chopped. Overhead the fuzzy white ball swung unhurriedly. It was sensate, it saw, felt, planned with a vegetable consciousness, calm, fearless, single-purposed. Its tendrils snaked, twisted, squeezed, returned to drain. And the Son of the Tree soared, swelled.

Panting survivors of the crowd fell back, staring helplessly at the corpse-strewn ground. Harry motioned to one of his personal guard. "Bring out a heat-gun."

The Arch-Thearchs came forward, protesting. "No, no, that is the Sacred Shoot, the Son of the Tree."

Harry paid them no heed. Gameanza clutched his arm with panicky insistence. "Recall your soldiers. Feed it nothing but criminals and slaves. In ten years it will be tremendous, a magnificent Tree."

Harry shook him off, jerked his head at a soldier. "Take this maniac away."

A projector on wheels was trundled from behind the Residence, halted fifty feet from the Son. Harry nodded. A thick white beam of energy spat against the Son. *"Aaah!"* sighed the crowd, in near-voluptuous gratification. The exultant sigh stopped short. The Son drank in the energy like sunshine, expanded, luxuriated, and grew. A hundred feet the fuzzy white ball towered.

"Turn it against the top," said Harry anxiously.

The bar of energy swung up the slender stalk, concentrated on the head of the plant. It coruscated, spattered, ducked away.

"It doesn't like it!" cried Harry. *"Pour it on!"*

The Arch-Thearchs, restrained in the rear, howled in near-personal anguish. *"No, no, no!"*

The white ball steadied, spat back a gout of energy. The projector exploded, blasting heads and arms and legs in every direction.

There was a sudden dead silence. Then the moans began. Then sudden screaming as the tendrils snapped forth to feed.

Joe dragged Elfane back and a tendril missed her by a foot. "But I am a Druid Priestess," she said in dull astonishment. "The Tree protects the Druids. The Tree accepts only the lay pilgrims."

"Pilgrims!" Joe remembered the Kyril pilgrims — tired, dusty, footsore, sick — entering the portal into the Tree. He remembered the pause at the portal, the one last look out across the gray land and up into the foliage before they turned and entered the trunk. Young and old, in all conditions, thousands every day...

Joe now had to crane his neck to see the top of the Son. The flexible central shoot was stiffening, the little white ball swung and twisted and peered over its new domain.

Harry came limping up beside Joe, his face a white mask. "Joe — that's the ungodliest creature I've seen on thirty-two planets."

"I've seen a bigger one — on Kyril. It eats the citizens by the thousand."

Harry said, "These people trust me. They think I'm some kind of god myself — merely because I know a little Earth engineering. I've got to kill that abomination."

"You're not throwing in with the Druids then?"

Harry sneered. "What kind of patsy do you take me for, Joe? I'm not throwing in with either one of 'em. A plague on both their houses. I've been holding 'em off, teasing 'em until I could get things straightened out. I'm still not satisfied — but I certainly didn't bargain for something like this. Who the hell brought the thing here?"

Joe was silent. Elfane said, "It was brought from Kyril by order of the Tree."

Harry stared. "My God, does the thing talk too?"

Elfane said vaguely, "The College of Thearchs reads the will of the Tree by various signs."

Joe scratched his chin.

"Hmph," said Harry. "Fancy decoration for a nice tight little tyranny. But that's not the problem. This thing's got to be killed!" And he muttered, "I'd like to get the main beast too, just for luck."

Joe heard — he looked at Elfane expecting to see her flare into anger. But she stood silent, looking at the Son.

Harry said, "It seems to thrive on energy...Heat's out. A bomb? Let's try blasting. I'll send down to the warehouse for some splat."

Gameanza tore himself loose, came running up with his gray robe flapping around his legs. "Excellency, we vehemently protest your aggressions against this Tree!"

"Sorry," said Harry, grinning sardonically. "I call it a murderous beast."

"Its presence is symbolic of the ties between Kyril and Ballenkarch," pleaded Gameanza.

"Symbolic my ankle. Clear that metaphysical rubbish out of your mind, man. That thing's a man-killer and I won't have it at large. I pity you for the king-size monster you've got on your own rock — although I suppose I shouldn't." He looked Gameanza up and down. "You've made pretty good use of the Tree. It's been your meal ticket for a thousand years. Well, this one is on its way out. In another ten minutes it'll be an acre of splinters."

Gameanza whirled on his heel, marched twenty feet away, where he conversed in low tones with Oporeto Implan. Ten pounds of explosive, packed with a detonator, was heaved against the Son's heavy trunk. Harry raised the radiation gun which would project trigger-frequencies.

On sudden thought, Joe jerked forward, caught his arm. "Just a minute. Suppose you make an acre of splinters — and each one of the splinters starts to grow?"

Harry put down the projector. "That's a grisly thought."

Joe gestured around the countryside. "All these farms, they look well taken care of, modern."

"Latest Earth techniques. So what?"

"You don't let your bully-boys pull all the weeds by hand?"

"Of course not. We've got a dozen different weed-killers — hormones…" He stopped short, clapped Joe on the shoulder. "Weed-killers! *Growth* hormones! Joe, I'll make you Secretary of Agriculture!"

"First," said Joe, "let's see if the stuff works on the Tree. If it's a vegetable it'll go crazy."

The Son of the Tree went crazy.

The tendrils twined, contorted, snapped. The fuzzy white head spat chattering arcs of energy in random directions.

The fronds hoisted to a grotesque two hundred feet in seconds, flopped to the ground.

Another heat projector was brought. Now the Son resisted only weakly. The trunk charred; the fronds crisped, blackened.

In minutes the Son of the Tree was an evil-smelling stump.

Prince Harry sat on his throne. The Arch-Thearchs Gameanza and Oporeto Implan stood with pallid faces muffled in their cowls. The Redbranch Mangs waited in a group to the side of the hall in a rigid system of precedence — first the Magnerru in his chased cuirass and scarlet robe, then Erru Kametin and behind him the two proctors.

Harry said in his light clear voice, "I haven't much to announce — except that for some months now there's been a widespread uncertainty as to which way Ballenkarch is going to jump — toward Mang or toward Kyril.

"Well," he shifted in his seat, put his hands along the arms of his throne, "the speculation has been entirely in the minds of the Druids and the Mangs; there was never any indecision here on Ballenkarch. Once and for all we will team up with neither planet.

"We'll develop in a different direction and I believe we'll end up with the finest world this side of Earth. Insofar as the Son of the Tree is concerned I hold no one personally responsible. You Druids acted, I believe, according to your best lights. You're victims of your beliefs, almost as much as your Laity.

"Another thing — while we won't enter any political commitments we're in business. We'll trade. We're building tools — hammers, saws, wrenches, welders. In a year we'll start building electrical equipment. In five years we'll have a space-yard down there on the shore of Lake Alan.

"In ten years we'll be running our cargo to every star you can see in the night and maybe a few more. So — Magnerru, you can return and convey my message to your Ampianu General and the Lathbon. As for you Druids I doubt if you'll wish to return. There might be quite some turmoil on Kyril by the time you'd arrive."

Gameanza asked sharply, "How is that?"

Harry's mouth twitched. "Call it a guess."

From Harry's private sundeck, the water of Lake Alan glowed in a thousand shades of sunset. Joe sat in a chair. Beside him sat Elfane, in a simple white gown.

Harry paced up and down, talking, gesticulating, boasting. New reduction furnaces at Palinth, a hundred new schools, power units for the new farmer class, guns for his army.

"They've still got that barbarian streak," said Harry. "They love fighting, they love the wildness, their spring festivals, their night fire-dancing. It's born and bred into 'em and I couldn't take it out of 'em if I tried."

He winked at Joe.

"The fire-breathers I send out against the clans of Vail Macrombie — that's the other continent. I kill two birds with one stone. They work off all their belligerence against the Macrombie cannibals and they're gradually winning the continent. It's bloody, yes — but it fills a need in their souls.

"The young ones we'll bring up differently. Their heroes will be the engineers rather than the soldiers and everything should work out about the same time. The new generation will grow up while their fathers are mopping up along Matenda Cape."

"Very ingenious," said Joe. "And speaking of ingenuity where's Hableyat? I haven't seen him for a day or so."

Harry dropped into a chair. "Hableyat's gone."

"Gone? Where?"

"Officially, I don't know — especially since we have Druids among us."

Elfane stirred.

"I'm — no longer a Druid. I've torn it out of me. Now I'm a —" she looked up at Joe "— a what?"

"An expatriate," said Joe. "A space-waif. A woman without a country." He looked back to Harry. "Less of the mystery. It can't be that important."

"But it is! Maybe."

Joe shrugged. "Suit yourself."

"No," said Harry, "I'll tell you. Hableyat, as you know, is in disgrace. He's out and the Magnerru Ippolito is in. Mang politics are complex and cryptic but they seem to hinge a great deal on prestige — on face. The Magnerru lost face here on Ballenkarch. If Hableyat can perform some remarkable feat he'll be back in the running. And it's to our advantage to have the Bluewaters in power on Mangtse."

"Well?"

"I gave Hableyat all the anti-weed hormone we had — about five tons of it. He had it loaded into a ship I made available to him and took off." Harry made a whimsical gesture. "Where he's going — I don't know."

Elfane hissed softly under her breath, shivered, looked away out over Lake Alan, pink, gold, lavender, turquoise in the sunset. "The Tree…"

Harry rose to his feet. "Time for dinner. If that's his plan — to spray the Tree with hormone — it should be quite a show."

The Houses of Iszm

Chapter I

IT WAS ASSUMED as a matter of course that visitors came to Iszm with a single purpose: to steal a female house. Cosmographers, students, babes-in-arms, notorious scoundrels: the Iszic cynically applied the same formula to all — microscopic inspection of mind and body, detailed surveillance.

Only the fact that they turned up so many house-thieves justified the procedure.

From a distance, it seemed simple enough to steal a house. A seed no larger than a grain of barley could be sewn into a strap; a seedling could be woven into the pattern of a shawl; a young shoot could be taped to a rocket-missile and launched into space. There were a thousand fool-proof ways to steal an Iszic house; all had been tried, and the unsuccessful thieves had been conducted to the Mad House, their Iszic escorts courteous to the last. As realists, the Iszic knew that some day — in a year, a hundred years, a thousand years — the monopoly would be broken. As fanatically secretive controllers of the monopoly they intended to postpone this day as long as possible.

Aile Farr was a tall, gaunt man in his thirties, with a droll corded face, big hands and feet; his skin, eyes, and hair a dust-colored monochrome. More important to the Iszic, he was a botanist, hence an automatic object of the utmost suspicion.

Arriving at Jhespiano Atoll aboard the Red Ball Packet *Eubert Honoré*, he encountered suspicion remarkable even in Iszm. Two of the Szecr, the elite police, met him at the exit hatch, escorted him down the gangway like a prisoner, ushered him into a peculiar one-way passage. Flexible spines grew from the walls in the direction of passage; a man could enter the hall, but could not change his mind and return. The end of the passage was closed by a sheet of clear glass; at this point Farr could move neither forward nor back.

An Iszic wearing bands of wine-red and gray stepped forward, examined him through the glass. Farr felt like a specimen in a case. The Iszic grudgingly slid the panel back, led Farr into a small private room. With the Szecr standing at his back, Farr turned over his debarkation slip, his health certificate, his bond of good character, his formal entry application. The clerk dropped the debarkation slip into a macerator, inspected and returned the certificate and bond, settled himself to a study of the application.

The Iszic eye, split into major and minor segments, is capable of double focus; the clerk read with the lower fraction of his eyes, appraising Farr with the top section.

"'Occupation' —" he turned both segments of his eyes on Farr, then flicking the bottom one back, read on in a cool monotone "— 'research associate. Place of business — University of Los Angeles, Department of Botany.'" He lay the application form to one side. "May I inquire your motives for visiting Iszm?"

Farr's patience was wearing thin. He pointed to the application. "I've written it all down."

The clerk read without taking his eyes from Farr, who watched in fascination, marvelling at the feat.

"'I am on sabbatical leave,'" read the clerk. "'I am visiting a number of worlds where plants contribute effectively to the welfare of man.'" The clerk focused both eye fractions on Farr. "Why do you trouble yourself to this extent? Surely the information is conveniently available on Earth?"

"I am interested in first-hand observations."

"To what purpose?"

Farr shrugged. "Professional curiosity."

"I expect that you are acquainted with our laws."

"How could I avoid it?" said Farr in irritation. "I've been briefed ever since the ship left Starholme."

"You understand that you will be allowed no special privileges — no exhaustive or analytical study... You understand?"

"Of course."

"Our regulations are stringent — I must emphasize this. Many visitors forget, and involve themselves with severe penalties."

"By now," said Farr, "I know your laws better than I know my own."

"It is illegal to lift, detach, cut, accept, secrete or remove any vegetable matter, vegetable fragment, seed, seedling, sapling or tree, no matter where you find it."

"I intend nothing illegal."

"Most of our visitors say the same," responded the clerk. "Kindly step into the next chamber, remove all your clothes and personal effects. These will be returned to you at your departure."

Farr looked at him blankly. "My money — my camera — my —"

"You will be issued Iszic equivalents."

Farr wordlessly entered a white enameled chamber where he undressed. An attendant packed his clothes in a glass box, pointed out that Farr had neglected to remove his ring.

"I suppose if I had false teeth you'd want them too," growled Farr.

The Iszic quickly scanned the form. "You assert quite definitely that your teeth are integral to your body, natural and without modification." The upper segments regarded Farr accusingly. "Is this an inaccuracy?"

"Of course not," protested Farr. "They are natural. I merely put forward as a hypothesis — a joke —"

The Iszic muttered into a mesh and Farr was taken into a side room where his teeth were given an exacting inspection. "I'll learn not to make jokes," Farr told himself. "These people have no sense of humor."

Eventually the medics, shaking their heads glumly, returned Farr to the outer chamber, where he was met by an Iszic in a tight white and gray uniform, carrying a hypodermic.

Farr drew back. "What's this!"

"A harmless radiant."

"I don't need any."

"It is necessary," said the medic, "for your own protection. Most visitors hire boats and sail out upon the Pheadh. Occasionally there are storms, the boats are blown off course. This radiant will define your position on the master panel."

"I don't want to be protected," said Farr. "I don't want to be a light on a panel."

"Then you must leave Iszm."

Farr submitted, cursing the medic for the length of the needle and the quantity of radiant.

"Now — into the next room for your tri-type, if you please."

Farr shrugged, walked into the next room.

"On the gray disk, Farr Sainh — palms forward, eyes wide."

He stood rigid; feeler-planes brushed down his body. In a glass dome a three-dimensional simulacrum of himself six inches high took form. Farr inspected it sourly.

"Thank you," said the operative. "Clothes and whatever personal effects you may need will be issued in the next room."

Farr dressed in visitor's uniform: white soft trousers, a gray and green striped smock, a loose dark-green velvet beret that fell low over his ear. "Now may I go?"

The attendant looked into a slot beside him. Farr could see a flicker of bright characters. "You are Farr Sainh the research botanist." It was as if he had said, "You are Farr, the admitted criminal."

"I'm Farr."

"There are several formalities awaiting you."

The formalities required three hours. Farr was once more given to the Szecr, who examined him carefully.

He was finally allowed his freedom. A young man in the yellow and green stripes of the Szecr escorted him to a gondola floating in the lagoon, a long slender craft grown from a single pod. Farr gingerly took a seat and was sculled across to the city of Jhespiano.

It was his first experience of an Iszic city, and it was far richer than his mental picture. The houses grew at irregular intervals along the avenues and canals — heavy gnarled trunks, supporting first the lower pods, then masses of broad leaves, half-submerging the upper pod-banks. Something stirred in Farr's memory; an association…Yeasts or mycetozoa under the microscope. *Lamproderma violaceum? Dictydium cancellatum?* There was the same proliferation of branches. The pods might have been magnified sporangia. There was the same arched well-engineered symmetry, the peculiar complex colors: dark blue overlaid with glistening gray down, burnt orange with a scarlet luster, scarlet with a purple over-glow, sooty green, white highlighted with pink, subtle browns and near-blacks. The avenues below drifted with the Iszic population, a quiet pale people, secure in the stratifications of their guilds and castes.

The gondola glided to the landing. A Szecr in a yellow beret with green tassels was waiting — apparently a man of importance. There was no formal introduction; the Szecr discussed Farr quietly between themselves.

Farr saw no reason to wait, and started up the avenue, toward one of the new cosmopolitan hotels. The Szecr made no attempt to stop him; Farr was now on his own, subject only to surveillance.

He relaxed and loafed around the city for almost a week. There were few other off-world visitors; the Iszic authorities discouraged tourism to the maximum degree allowed them by the Treaty of Access. Farr tried to arrange an interview with the Chairman of the Export Council, but an under-clerk turned him away politely but brusquely, upon learning that Farr wished to discuss the export of low-quality houses. Farr had expected no better. He explored the canals and the lagoon in gondolas, he strolled the avenues. At least three of the Szecr gave him their time, quietly following along the avenues, lounging in nearby pods on the public terraces.

On one occasion he walked around the lagoon to the far side of the island, a rocky sandy area exposed to the wind and the full force of the sun. Here the humbler castes lived in modest three-pod houses, growing in rows with strips of hot sand between. These houses were neutral in color, a brownish gray-green with a central tuft of large leaves casting black shade over the pods. Such houses were not available for export and Farr, a man with a highly developed social conscience, became indignant. A shame these houses could not be made available to the under-housed billions of Earth! A whole district of such habitations could be provided for next to nothing: the mere cost of seed! Farr walked up to one of the houses, peered into a low-hanging pod. Instantly a branch dropped down, and had Farr not jumped back he might have been injured. As it was, the heavy terminal frond slapped across his scalp. One of the Szecr, standing twenty yards distant, sauntered forward. "You are not advised to molest the trees."

"I wasn't molesting anything or anyone."

The Szecr shrugged. "The tree thought otherwise. It is trained to be suspicious of strangers. Among the lower castes —" the Szecr spat contemptuously "— feuds and quarrels go on, and the trees become uneasy at the presence of a stranger."

Farr turned to examine the tree with new interest. "Do you mean that the trees have a conscious mind?"

The Szecr's answer was no more than an indifferent shrug.

Farr asked, "Why aren't these trees exported? There would be an enormous market; many people need houses who can afford nothing better than these."

"You have answered yourself," responded the Szecr. "Who is the dealer on Earth?"

"K. Penche."

"He is a wealthy man?"

"Exceedingly wealthy."

"Would he be equally wealthy selling hovels such as these?"

"Conceivably."

The Szecr turned away. "In any case, we would not profit. These houses are no less difficult to root, nurture, pack and ship than the Class AA houses we choose to deal in…I advise you not to investigate another strange house so closely. You might well suffer serious injury. The houses are not so tolerant of intruders as their inhabitants."

Farr continued around the island, past orchards bearing fruit and low coarse shrubs like Earth century plants, from the center of which sprouted a cluster of ebony rods as much as an inch in diameter and ten feet tall: smooth, glossy, geometrically straight. When Farr went to investigate the Szecr interfered.

"These are not house trees," Farr protested. "In any event, I plan no damage. I am a botanist and interested in strange plants."

"No matter," said the Szecr lieutenant. "Neither the plants nor the craft which has developed them are your property, and hence should be of complete disinterest to you."

"The Iszics seem to have small understanding of intellectual curiosity," observed Farr.

"To compensate, we have a large understanding of rapacity, larceny, brain-picking and exploitation."

Farr had no answer, and grinning wryly continued around the beach and so back to the rich-colored fronds, pods and trunks of the town.

One phase of the surveillance puzzled Farr. He approached the lieutenant, indicated an operative a few yards away. "Why does he mimic me? I sit down, he sits down. I drink, he drinks. I scratch my nose, he scratches his nose."

"A special technique," explained the Szecr. "We divine the pattern of your thinking."

"It won't work," said Farr.

The lieutenant bowed. "Farr Sainh may be quite correct."

Farr smiled indulgently. "Do you seriously think you can predict my plans?"

"We can only do our best."

"This afternoon I plan to rent a sea-going boat. Were you aware of that?"

The lieutenant produced a paper. "I have the charter ready for you. It is the *Lhaiz*, and I have arranged a crew."

Chapter II

THE *LHAIZ* WAS A two-masted barque the shape of a Dutch wooden shoe, with purple sails and a commodious cabin. It had been grown on a special boat-tree, one piece even to the main-mast, which originally had been the stem of the pod. The foremast, sprit, booms and rigging were fabricated parts, a situation as irking to the Iszic mind as mechanical motion to an Earth electronics engineer. The crew of the *Lhaiz* sailed west; atolls rose over the horizon, sank astern. Some were deserted little gardens; others were given to the breeding, seeding, budding, grafting, sorting, packing and shipping of houses.

As a botanist, Farr was most strongly interested in the plantations, but here the surveillance intensified, became a review of his every motion.

At Tjiere Atoll irritation and perversity led Farr to evade his guards. The *Lhaiz* sailed up to the pier; two of the crew passed lines ashore; the others furled sail, cradled booms. Aile Farr jumped easily from the after-deck down to the pier, set off toward the shore. A mutter of complaints came from behind; these gave Farr malicious amusement.

He looked ahead to the island. The beach spread wide to either side, pounded by surf, and the slopes of the basalt ridge were swathed in green, blue and black vegetation — a scene of great peace and beauty. Farr controlled the urge to jump down on the beach to disappear under the leaves. The Szecr were polite, but very quick on the trigger.

A tall strong man appeared upon the dock ahead. Blue bands circled his body and limbs at six inch intervals, the pallid Iszic skin showing between. Farr slackened his pace. Freedom was at an end.

The Iszic lifted a single-lensed lorgnette on an ebony rod: the viewer habitually carried by high-caste Iszic, an accessory almost as personal as one of their organs. Farr had been viewed many times; it never failed to irritate him. Like any other visitor to Iszm, like the Iszic themselves, he had no choice, no recourse, no defense. The radiant injected into his shoulder had labeled him; he was now categorized and defined for anyone who cared to look.

"Your pleasure, Farr Sainh?" The Iszic used the dialect which children spoke before they learned the language of their caste.

Farr resignedly made the formal reply. "I await your will."

"The dock-master was sent to extend proper courtesy. You perhaps became impatient?"

"My arrival is a small matter; please don't trouble yourself."

The Iszic flourished his viewer. "A privilege to greet a fellow-scientist."

Farr said sourly, "That thing even tells you my occupation?"

The Iszic viewed Farr's right shoulder. "I see you have no criminal record; your intelligence index is 23; your persistence level is Class 4... There is other information."

"Who am I privileged to address?" asked Farr.

"I call myself Zhde Patasz; I am fortunate enough to cultivate on Tjiere Atoll."

Farr re-appraised the blue-striped man. "A planter?"

Zhde Patasz twirled his viewer. "We will have much to discuss. I hope you will be my guest."

The dock-master came puffing up; Zhde Patasz flourished his viewer and drifted away.

"Farr Sainh," said the dock-master. "Your modesty leads you to evade your entitled escort; it saddens us deeply."

"You exaggerate."

"Hardly possible. This way, Sainh."

He marched down the concrete incline into a wide trench, with Farr sauntering behind so leisurely that the dock-master was forced to halt and wait at hundred-foot intervals. The trench led under the basalt ridge, became a subterranean passage. Four times the dock-master slid aside plate-glass panels; four times the doors swung shut behind. Farr realized that search-screens, probes, detectors, analyzers were feeling him, testing his radiations, his mass, metallic content. He strolled along indifferently. They would find nothing. All his clothing and personal effects had been impounded; he was still wearing the visitor's uniform, trousers of white floss, a jacket striped gray and green, the loose dark-green velvet beret.

The dock-master rapped at a door of corrugated metal. It parted in the middle into two interlocking halves, like a medieval portcullis; the passage opened into a bright room. Behind a counter sat a Szecr in the usual yellow and green stripes.

"If the Sainh pleases — his tri-type for our records."

Farr patiently stood on the disk of gray metal.

"Palms forward, eyes wide."

Farr stood quietly. Feeler-planes brushed down his body.

"Thank you, Sainh."

Farr stepped up to the counter. "That's a different type to the one at Jhespiano. Let's see it."

The clerk showed him a transparent card with a manlike brownish splotch on its middle. "Not much of a likeness," said Farr.

The Szecr dropped the card into a slot. On the counter-top appeared a three-dimensional replica of Farr. It could be expanded a hundred times, revealing finger-prints, cheek-pores, ear and retinal configuration.

"I'd like to have this as a souvenir," said Farr. "It's dressed. The one at Jhespiano showed my charms to the world."

The Iszic shrugged. "Take it."

Farr put the replica in his pouch.

"Now, Farr Sainh, may I ask an impertinent question?"

"One more won't hurt me."

Farr knew there was a cephaloscope focused on his brain; any pulse of excitement, any flush of fear would be recorded on a chart. He brought the image of a hot bath to the brink of his mind.

"Do you plan to steal houses, Farr Sainh?"

Now: *the placid cool porcelain, the feel of warm air and water, the scent of soap.*

"No."

"Are you aware of, or party to, any such plan?"

Warm water, lie back, relax.

"No."

The Szecr sucked in his lips, a grimace of polite skepticism. "Are you aware of the penalties visited upon thieves?"

"Oh yes," said Farr. "They go to the Mad House."

"Thank you, Farr Sainh; you may proceed."

Chapter III

THE DOCK-MASTER relinquished Farr to a pair of under-Szecr in pale yellow and gold bands.

"This way, if you please."

They climbed a ramp, stepped out into an arcade with a glassed-in wall.

Farr stopped to survey the plantation; his guides made uneasy motions, anxious to proceed.

"If Farr Sainh desires —"

"Just a minute," said Farr irritably. "There's no hurry."

On his right hand was the town, a forest of intricate shapes and colors. To the back grew the modest three-pod houses of the laborers; they could hardly be seen through the magnificent array along the lagoon — houses of the planters, the Szecr, the house-breeders and house-breakers. Each was different, trained and shaped by secrets the Iszic withheld even from each other.

They were beautiful, thought Farr, but in a weird indecisive way they puzzled him; just as sometimes the palate falters on a new flavor. He decided that environment influenced his judgment. Iszic houses on Earth looked habitable enough. This was Iszm; any attribute of a strange planet shared the basic strangeness.

He turned his attention to the fields. They spread off to his left: various shades of brown, gray, gray-green, green, according to the age and variety of the plant. Each field had its long low shed where mature seedlings were graded, labeled, potted and packed for destinations around the universe.

The two young Szecr began to mutter in the language of their caste; Farr turned away from the window.

"This way, Farr Sainh."

"Where are we going?"

"You are the guest of Zhde Patasz Sainh."

Excellent, thought Farr. He had examined the houses exported to Earth, the Class AA houses sold by K. Penche. They would compare poorly with the houses the planters grew for themselves.

He became aware of the two young Szecr. They were standing like statues, staring at the floor of the arcade.

"What's the matter?" asked Farr.

They began to breathe heavily. Farr looked at the floor. A vibration, a low roar. Earthquake! thought Farr. The sound grew louder; the windows rumbled in resonance. Farr felt a sudden wildness, a sense of emergency; he looked out the window. In a nearby field the ground broke up, took on a crazy hump, erupted. Tender seedlings crushed under tons of dirt. A metal snout protruded, grinding up ten feet, twenty feet. A door clanged open; squat heavy-muscled brown men leapt out, ran into the fields, began to uproot young plants. In the door a man, grinning in the extremity of tension, roared out incomprehensible orders.

Farr watched in fascination; a raid of tremendous scope! Horns rang out from Tjiere Town; the vicious *fwipp-hiss* of shatter-bolts sounded. Two of the brown men became red clots; the man in the doorway bellowed, the others retreated to the metal snout.

The port clanged shut; but one raider had waited too long. He beat his fists on the hull, to no avail; he was ignored. Frantically he pounded and the seedlings he had gathered crushed in his grip.

The snout vibrated, lifted higher from the ground. The shatter-bolts from the Tjiere fort began to chip off flakes of metal. A bull's-eye port in the hull snapped open; a weapon spat blue flame. In Tjiere a great tree shattered, sagged. Farr's head swam to a tremendous soundless scream; the young Szecr dropped gasping to their knees.

The tree toppled; the great pods, the leaf-terraces, the tendrils, the careful balconies — they whistled through the air, crashed — a pitiful tangle. Iszic bodies hurtled from the ruins, kicking and twisting, others limp.

The metal snout ground up another ten feet. In a moment it would shake loose the soil, blast up and out into space. The brown man left outside fought for footing on the heaving soil, still pounding on the hull, but now without hope.

Farr looked at the sky. Three monitors were slipping down from the upper air — ugly awkward craft, metal scorpions.

A shatter-bolt smashed a crater in the soil beside the hull. The brown man was flung a looping sixty feet; he turned three cartwheels and landed on his back.

The metal hull began to churn back down into the soil, settling slowly at first, then faster and faster. Another shatter-bolt rang on the prow like a great hammer. The metal shriveled, fragmented into ribbons. The hull was under the surface; clods of soil caved in on top.

Another shatter-bolt threw up a gout of dust.

The two young Szecr had risen to their feet; they stared out across the devastated field, crying out in a tongue meaningless to Farr. One grasped Farr's arm.

"Come, we must secure you. Danger, danger!"

Farr shook them off. "I'll wait here."

"Farr Sainh, Farr Sainh," they cried. "Our orders are to see to your safety."

"I'm safe here," said Farr. "I want to watch."

The three monitors hung over the crater, drifting back and forth.

"Looks like the raiders got away," said Farr.

"No! Impossible," cried the Szecr. "It's the end of Iszm!"

Down from the sky dropped a slender ship, smaller than the monitors. If the monitors were scorpions, the new vessel was a wasp. It settled over the crater, sank into the loose dirt — slowly, gingerly, like a probe. It began to roar, to vibrate; it churned out of sight.

Along the arcade came a dozen men, running with the sinuous back-leaning glide of the Iszic. Farr on an impulse fell in behind them, ignoring the distress of the two young Szecr.

The Iszic fled across the field toward the crater; Farr followed. He passed the limp body of the brown man, slowed, halted. The man's hair was heavy, leonine; his features were broad, blunt; his hand still clenched the seedlings he had uprooted. The fingers fell limp even as Farr came to a halt; at the same time the eyes opened. They held full intelligence; Farr bent forward half in pity, half in interest.

Hands gripped him; he saw yellow and green stripes, furious faces with lips drawn back to show the pallid Iszic mouth, the sharp teeth.

"Here!" cried Farr, as he was hustled off the field. "Let go!"

The Szecr fingers bit into his arms and shoulders; they were obsessed by a murderous madness, and Farr held his tongue.

Underfoot sounded a deep far rumble; the ground heaved.

The Szecr ran Farr toward Tjiere, then turned aside. Farr began to struggle, to drag his feet. Something hard struck the back of his neck; half-stunned, he made no further resistance. They took him to an isolated tree near the basalt scarp. It was very old, with a gnarled black trunk, a heavy umbrella of leaves, two or three withered pods. An irregular hole gaped into the trunk; without ceremony they thrust him through.

Chapter IV

AILE FARR, SCREAMING HOARSELY, fell through the dark. He kicked, clawed at the air. His head scraped against the side of the shaft; then his shoulder struck, then his hip, then he was in full contact. The fall became a slide as the tube curved. His feet struck a membrane that seemed to collapse, then another and another. Seconds later he struck a resilient wall. The impact stunned him. He lay quiet, collecting his wits, feeling very sorry for himself.

He moved, felt his head. The scrape on his scalp smarted. He heard a peculiar noise, a hissing bumping rush; an object sliding down the tube. Farr scrambled to the side. Something hard and heavy struck him in the ribs; something struck the wall with a thump and a groan. There was silence except for the sound of shallow breathing.

Farr said cautiously, "Who's there?"

No answer.

Farr repeated the question in all his languages and dialects — still no answer. He hunched himself up uneasily. He had no light, no means of making fire.

The breathing became stertorous, labored. Farr groped through the dark, felt a crumpled body. He rose to his knees, laid the unseen figure flat, straightening the arms and legs. The breathing became more regular.

Farr sat back on his haunches, waiting. Five minutes passed. The walls of the room gave a sudden pulse; Farr heard a deep sound like a distant explosion. A minute or two later the sound and the pulse occurred again. The underground battle was raging, thought Farr. Wasp against mole, an underground battle to the death.

A wave of pressure and sound rocked him; the walls heaved. An explosion that had a feeling of finality. The man in the dark gasped, coughed.

"Who's there?" Farr called.

A bright eye of light winked into his face; Farr winced, moved his head. The light followed.

"Turn that damn thing away!" growled Farr.

The light moved up and down his body, lingering on the striped visitor's shirt. In the reflected glow Farr saw the brown man, dirty, bruised, haggard. The light issued from a clasp on the shoulder of his tunic.

The brown man spoke in a slow hoarse voice; the language was unknown to Farr and he shook his head in incomprehension. The brown man regarded him a moment or two longer in careful, if dubious, appraisal. Then he lurched painfully to his feet and ignoring Farr minutely examined the walls, floor and ceiling of the cell. Inaccessibly above was the opening by which they had entered; to the side was a tightly knotted sphincter. Farr felt sullen and resentful, and the cut on his head smarted. The brown man's activity irritated him. Obviously there would be no easy escape; the Szecr were nothing if not painstaking in matters of this sort.

Farr watched the brown man and presently decided him to be a Thord, the most manlike of the three Arcturian races. Regarding the Thord there were various disturbing rumors, and Farr was not too easy at having one of the race for a cell-mate — especially in the dark.

The Thord completed his study of the walls, and returned his attention to Farr. His eyes glowed softly, deep, cool and yellow, like cabochons of topaz. He spoke once again in his halting husky voice. "This is not a true prison."

Farr was startled. Under the circumstances the remark seemed more than peculiar. "Why do you say that?"

The Thord studied him a full ten seconds before making a reply. "There was great excitement. The Iszt dropped us here for safekeeping. Soon they will take us elsewhere. There are no spy-holes here, nor sound receptors. This is a storage chamber."

Farr looked dubiously at the walls. The Thord uttered a low moaning sound which caused Farr new startlement, until he understood that the Thord was merely expressing some unearthly variety of amusement.

"You wonder how I can be sure of this," said the Thord. "It is my ability to feel the weight of attention."

Farr nodded politely. The Thord's unwavering scrutiny was becoming oppressive. Farr turned half-away. The Thord began to mutter to himself: a crooning monotonous sound. A lament? a threnody? The light dimmed but the Thord's lugubrious murmur continued. Farr eventually became drowsy and fell asleep. It was a troubled restless sleep. His head seemed to smart and burn. He heard confidential voices and hoarse cries; he was home on Earth, and on his way to see — someone. A friend. Who? In his sleep Farr twisted and muttered. He knew he was asleep; he wanted to wake up.

The hollow voices, the footsteps, the restless images dwindled, and he slept soundly.

Light streamed in through an oval gap, silhouetting the frames of two Iszic. Farr awoke. He was vaguely surprised to find the Thord gone. In fact, the entire room seemed different; he was no longer in the root of the gnarled black tree.

He struggled up in a sitting position. His eyes were dim and watery; he found it hard to think. There was no anchor for his thoughts; it was as if all the faculties of his mind were separate pieces falling free through the air.

"Aile Farr Sainh," said one of the Iszic, "may we trouble you to accompany us?" They wore bands of yellow and green: Szecr.

Farr struggled to his feet, stumbled through the oval door. With one of the Szecr ahead and one behind he walked along a twisting corridor. The foremost Szecr slid back a panel; Farr found himself in the arcade he had traversed before.

They took him out into the open, under the night sky. The stars glittered; Farr noticed Home Sun a few degrees below a star he knew to be Beta Aurigae; it aroused no pang, no home-sickness. He felt emotion toward nothing. He saw without attention; he felt light, easy, relaxed.

They skirted the tangle of the fallen house, approached the lagoon. Ahead a great trunk grew from a carpet of soft moss.

"The house of Zhde Patasz Sainh," said the Szecr. "You are his guest; he holds to his word."

The door slid aside; Farr stepped into the trunk on flexible legs.

The door slid quietly shut. Farr stood alone in a tall circular foyer. He clutched at the wall to steady himself, faintly annoyed with the looseness of his perceptions. He made an effort; his faculties drifted closer together, coalesced one by one.

A young Iszic woman came forward. She wore black and white bands, a black turban. The skin between the bands flushed faintly rose-violet; a black line around her head accented the horizontal division of her eyes. Farr became suddenly aware of his disheveled, dirty, unshaven condition.

"Farr Sainh," said the woman, "indulge me with your company."

She led him to an elevator duct. The disk lifted them a hundred feet; Farr's head swam with the movement. He felt the cool hand of the woman.

"Through here, Farr Sainh."

Farr stepped forward, halted, leaned against the wall until his vision cleared.

The woman waited patiently.

The blur lifted. He stood in the core of a branch; the woman supporting him with an arm around his wrist. He looked into the pale segmented eyes. She regarded him with indifference.

"Your people drugged me," muttered Farr.

"This way, Farr Sainh."

She started down the corridor with the sinuous gait that seemed to float her upper body. Farr followed slowly. His legs were stronger; he felt a little better.

The woman stopped by the terminal sphincter, turned, made a wide ceremonial sweep of her two arms. "Here is your chamber. You shall want for nothing. To Zhde Patasz, all of dendrology is an open book. His groves fulfill every want. Enter and rejoice in the exquisite house of Zhde Patasz."

Farr entered the chamber, one of four connecting compartments in the most elaborate pod he had yet seen. This was an eating chamber; from the floor a great rib grew up and splayed to either side to form a table, which supported a dozen trays of food.

The next chamber, swathed in fibrous blue hangings, appeared to be a rest chamber, and beyond was a chamber ankle deep in pale

green nectar. Behind Farr suddenly appeared a small obsequiously
sighing Iszic, in the pink and white bands of a house servitor. Deftly
he removed Farr's soiled garments; Farr stepped into the bath and
the servant tapped at the wall. From small orifices issued a spray of
fresh-smelling liquid which tingled coolly upon Farr's skin. The servant
scooped up a ladle of the pale green nectar, poured it over Farr's head,
and he was instantly covered with a prickling effervescent foam, which
presently dissolved, leaving Farr's skin fresh and soft.

The servant approached with a husk full of a pale paste; this he
carefully rubbed upon Farr's face with a wisp of bast, and Farr's beard
melted away.

Directly overhead a bubble of liquid had been forming in a sac of
frail membrane. It grew larger, swaying and trembling; now the servant reached up with a sharp thorn; the sac burst; a soft aromatic
liquid smelling of cloves drenched Farr, and quickly evaporated. Farr
stepped into the fourth chamber where the servant draped fresh garments upon him, and then fixed a black rosette to the side of his leg.
Farr knew something of Iszic folkways and was vaguely surprised. As
the personal insignia of Zhde Patasz, the rosette conveyed a host of
significances. Farr had been acknowledged the honored house-guest
of Zhde Patasz, who thereupon undertook his protection against any
and all of Farr's enemies. Farr was given liberty of the house, with a
dozen prerogatives otherwise reserved to the house owner. Farr could
manipulate any of the house's nerves, reflexes, triggers and conduits; he
could make himself free of Zhde Patasz's rarest treasures, and in general
was made an alter ego of Zhde Patasz himself. The honor was unusual,
and for an Earthman perhaps unique: Farr wondered what he had
done to deserve such a distinction. Perhaps it came by way of apology
for the rude treatment Farr had experienced during the Thord raid...
Farr pondered. Yes, this must be the explanation. He hoped that Zhde
Patasz would overlook his ignorance of the highly complex rituals of
Iszic courtesy.

The woman who had conducted Farr to the chamber reappeared.
She performed an elaborate genuflection. Farr was insufficiently familiar with the subtleties of Iszic mannerisms to decide whether or not
there might be irony in the gesture, and he reserved judgment. His

sudden change in status seemed highly remarkable... A hoax? Unlikely. The Iszic sense of humor was non-existent.

"Aile Farr Sainh," declared the woman. "Now that you have refreshed yourself, do you wish to associate with your host, Zhde Patasz?"

Farr smiled faintly. "At any time."

"Then allow me to lead the way; I will take you to the private pods of Zhde Patasz Sainh, where he waits with great restlessness."

Farr followed her along the conduit, up an incline where the branch drooped, by elevator up the central trunk, and off along another passage. At a sphincter she paused, bowed, swept wide her arms. "Zhde Patasz Sainh awaits you."

The sphincter expanded, Farr stepped dubiously into the chamber. Zhde Patasz was not immediately to be seen. Farr moved forward slowly, looking from right to left. The pod was thirty feet long, opening on a balcony with a waist-high balustrade. The walls and domed ceiling were tufted with trefoils of a silky green fiber; the floor was heavy with plum-colored moss; quaint lamps grew out of the wall. There were four magenta pod-chairs against one wall; in the middle of the floor stood a tall cylindrical vase containing water, plants and black dancing eels. There were pictures on the walls by ancient Earth masters, colorful curios from a strange world.

Zhde Patasz came in from the balcony. "Farr Sainh, I hope you feel well?"

"Well enough," said Farr cautiously.

"Will you sit?"

"As you command." Farr lowered himself upon one of the frail magenta bladders. The smooth skin stretched, fitted itself to his body.

His host languidly seated himself nearby. There was a moment of silence, while each surveyed the other. Zhde Patasz wore the blue stripes of his caste and today, the pale narrow cheeks were decorated with glossy red disks. These were not haphazard decorations, Farr realized: every outward attribute of the Iszic was meaningful to some degree. Zhde Patasz today was without the usual loose beret; the knob and ridges along the top of his scalp formed almost a crest: an indication of aristocratic lineage across thousands of years.

"You are enjoying your visit to Iszm?" inquired Zhde Patasz at last.

Farr considered a moment, then spoke formally. "I see much to interest me. I have also suffered molestation, which I hope will cause me no permanent harm." He gingerly felt his scalp. "Only the fact of your hospitality compensates for the ill treatment I have received."

"This is sorry news," said Zhde Patasz. "Who has wronged you? Provide me their names and I will have them drowned."

Farr admitted that he could not precisely identify the Szecr who had thrust him into the dungeon. "In any event they were excited by the raid, and I bear them no malice on this account. But afterward I seem to have been drugged, which I consider very poor treatment."

"Your remarks are well taken," Zhde Patasz replied in the most bland of voices. "The Szecr would normally administer a hypnotic gas to the Thord. It seems that through a stupid error you had been conveyed to the same cell, and so shared this indignity. Undoubtedly the parties responsible are at this moment beside themselves with remorse."

Farr tried to speak with indignation. "My legal rights have been totally ignored. The Treaty of Access has been violated."

"I hope you will forgive us," said Zhde Patasz. "Of course you realize that we must protect our fields."

"I had nothing to do with the raid."

"Yes. We understand that."

Farr smiled bitterly. "While I was under hypnosis you siphoned out everything I know."

Zhde Patasz performed the curious contraction of the filament dividing the segments of his eyes which Farr had come to recognize as a manifestation of Iszic amusement. "By chance I was informed of your misadventure."

" 'Misadventure'? An outrage!"

Zhde Patasz made a soothing gesture. "The Szecr would naturally plan to subdue the Thord by use of a hypnotic atmosphere; the race has powerful capabilities, both physical and psychic, as well as notorious moral deficiencies, which presumably is why they were recruited to conduct the raid."

Farr was puzzled. "You think the Thord weren't acting on their own?"

"I think not. The organization was too precise, the planning too exact. The Thord are an impatient race and while it is not impossible that they mounted the expedition, we are inclined to think otherwise, and are extremely anxious to identify the instigator of the raid."

"So you examined me under hypnosis, violating the Treaty of Access."

"I assume the questioning covered only matters pertaining to the raid." Zhde Patasz was trying to conciliate Farr. "The Szecr were perhaps over-assiduous, but you appeared a conspirator; you must recognize that."

"I'm afraid I don't."

"No?" Zhde Patasz seemed surprised. "You arrive at Tjiere on the day of the assault. You attempt to evade your escort at the dock. During an interview you make pointless attempts to control your reactions. Forgive me if I show you your errors."

"Not at all; go right ahead."

"In the arcade you once more evade your escort; you race out on the field: an apparent effort to take part in the raid."

"This is all nonsense," said Farr.

"We are satisfied of this," said Zhde Patasz. "The raid has ended in disaster for the Thord. We destroyed the mole at a depth of eleven hundred feet; there were no survivors except the person with whom you shared a cell."

"What will happen to him?"

Zhde Patasz hesitated; Farr thought to detect uncertainty in his voice. "Under normal conditions he would have been perhaps the least lucky of all." He paused, forming his thoughts into words. "We have faith in the deterrent effect of punishment. He would have been confined to the Mad House."

"What happened to him?"

"He killed himself in the cell."

Farr felt suddenly bewildered, as if this were an unexpected development. Somehow the brown man was obligated to him; something was lost...

Zhde Patasz said in a voice full of solicitude, "You appear shocked, Farr Sainh."

"I don't know why I should be."

"Are you tired, or weak?"

"I'm collecting myself a little at a time."

The Iszic woman came with a tray of food — spice-nuts, a hot aromatic liquid, dried fish.

Farr ate with pleasure; he was hungry. Zhde Patasz watched him curiously. "It is strange. We are of different worlds, we evolved from different stock. Yet we share a number of similar ambitions, similar fears and desires. We protect our possessions, the objects which bring us security."

Farr felt the raw spot on his scalp; it still smarted and pulsed; he nodded thoughtfully.

Zhde Patasz strolled to the glass cylinder, looked down at the dancing eels. "Sometimes we are over-anxious, of course, and our fears cause us to over-reach ourselves." He turned. They surveyed each other a long moment: Farr half-submerged in the chair-pod, the Iszic tall and strong, the double eyes large in his thin aquiline head.

"In any event," said Zhde Patasz, "I hope you will forget our mistake. The Thord and their mentor or mentors are responsible. But for them the situation would not have arisen. And please don't overlook our intense concern. The raid was of enormous scope and a near-success. Who conceived, who planned so complex an operation? We must learn this. The Thord worked with great precision. They seized both seeds and seedlings from specific plots evidently charted beforehand by a spy in the guise of a tourist like yourself." And Zhde Patasz inspected Farr somberly.

Farr laughed shortly. "A tourist unlike myself. I don't care to be associated with the affair even indirectly."

Zhde Patasz bowed politely. "A creditable attitude. But I am sure you are generous enough to understand our agitation. We must protect our investment; we are businessmen."

"Not very good businessmen," said Farr.

"An interesting opinion. Why not?"

"You have a good product," said Farr, "but you market it uneconomically. Limited sale, high mark-up."

Zhde Patasz brought out his viewer, waved it indulgently. "There are many theories."

"I've studied several analyses of the house trade," said Farr. "They disagree only in detail."

"What is the consensus?"

"That your methods are inefficient. On each planet a single dealer has the monopoly. It's a system which pleases only the dealer. K. Penche is a hundred times a millionaire and he's the most hated man on Earth."

Zhde Patasz swung his viewer thoughtfully. "K. Penche will be an unhappy man as well as a hated one."

"Glad to hear it," said Farr. "Why?"

"The raid destroyed a large number of his quota."

"He won't get any houses?"

"Not of the kind he ordered."

"Well," said Farr, "it makes little difference. He sells everything you send him anyway."

Zhde Patasz showed a trace of impatience. "He is an Earther — a mercantilist. We are Iszic; house-breeding is in our blood: a basic instinct. The line of planters began two hundred thousand years ago when Diun, the primordial anthrophib, crawled out of the ocean. With salt-water still draining from his gills he took refuge in a pod. He is my ancestor. We have gained mastery over houses; we shall not dissipate this accumulated lore, or permit ourselves to be plundered."

"The knowledge eventually will be duplicated," said Farr, "whether you like it or not. There are too many homeless people in the universe."

"No." Zhde Patasz snapped his viewer. "The craft cannot be induced rationally; an element of magic still exists."

"Magic?"

"Not literally. The trappings of magic. For instance — we sing incantations to sprouting seeds. The seeds sprout and prosper. Without incantations they fail. Why? Who knows? No one on Iszm. In every phase of growing, training and breaking the house for habitation, this special lore makes the difference between a house and a withered useless vine."

"On Earth," said Farr, "we would begin with the elemental tree. We would sprout a million seeds, we would explore a million primary avenues."

"After a thousand years," said the Iszic, "you might control the number of pods on a tree." He walked to the wall, stroked the green fiber.

"This floss — we inject a liquid into an organ of the rudimentary pod. The liquid comprises substances such as powdered ammonite nerve, ash of the frunz bush, sodium isochromyl acetate, powder from the Phanodano meteorite. The liquid undergoes six critical operations, and must be injected through the proboscis of a sea-lympid. Tell me," he glanced at Farr through his viewer, "how long before your Earth researchers could grow green floss into a pod?"

"Perhaps we'd never try. We might be satisfied with five or six-pod houses the owners could furnish as they liked."

Zhde Patasz's eyes snapped. "But this is crudity! You understand, do you not? A dwelling must be all of a unit — the walls, the drainage, the décor grown in! What use is our vast lore, our two hundred thousand years of effort, otherwise? Any ignoramus can paste up green floss; only an Iszic can grow it!"

"Yes," said Farr. "I believe you."

Zhde Patasz continued, passionately waving his viewer. "And if you stole a female house, and if you managed to breed a five-pod house, that is only the beginning. It must be entered, mastered, trained. The webbings must be cut; the nerves of ejaculation must be located and paralyzed. The sphincters must open and close at a touch.

"The art of house-breaking is almost as important as house-breeding. Without correct breaking a house is an unmanageable nuisance — a menace."

"K. Penche breaks none of the houses you send to Earth."

"Pah! Penche's houses are docile, spiritless. They are without interest; they lack beauty, grace." He paused. "I cannot speak. Your language has no words to tell what an Iszic feels for his house. He grows it, grows into it; his ashes are given it when he dies. He drinks its ichor; it breathes his breath. It protects him; it takes on the color of his thoughts. A spirited house will repel a stranger. An injured house will kill. And a Mad House — that is where we take our criminals."

Farr listened in fascination. "That's all very well — for an Iszic. An Earther isn't so particular — at least, a low income Earther. Or as you would put it, a low-caste Earther. He just wants a house to live in."

"You may obtain houses," said Zhde Patasz. "We are glad to provide them. But you must use the accredited distributors."

"K. Penche?"

"Yes. He is our representative."

"I think I will go to bed," said Farr. "I am tired and my head hurts."

"A pity. But rest well, and tomorrow, should you choose, we will inspect my plantation. In the meantime, my house is yours."

The young woman in the black turban conducted Farr to his chambers. She ceremoniously bathed his face, his hands, his feet, sprayed the air with an aromatic scent, departed.

Farr fell into a fitful slumber. He dreamt of the Thord. He saw the blunt brown face, heard the heavy voice. The abrasion on his scalp stung like fire, and Farr twisted and turned.

The brown man's face disappeared like an extinguished light. Farr slept in peace.

Chapter V

THE FOLLOWING DAY Farr awoke to the sighing whispering sounds of Iszic music. Fresh clothing hung close at hand, which he donned and then went out on the balcony. The scene was one of magnificent eery beauty. The sun, Xi Aurigae, had not yet risen, the sky was an electric blue, the sea was a plum-colored mirror, darkening to a tarnished black at the horizon. To right and left stood the vast and intricate houses of the Tjiere aristocrats, the foliage in silhouette against the sky; the pods showing traces of muted colors: dark blue, maroon, deep green, like old velvet. Along the canal drifted dozens of gondolas; beyond spread the Tjiere bazaar where goods and implements from the industrial systems of South Continent and a few off-world items were distributed by some apparently casual means of exchange not completely clear to Farr.

From within the apartment came the sound of a plucked string; Farr turned to find two attendants carrying in a tall compartmented buffet laden with food. Farr ate wafers, fruits, marine tubers and pastes while Xi Aurigae bulged gradually over the horizon.

When he finished, the attendants reappeared with a promptitude which caused Farr a twinge of wry amusement. They removed the buffet, and now entered the Iszic woman who had greeted Farr the previous evening. Today her normal costume of black ribbons was augmented by a complicated head-dress of the same black ribbons which concealed the knobs and ridges of her scalp and gave her an unexpectedly attractive semblance. After performing an elaborate ceremonial salute she announced that Zhde Patasz awaited Farr Sainh's pleasure.

Farr accompanied her to the lobby at the base of the great trunk. Here Zhde Patasz waited in the company of an Iszic whom he introduced as Omon Bozhd, a general agent for the house-growers' cooperative.

Omon Bozhd was taller than Zhde Patasz; his face was rather broader and less keen, his manner was almost imperceptibly brisker and more direct. He wore bands of blue and black, with black cheek disks: a costume Farr vaguely understood to indicate one of the upper castes. Zhde Patasz's manner toward Omon Bozhd seemed a peculiar mixture of condescension and respect, insofar as Farr could define it, and he ascribed it to the discord between Omon Bozhd's caste and his pallid white skin, which was that of a man from one of the southern archipelagoes, or even South Continent, and which lacked the pale blue tinge distinguishing the aristocratic planters of the Pheadh. Farr, sufficiently perplexed by the extraordinary attention he was receiving, gave him no great attention.

Zhde Patasz conducted his guests to a charabanc with padded benches, supported by a hundred near-silent whorls of air. There was no attempt at embellishment or decoration, but the pale shell of the structure, grown in one piece along with the curved and buttressed railings, the arched seats and the dangling fringe of dark brown fiber, were sufficiently striking in themselves. A servant in red and brown bands straddled a prong protruding forward and worked the controls. On a low bench to the rear sat two other servants who carried the various instruments, emblems and accoutrements of Zhde Patasz, serving purposes which Farr for the most part could not guess.

At the last minute a fourth Iszic joined the group, a man in blue and gray bands whom Zhde Patasz introduced as Uder Che, his 'chief architect'.

"The actual Iszic word," said Zhde Patasz, "of course is different, and includes an array of other meanings or resonants: biochemist, instructor, poet, precursor, one who lovingly nurtures, much else. The end effect nonetheless is the same, and describes one who creates new sorts of houses."

Behind, as a matter of course, came a trio of the ubiquitous Szecr riding another smaller platform. Farr thought to recognize one of the group as his escort at the time of the Thord raid, the author of the various indignities to which he had been subjected. But he could not be certain: to his alien eye all Iszic looked alike. He toyed with the idea of denouncing the man to Zhde Patasz, who had sworn to have him drowned. Farr restrained the urge; Zhde Patasz might feel impelled to make good his word.

The platform glided off under the massive tree-dwellings at the center of town, out along a road which led beside a series of small fields. Here grew the gray-green shoots Farr recognized as infant houses. "Class AAA and AABR houses for the work-supervisors of South Continent," explained Zhde Patasz with a rather patronizing air. "Yonder are four- and five-pod trees for the artisans. Each district has its unique requirements, the description of which I will not burden you. Our off-world exports of course are not of such critical concern, since we only sell a few standard and easily grown structures."

Farr frowned. It seemed that Zhde Patasz's patronizing manner had become more pronounced. "You could increase your off-world sales tremendously if you chose to diversify."

Zhde Patasz and Omon Bozhd both exhibited signs of amusement. "We sell as many trees off-world as we choose. Why strive further? Who appreciates the unique and exceptional qualities of our houses? You yourself tell us that the Earther regards his house as hardly more than a cubicle to ward off the weather."

"You misunderstood me — or perhaps I expressed myself poorly. But even if this were wholly true — which it isn't — the need still exists for a whole variety of houses, on Earth as well as on the other planets to which you sell houses."

Omon Bozhd spoke. "You really are irrational, Farr Sainh, if I may invest the word with its least offensive aura of meaning. Let me expatiate. On Earth you claim that a need exists for housing. On Earth there is also a surplus of wealth — a surplus so great that vast projects are generated by the impounded energy. This wealth could solve the problem of deficient housing in the twinkling of an eye — if those who controlled the wealth so desired. Since you understand this course of events to be unlikely, you turn your eye speculatively upon us relatively poor Iszics, hoping that we will prove less obdurate than the men of your own planet. When you find that we are absorbed in our own interests, you become resentful — and herein lies the irrationality of your position."

Farr laughed. "This is a distorted reflection of reality. We are wealthy, true enough. Why? Because we constantly try to maximize production and minimize effort. The Iszic houses represent this minimizing of effort."

"Interesting," murmured Zhde Patasz. Omon Bozhd nodded sagely. The glide-car turned, rose to drift above a tangle of spiky gray bushes overgrown with black spheres. Beyond, across a fringe of beach, lay the calm blue world-ocean, the Pheadh. The glide-car nosed out over the low surf, slid out toward an off-shore islet.

Zhde Patasz spoke in a solemn, almost sepulchral, voice. "You are now to be shown what very few are permitted to see: an experimental station where we conceive and develop new houses."

Farr tried to make a suitable reply, expressing interest and appreciation, but Zhde Patasz had withdrawn his attention and Farr became silent.

The platform heaved across the water, the whorls of air creating a seethe of white spume astern. Light from Xi Aurigae glittered on the blue water and Farr thought what an Earthly scene this might have been — but for the oddly-shaped glide-car, the tall milky-white men in stripes beside him, the peculiar aspect of the trees on the island ahead. Those visible were of a type he had not seen previously: heavy, low, with densely matted black branches. The foliage, fleshy strips of brown tissue, seemed in constant motion.

The glide-car slowed, coasted toward the beach, halted twenty feet offshore, whereupon Uder Che, the architect, jumped into the knee-deep water, cautiously walked ashore, carrying a black box. The trees reacted to his presence, at first leaning toward him, then recoiling and unlacing their branches. After a moment there was a gap wide enough for the glide-car, which now proceeded across the beach and through the gap. Uder Che followed, boarded the car; the trees once more joined branches to create an impenetrable tangle.

Zhde Patasz explained. "The trees will kill anyone who attempts to pass without manifesting the proper safe-signal, which is radiated from the box. In the past, planters often mounted expeditions against each other — no longer the case, of course, and the sentry trees are perhaps not strictly necessary. But we are a conservative lot and maintain our old customs."

Farr looked around him, making no attempt to conceal his interest.

Zhde Patasz watched him with patient amusement. "When I came to Iszm," said Farr at last, "I hoped for an opportunity like this, but never expected it. I admit that I'm puzzled. Why do you show me these things?" He searched the pale ridged face, but inevitably could read nothing from the Iszic's expression.

Zhde Patasz reflected a moment before he answered: "Conceivably you demand reasons where none exist, beyond the normal solicitude of a host for an honored guest."

"This is a possibility," admitted Farr. He smiled politely. "But perhaps other motivations also exist?"

"Conceivably. The raid of the Thords still troubles us and we are anxious for more information. But let us not concern ourselves with such matters today. As a botanist, I believe you will be interested in the contrivances of myself and Uder Che."

"Oh indeed." And for the next two hours Farr examined houses with buttressed pods for the high-gravity worlds of Cleo 8 and Martinon's Fort; loose complex houses with pods like balloons for Fei, where gravity was only half that of Iszm. There were trees comprised of a central columnar trunk and four vast leaves, arching out and over to the ground to form four domed halls illuminated by the pale green transmitted light. There was a tough-trunked tree supporting a single turret-like pod, with lanceolate foliage spiking outward at the base: a watch-tower for the feuding tribesmen of Eta Scorpionis. In a walled enclosure were trees with varying degrees of motility and awareness. "A new and adventurous area of research," Zhde Patasz told Farr. "We play with the idea of growing trees to perform special tasks, such as sentry duty, garden supervision, mineral exploration, simple machine tending. As I say, we are merely amusing ourselves at the moment. I understand that on Duroc Atoll, the master planter in residence has created a tree which first produces colored fibers, and from these weaves rugs of characteristic pattern. We ourselves have performed our share of bizarre feats. For instance, in yonder cupola, we have achieved a conjunction which might be thought impossible, if one did not understand the basis of the adaptation."

Farr made a polite sound of wonder and admiration. He noted that both Omon Bozhd and Uder Che were giving particularly respectful

attention to the planter's words, as if they signified something porten-
tous. And suddenly Farr realized that whatever the motive for Zhde
Patasz's elaborate hospitality, it was now about to be made clear to him.

Zhde Patasz continued in the harsh crisp accent of the aristocratic
Iszic: "The mechanism, if I may call it that, of this conjoining is in
theory not difficult. The animal corpus depends upon food and oxygen,
plus a few subsidiary compounds. The vegetable system, of course,
produces these substances, and recycles the waste products of the
animal. It is tempting to try for a closed system, requiring only energy
from an external source. Our achievements, while I think you will find
them dramatic, still fall far short of elegance. There is little real mingling
of tissue: all interchange is done across semi-permeable membranes
which isolate plant fluids and animal fluids. Nevertheless a start has
been made." As Zhde Patasz spoke he had been moving toward a pale
yellow-green hemisphere above which tall yellow fronds swung and
fluttered. Zhde Patasz gestured toward an arched opening. Omon
Bozhd and Uder Che stayed discreetly to the rear. Farr looked dubiously from one to the other.

Zhde Patasz bowed once more. "As a botanist I am sure you will be
fascinated by our achievement."

Farr studied the opening, trying to assess its implications. Within
was something which the Iszics intended him to see, some stimulus
which they intended him to experience…Danger? They had no need
to trick him; he was in any case at their mercy. Zhde Patasz moreover
was bound by the universal laws of hospitality, as firmly as any Bedouin
sheikh. Danger there would be none. Farr stepped forward, passed into
the interior of the dome. At the center was a slightly raised bed of rich
soil, on which rested a large bubble, a sac of yellow gum. The surface
of this sac was veined with glistening white strings and tubes of membrane which at the apex merged to form a pale gray trunk, which in turn
supported a symmetrical crown of branches and wide heart-shaped
black-green leaves. So much Farr glimpsed in an instant, though from
the moment of his entry his attention was fixed on that which was con-
tained in the capsule of gum: a naked Thord body. The feet rested in a
dark yellow sediment at the bottom of the sac, the head was close up
under the trunk; the arms were raised shoulder high and terminated,

not in hands, but in tangled balls of gray fiber which then became ropes rising into the trunk. The top of the scalp was removed, revealing the mass of orange spherules which comprised the Thord brain. About the exposed brain hung a nimbus which Farr, moving step by fascinated step closer, saw to be a mesh of near-invisible threads, likewise knotting into a rope and disappearing into the trunk. The eyes were covered by the shutter of a dark brown membrane which served the Thord for eyelids.

Farr took a deep breath, fighting to control intense revulsion mingled with pity and a peculiar urgency he could not define... He became aware of the attention of the Iszics, and turned sharply. The double-segmented eyes of all three were riveted upon him.

Farr suppressed his emotions as best he could. Whatever the Iszics expected, he would make certain to disappoint them. "This must be the Thord with whom I was locked up."

Zhde Patasz came slowly forward, his lips twisting in and out. "You recognize him?"

Farr shook his head. "I hardly saw him. He is an alien, and looks to me much like any other of his race." He peered more closely into the sac of amber gum. "Is he alive?"

"To a certain degree."

"Why do you bring me here?"

Zhde Patasz was almost certainly disturbed, perhaps even angry. Farr wondered what sort of complex plan had gone awry. He stared into the sac. The Thord — had it moved? Omon Bozhd, standing at his left, apparently had noticed the same almost imperceptible twitch of muscle. "The Thord have great psychic resources," said Omon Bozhd, moving forward.

Farr turned to Zhde Patasz. "It was my understanding that he had died."

"So he has," said Zhde Patasz, "for all practical purposes. He is no longer Chayen, Fourteenth of Tente, Baron of Binicristi Castle. His personality is departed, he is now an organ, or a nodule, attached to a tree."

Farr looked back to the Thord. The eyes had opened, the face had taken on an odd expression. Farr wondered if the Thord could hear words, could understand. In Omon Bozhd beside him, there was a tension, a straining of perplexity. A quick glance showed the same rigidity now in Zhde Patasz and Uder Che: all stared in wonder at the Thord. Uder Che uttered a sudden staccato burst of Iszic, pointed to the foliage. Farr looked up to find that the leaves were shivering. There were no draughts, no currents of air within the dome. Farr looked back to the Thord, to find the eyes fixed on his own. The face strained, the muscles around the mouth had corded. Farr could not tear his gaze away. Now the mouth drooped, the lips quivered; overhead the heavy branches creaked and groaned.

"Impossible!" croaked Omon Bozhd. "This is not a correct reaction!"

The branches swayed and lurched, there was a terrifying crack; down swept a whistling mass of foliage, to fall upon Zhde Patasz and Uder Che. There was another groaning of tortured wood; the trunk split, the entire tree wavered and toppled. The sac burst, the Thord sprawled out upon the floor, half-supported by the fiber bundles into which his arms terminated. His head lolled back, his mouth split into a ghastly grin. "I am no tree," he croaked in a throaty gurgling voice. "I am Chayen of Tente." Trickles of yellow lymph oozed from his mouth. He coughed convulsively and fixed his gaze upon Farr. "Get hence, get hence. Leave these cursed tree-dwellers. Go; do what you must."

Omon Bozhd had leapt to assist Zhde Patasz from under the toppled tree; Farr looked toward them uncertainly. The Thord sank back. "Now I die," he said in a guttural whisper. "I die not as a tree of Iszm, but as a Thord, as Chayen of Tente."

Farr turned away, and gave assistance to Omon Bozhd and Zhde Patasz who were trying to extricate Uder Che from under the foliage. But to no avail. A broken branch had driven through the architect's neck. Zhde Patasz gave a cry of despair. "The creature has wounded me in death as he troubled me in life; he has killed the most accomplished of architects." Zhde Patasz turned away, and strode from the dome. Omon Bozhd and Farr followed.

The party returned to Tjiere Town, in gloom and silence. Zhde Patasz conducted himself toward Farr with no more than bare civility. When the glide-car slid into the central avenue, Farr said, "Zhde Patasz

Sainh, the events of this afternoon have troubled you deeply, and I think it best that I no longer trespass on your hospitality."

Zhde Patasz responded curtly. "Farr Sainh must do as he thinks best."

"I will carry with me forever the memory of my stay on Tjiere Atoll," said Farr fulsomely. "You have given me an insight into the problems of the Iszic planter, and for this I thank you."

Zhde Patasz bowed. "Farr Sainh may rest assured that we, on our part, will keep him ever fresh in our minds."

The glide-car stopped at the plaza beside which grew the three hotels; Farr alighted. After a moment's hesitation Omon Bozhd did likewise. There was a final exchange of formal thanks and equally formal disclaimers, and then the glide-car moved on.

Omon Bozhd went up to Farr. "And what are your plans now?" he inquired gravely.

"I will rent a room at the hotel," said Farr.

Omon Bozhd nodded, as if Farr had uttered a truth of great profundity. "And then?"

"My boat is still under charter," said Farr. He frowned. He had little desire to investigate the plantations of other atolls. "I'll probably return to Jhespiano. And then —"

"And then?"

Farr shrugged fretfully. "I'm not sure."

"In any event, I wish you a pleasant voyage."

"Thank you."

Farr crossed the plaza, registered at the largest of the hotels, and was shown to a suite of pods similar to those which he had occupied at the house of Zhde Patasz.

When he came down to the restaurant for his evening meal, the Szecr were once more in evidence, and Farr felt stifled. After the meal, a typical Iszic repast of marine and vegetable pastes, Farr walked down the avenue to the waterfront, where he ordered the *Lhaiz* made ready for immediate sailing. The captain was not aboard; the boatswain protested that dawn of the following day was the earliest possible time of departure, and Farr had to be content. To pass the evening he went to walk along the beach. The surf, the warm wind, the sand were like those of Earth; but the silhouettes of the alien trees and the two Szecr padding behind threw everything into a different context, and Farr felt a pang of homesickness. He had journeyed enough; it was time to return to Earth.

Chapter VI

FARR BOARDED THE *LHAIZ* before Xi Aurigae had fully cleared the horizon, and with the freedom of the Pheadh before him his spirits lifted. The crew was at work, reeving halyards, unfolding sails; there was about the *Lhaiz* the electric sense of immediacy of a ship about to sail. Farr tossed his meager luggage into the after cabin, looked about for the captain, and gave orders to sail. The captain bowed, called various orders to the crew. Half an hour passed, but the *Lhaiz* had not yet cast off. Farr went to the captain, who stood far forward. "Why the delay?"

The captain pointed below, to where a seaman in a punt worked on the hull. "A leak is being repaired, Farr Sainh; we will soon be underway."

Farr returned to the elevated fan-tail, seated himself in the shade of an awning. Another fifteen minutes went by. Farr relaxed and began to take pleasure in the surroundings, the activity of the waterfront, the passers-by in their stripes and bands of various colors…Three Szecr approached the *Lhaiz*, came aboard. They spoke to the captain, who turned and gave orders to the crew.

Sails bellied to the wind, mooring lines were cast off, rigging creaked. Farr jumped from his chair, suddenly furious. He started forward to order the Szecr ashore, then restrained himself: an exercise in pure futility. Fuming with repressed rage, Farr returned to his chair. Bubbling, breasting through the blue water, the *Lhaiz* put out to sea. Tjiere Atoll dwindled, became a shadow on the horizon, vanished. The *Lhaiz* scudded west, with the wind astern. Farr frowned. To the best of his recollection he had given no instructions as to their destination. He summoned the captain.

"I have given you no orders; why do you sail west?"

The captain shifted the gaze of one segment of his eyes. "Our destination is Jhespiano; is this not Farr Sainh's desire?"

"No," said Farr from sheer perversity. "We will head south, toward Vhejanh."

"But, Farr Sainh, should we not make directly for Jhespiano, you may well miss the departure of the spaceship!"

Farr could hardly speak for astonishment. "What is this to you?" he said at last. "Have I expressed a desire to board the spaceship?"

"No, Farr Sainh. Not to my hearing."

"Then kindly make no further assumptions regarding my wishes. We will sail for Vhejanh."

The captain hesitated. "Your orders, Farr Sainh, of course must be weighed carefully. There are also the commands of the Szecr to be considered. They desire that the *Lhaiz* proceed to Jhespiano."

"In that case," said Farr, "the Szecr can pay the charter fee. You will collect nothing from me."

The captain turned slowly away, went to consult the Szecr. There was a brief discussion, during which the captain and the Szecr turned to examine Farr who sat aloof on the fan-tail. At last the *Lhaiz* swung south on a reach, and the Szecr went angrily forward.

The voyage proceeded. Farr's relaxation soon vanished. The crew was as vigilant as ever, and less punctilious. The Szecr watched his every move and searched his cabin with an insolent casualness. Farr felt more like a prisoner than a tourist. It was almost as if he were being subjected to deliberate provocation, as if the aim were to make him disgusted with Iszm. "No difficulty in that case," Farr told himself grimly. "The day I leave this planet will be the happiest day of my life."

Vhejanh Atoll rose above the horizon: a group of islands which might have been the twin of Tjiere. Farr forced himself to go ashore but found nothing more interesting to do than sit on the terrace of the hotel with a goblet of *narciz*, a sharp, faintly salty beverage derived from seaweed, consumed in quantities by the Iszics of the Pheadh. As he departed he noticed a placard displaying a photograph of a spaceship, and a schedule of arrivals and departures. The SS *Andrei Simic* was scheduled to leave Jhespiano in three days. There were no other scheduled departures for four months. Farr considered the placard with great interest. He then returned to the dock, resigned his charter of the *Lhaiz*, after which he took air passage to Jhespiano.

He arrived the same evening, and at once booked passage aboard the SS *Andrei Simic* to Earth, whereupon he felt great comfort and peace of mind. "Ridiculous situation," he told himself in half-humorous self-contempt. "Six months ago I could think of nothing but travel to strange planets; now all I want is to go home to Earth."

The Spaceport Hotel at Jhespiano was an enormous rambling growth of a dozen interlinked trees. Farr was assigned a pleasant pod overlooking the canal leading from the lagoon into the heart of Jhespiano Town. With the time of his departure established Farr once more began to enjoy himself. His meals at the restaurant, pre-packaged and imported, were again palatable; the guests were a varied group, with representatives of most of the anthropoid races, including a dozen Earthers.

The sole annoyance was the continued surveillance by the Szecr, which became so pervasive that Farr complained first to the hotel management, then to the Szecr lieutenant, in both cases receiving only bland shrugs for his trouble. He finally marched across the compound to the little concrete bungalow which housed the office of the District Treaty Administrator, one of the few non-organic buildings on Iszm. The Administrator was a pudgy little Earther with a beak nose, a ruff of black hair and a fussy manner, to whom Farr took an immediate aversion. Nevertheless he explained his grievance in a reasonable measured manner and the Administrator promised to make inquiries.

Farr called the next day at the Administrative Mansion, a massive and dignified house overhanging the central canal. On this second visit the Administrator was only formally cordial, although he grudgingly asked Farr to lunch. They ate on a balcony, with boat-pods laden with fruit and flowers passing along the canal below.

"I called the Szecr Central about your case," the Administrator told Farr. "They're ambiguous, which is unusual. Usually they say bluntly, so-and-so is objectionable; he has been spying."

"I still don't understand why they should persecute me so intensely."

"Apparently you were present when a company of Arcturians —"

"Thord."

The Administrator acknowledged the correction. "—when the Thord made a massive raid on Tjiere plantation."

"I was there, certainly."

The Administrator fiddled with his coffee cup. "This has been enough, evidently, to arouse their suspicions. They believe that one or more spies in the guise of tourists have planned and controlled the raid, and apparently have selected you as one of the responsible parties."

Farr leaned back in his chair. "That's incredible. The Szecr dosed me with hypnotics, questioned me. They know everything I know. And afterwards the head planter at Tjiere had me as his house-guest. They *can't* believe that I'm involved! It's unreasonable!"

The Administrator gave a wry noncommittal shrug. "This may be. The Szecr admit they have no special charge to bring against you. But, in some way or another you've managed to make yourself an object of suspicion."

"And so, guilty or innocent, I have to be molested by their attentions? This isn't either the letter or the spirit of the Treaty."

"That may well be." The Administrator was annoyed. "I fancy that I am as familiar with the provisions of the Treaty as you are." He passed Farr a second cup of coffee, darting a curious glance at him as he did so. "I assume you're not guilty... But perhaps there's something you know. Did you communicate with anyone they might suspect?"

Farr made an impatient motion. "They threw me into a cell with one of the Thord. I hardly spoke to him."

The Administrator was obviously unconvinced. "There must be something you've done to bother them. The Iszics, no matter what you care to say, have no interest in harassing you or anyone else from sheer caprice."

Farr lost his temper. "Who are you representing? Me? Or the Szecr?"

The Administrator said coldly, "Try to see the situation from my viewpoint. After all it's not impossible that you are what they seem to think you are."

"First they have to prove it. And even then you are my legal representative. What else are you here for?"

The Administrator evaded the question. "I only know what you've told me. I spoke to the Iszic Commandant. He is noncommittal. Perhaps they regard you as a dupe, a decoy, a messenger. They may be waiting for you to make a false move or lead them to someone who will."

"They'll have a long wait. In fact, I'm the aggrieved party, not the Iszics."

"In what sense?"

"After the raid, they dropped me into a cell. I mentioned that they imprisoned me — threw me down a hollow root into an underground cell. I banged my head rather badly; in fact I'm still wearing scabs." He felt his scalp, where hair at last was beginning to grow, and sighed. It was evident that the Administrator would take no action. He looked around the balcony. "This place must be tapped for sound."

"I have nothing to conceal," said the Administrator stiffly. "They can listen night and day. They probably do." He rose to his feet. "When does your ship leave?"

"In two or three days, depending on cargo."

"My advice is to tolerate the surveillance, make the best of it."

Farr extended perfunctory thanks and departed. The Szecr were waiting; they bowed politely as Farr stepped out into the street. Farr drew a deep breath of resignation. Since there would evidently be no amelioration to the situation, he might as well make the best of it.

He returned to the hotel, showered in the translucent nodule attached to his pod. The liquid was a cool fresh-scented sap, issuing from a nozzle disturbingly like a cow's udder. After dressing in fresh garments provided by the hotel, Farr descended to the terrace. Bored with his own company he looked around the tables. He had formed some slight acquaintance with the other guests: Mr. and Mrs. Anderview, a pair of peripatetic missionaries; Jonas Ralf, and Wilfred Willeran, engineers returning to Earth from Capella XII's great Equatorial Highway and who were sitting now with a group of touring school teachers only just arrived on Iszm; three round Monagi commercial travelers, Earth stock, but after a hundred and fifty years, already modified by the environment of Monago, or Taurus 61 III, to a characteristic somatic type. To their right were three Nenes, tall slender near-men, agile, voluble and clairvoyant, then a pair of young Earthers Farr understood to be students, then a group of Great Arcturians, the stock from which, after a million years on a different planet, the Thord had evolved. To the other side of the Monagis sat four Iszic in red and purple stripes, the significance of which Farr was ignorant, and not far distant, drinking a goblet of *narciz* with an air of intense preoccupation, another Iszic in blue, black and white. Farr stared. He could not be sure — all Iszic seemed much alike — but this individual almost certainly was Omon Bozhd.

Seeming to sense Farr's attention the man turned his head, nodded politely to Farr, then rose to his feet, came across the terrace. "May I join you?"

Farr indicated a chair. "I had not expected the pleasure of renewing our acquaintance so soon," he said dryly.

Omon Bozhd performed one of the bland Iszic gestures the significance of which was beyond Farr's understanding. "You did not know of my plans to visit Earth?"

"No, certainly not."

"Curious."

Farr said nothing.

"Our friend Zhde Patasz Sainh has asked me to convey to you a message," said Omon Bozhd. "First he transmits through me a correct Type 8 salute and the sense of his shame that disturbance marred your last day at Tjiere. That the Thord had psychic force sufficient for such an act is still almost incredible to us. Secondly, he counsels you to choose your associates with great caution during the next few months; and thirdly, he commends me to your care and hospitality on Earth, where I will be a stranger."

Farr mused. "How could Zhde Patasz Sainh know that I planned to return to Earth? When I left Tjiere this was not my intent."

"I spoke with him only last night by telecom."

"I see," said Farr grudgingly. "Well, naturally I'll do what I can to help you. Which part of Earth will you visit?"

"My plans are not yet complete. I go to inspect Zhde Patasz's houses at their various plantings, and no doubt will travel considerably."

"What do you mean 'choose my associates with caution'?"

"Just that. It seems that rumors of the Thord raid have reached Jhespiano, and have been enlarged in the process. Certain criminal elements might on this account be interested in your activities — but then,

I speak too freely." Omon Bozhd rose to his feet, bowed, departed. Farr stared after him in utter perplexity.

On the next evening the hotel management, taking cognizance of the large number of Earther guests, arranged a musical soiree, with Earth-style music and Earth-style refreshments. Almost all the guests, Earthers and otherwise, attended.

Farr became mildly intoxicated on Scotch-and-soda, to the extent that he found himself behaving with great gallantry toward the youngest and prettiest of the touring school-teachers. She seemed to return his interest and they strolled arm in arm along the promenade overlooking the beach. There was small talk, then suddenly she turned him an arch look. "If I may say so, you certainly don't seem the type."

" 'Type'? What type?"

"Oh — you know. A man capable of fooling the Iszics and stealing trees right out from under their very noses."

Farr laughed. "Your instincts are correct. I'm not."

Again she turned him a quick sidewise look. "I've heard differently on ever so reliable authority."

Farr tried to keep his voice light and casual. "So? What did you hear?"

"Well — naturally it's supposed to be secret, because if the Iszics knew, you'd be sent to the Mad House, so obviously you wouldn't be particularly keen to talk about it — but the person who told me is quite reliable, and of course I'd never say a word to anyone; in fact, my reaction is, cheers!"

"I haven't the slightest idea what you're talking about," said Farr in an edgy voice.

"No, I suppose you'd never really dare admit it," said the young woman regretfully. "After all, I might be an Iszic agent — they do have them, you know —"

"Once and for all," said Farr, "I don't know what you're talking about."

"The raid on Tjiere," said the young woman. "It's going around that you're the brains behind the raid. That you're smuggling trees out of Iszm for delivery on Earth. Everybody is talking about it."

Farr laughed sadly. "What utter nonsense. If this were true, do you imagine I'd be at large? Of course not. The Iszics are considerably more clever than you give them credit for... How did this ridiculous idea get started?"

The young woman was disappointed. She would have preferred a daring tree-thief to plain ordinary innocent Aile Farr. "I'm sure I don't know."

"Where did you hear it?"

"At the hotel. Some of the people were talking about it."

"Anything for a sensation," said Farr.

The young woman sniffed and her demeanor was noticeably cooler as they returned to the terrace.

No sooner had they seated themselves than four Szecr, with head-dresses betokening high rank, marched across the room. They stopped at Farr's table, bowed curtly. "If Farr Sainh pleases, his presence is requested elsewhere."

Farr sat back, half of a notion to defy the group. He looked around the terrace, but saw only averted faces. The school-teacher was in a transport of excitement.

"Where is my presence desired?" demanded Farr in a voice stiff with fury. "And why?"

"There are a few routine inquiries to be made, in connection with your professed business on Iszm."

"Can't it wait till tomorrow?"

"No, Farr Sainh. Please come at once."

Seething with indignation Farr rose to his feet, and surrounded by the Szecr, walked from the terrace.

He was taken a quarter-mile to a small three-pod tree near the beach. Within an old Iszic sat on a divan. He motioned Farr to sit opposite, and introduced himself as Usimr Adislj, of the caste comprising savants, theoreticians, philosophers and other formulators of abstract principles. "Learning of your presence in Jhespiano, and your almost immediate departure, I felt it my duty to make your acquaintance as expeditiously as possible. I understand that on Earth you are professionally connected with the field of knowledge that is one of our major preoccupations?"

"That is true," said Farr shortly. "I am immensely flattered by your attention, but I could have wished for its manifestation in less emphatic terms. Everyone at the hotel is certain I have been arrested by the Szecr for the crime of house-stealing."

Usimr Adislj gave an uninterested shrug. "This craving for morbid sensation is a general trait of those hominids of simian descent. It is an emotion I believe may best be countered by lofty contempt."

"Indeed," said Farr. "I agree. But was it necessary to send four Szecr with your invitation? It was less than discreet."

"No matter. Men of our stature cannot be bothered with such trifles. Now tell me of your background and your special interests."

For four hours he and Usimr Adislj discussed Iszm, Earth, the universe, the variations of man and the direction of the future; and when the Szecr, their number and quality now reduced to a pair of underlings, finally escorted Farr back to the hotel, he felt that he had passed a highly rewarding evening.

The next morning, when he appeared on the terrace for breakfast, he was greeted with something like awe. Mrs. Anderview, the pretty young wife of the missionary, said, "We thought for sure you'd been taken away — to jail. Or even the Mad House. And we wondered if we shouldn't arouse the Administrator immediately."

"It was unimportant," said Farr. "Just a mistake. But thank you for your interest."

The Monagi also questioned him. "Is it a fact that you and the Thord have completely outwitted the Szecr? Because if so, we can make you a very handsome offer for any female tree of which you chance to find yourself in possession."

"I am capable of outwitting no one," declared Farr. "I own no female tree, by chance or otherwise."

The Monagi nodded and winked knowingly. "Naturally, naturally, not on Iszm where even the grass has ears."

The next day the SS *Andrei Simic* dropped down from the sky, and departure hour was posted precisely: nine o'clock of the morning two days hence. During these final two days Farr found the Szecr possibly even more assiduous in their watchfulness. The night before departure one of them approached and with great punctilio delivered a message. "If Farr Sainh can spare the time, he is asked to call at the embarkation office."

"Very well," said Farr, resigning himself to the worst. He dispatched his luggage to the space-terminal, and presented himself at the embarkation office, expecting an examination to end all examinations.

The Szecr completely confounded him. He was conducted into the pod of the Szecr sub-commandant, who spoke bluntly and to the point.

"Farr Sainh — you may have sensed our interest during the last few weeks."

Farr expressed agreement.

"I may not divulge the background to the case," said the Szecr. "The surveillance was motivated by concern for your safety."

"Ha, ha! My safety?"

"We suspect that you are in danger."

"Danger? Ridiculous."

"Not so. Quite the contrary. On the night of the musicale, we removed a poisoned thorn from your seat. On yet another occasion, while you drank on the terrace, poison was introduced into your goblet."

Farr's mouth dropped in astonishment. Somewhere, somehow, a terrible mistake was being made. "How can you be sure of all this? It seems — incredible!"

The Iszic flickered the filament dividing his double eyes in amusement. "You remember formalities connected with arrival at Iszm. They allow us to maintain a quarantine upon the import of weapons. Poison is a different matter. A speck of dust can be infected with ten million virulent bacteria, and can be concealed without difficulty. Hence, any outworlder planning murder must employ strangulation or poison. The vigilance of the Szecr prohibits acts of physical violence, so we must only be alert for poison. What are the vehicles? Food, drink, injection. When we classify the various means and devices to achieve these ends, we find one of the subdivisions to read: 'Poisoned thorn, splinter, or barb, calculated to penetrate or puncture the thigh, haunch, or buttock, through vertical impingement under force of gravity'. Hence, our surveillance at all times includes the chair or benches where you are likely to sit."

"I see," said Farr in a subdued voice.

"Poison in your drink we detect by means of a reagent which darkens when a change of any sort is made in the mother solution. When one of your Scotch-and-sodas became unusually murky, we removed it and provided a substitute."

"This is extremely bewildering," said Farr. "Who would want to poison me? For what reason?"

"I have been authorized to communicate only this warning."

"But — what are you warning me against?"

"The details will contribute nothing to your safety."

"But — I've done nothing!"

The Szecr sub-commandant twirled his viewer. "The universe is eight billion years old, the last two billion of which have produced intelligent life. During this time not one hour of absolute equity has prevailed. It should be no surprise to find this basic condition applying to your personal affairs."

"In other words —"

"In other words — tread soundlessly, look around corners, follow enticing females into no dark chambers." He plucked a taut string; a young Szecr appeared. "Conduct Aile Farr Sainh aboard the *Andrei Simic*; we are waiving all further examinations."

Farr stared in disbelief.

"Yes, Farr Sainh," said the Szecr. "We feel you have demonstrated your honesty."

Farr left the pod in a daze of perplexity. Something was wrong. The Iszic waived examination of no one and nothing.

Alone in his cubicle aboard the *Andrei Simic*, he eased himself down on the elastic panel that served as his bed. He was in danger. The Szecr had said so. It was an unsettling idea. Farr had a normal quota of courage; fighting tangible enemies he would not disgrace himself. But to learn that his life might be taken, to be ignorant of the hows and whys and wherefores — it brought a queasy turmoil to his stomach...Of course, reasoned Farr, the Szecr sub-commandant might be in error; or he might have used the mysterious threat to speed Farr away from Iszm.

He rose to his feet, searched his cabin. He found no overt mechanisms, no spy-cells. He arranged his possessions in such a way that he would notice a disturbance; then, sliding aside the fiber panel, he looked out upon the catwalk. It was a ribbon of striated gray glass — empty. Farr stepped out, walked hurriedly to the lounge.

He examined the roster. There were twenty-eight passengers including himself. Some of the names he recognized: Mr. and Mrs. Anderview, Jonas Ralf, Wilfred Willeran and Omon Bozhd; others, approximate renderings of alien phonemes, meant nothing.

Farr returned to his cabin, locked the door, and lay down on the bed...

Chapter VII

NOT TILL THE *ANDREI SIMIC* was space-borne and the captain came to the lounge for the routine reading of the ship's regulations did Farr see his fellow passengers. There were seven Iszic, nine Earthers, the three Monagi savants, three Codain monks performing a ritual pilgrimage around the worlds, five others of assorted worlds, most of whom had arrived at Iszm with the ship. Except for Omon Bozhd the Iszic wore the gold and black stripes of planter's agents, high-caste austere men, more or less of a type. Farr presumed that two or perhaps three were Szecr. The Earthers included a pair of talkative young students and a grizzled sanitary engineer on leave to Earth; the Anderviews; Ralf and Willeran; Carto and Maudel Wlewska, a young couple on tour.

Farr assessed the group, trying to picture each in the role of a potential assassin, and finally admitted himself at a loss. Those who had already been aboard the ship seemed automatically eliminated from suspicion, as did the Codain monks and the cherubic Monagi. It was wildly unreasonable to suspect the Iszics, which more or less left the Earthers — but why should any of these seek to harm him? Why should he expect harm from anyone? He scratched his head in perplexity, disturbing the scab he still carried from his slide down the Tjiere root-tube.

The voyage settled into routine — steady identical hours broken by meals and sleep-periods at whatever rhythm the passenger chose. To while away the tedium, or perhaps because the tedium provided nothing else to think of, Farr began an innocent flirtation with Mrs. Anderview. Her husband was engrossed in writing a voluminous report regarding the achievements of his mission at Dapa Doory, on the planet Mazen, and was seen only at meal-times, leaving Mrs. Anderview much to herself — and to Farr. She was a graceful woman, with a rich mouth and a provocative half-smile. Farr's part in the affair extended no further than a frame of mind, a warmth of tone, a significant glance or two — a lukewarm matter at best. He was correspondingly surprised when Mrs. Anderview, whose first name he did not know, came quietly into his cabin one evening, smiling with a kind of shy recklessness.

Farr sat up blinking.

"May I come in?"

"You're already in."

Mrs. Anderview nodded slowly and slid the panel shut behind her. Farr noticed suddenly that she was far prettier than he had let himself observe, that she wore a perfume of indefinable sweetness: aloes, cardamon, limone.

She sat beside him. "I grow so bored," she complained. "Night after night Merritt writes, it's always the same. He thinks of nothing but his budget. And I — I like fun."

The invitation could hardly have been more explicit. Farr examined first one side of the situation then the other. He cleared his throat, while Mrs. Anderview, blushing a little, watched him.

There was a rap at the door. Farr jumped to his feet, as if he were already guilty. He eased the panel open. Waiting outside was Omon Bozhd.

"Farr Sainh, may I consult you for a moment? I would consider it a great favor."

"Well," said Farr, "I'm busy right now."

"The matter transcends business."

Farr turned to the woman. "Just a minute; I'll be right back."

"Hurry!" She seemed very impatient; Farr looked at her in surprise, started to speak.

"Sh," she warned him. Farr shrugged, stepped out into the corridor.

"What's the trouble?" he asked Omon Bozhd.

"Farr Sainh — would you like to save your life?"

"Very much indeed," said Farr, "but —"

"Invite me into your cabin." Omon Bozhd took a step forward.

"There's hardly room," said Farr. "And anyway —"

The Iszic said earnestly, "You understand the pattern, do you not?"

"No," said Farr. "I'd like to — but I'm afraid I don't."

Omon Bozhd nodded. "Your gallantry must be forgotten. Let us enter your cabin; there is not much time." He slid back the panel, stepped through. Farr followed, sure he was a fool, but not sure exactly what kind of fool.

Mrs. Merritt Anderview jumped to her feet. "Oh," she gasped, flushing. "Mr. Farr!"

Farr held out his hands helplessly. Mrs. Anderview started to march from the cabin; Omon Bozhd stood in her way. He grinned; his pale mouth split, showing his gray palate, his arch of pointed teeth.

"Please, Mrs. Anderview, do not leave; your reputation is safe."

"I have no time to waste," she said sharply. Farr saw suddenly that she was not pretty, that her face was pinched, her eyes angry and selfish.

"Please," said Omon Bozhd, "not just yet. Sit down, if you will."

A rap-rap on the door. A voice hoarse with fury. "Open up, open up in there!"

"Certainly," said Omon Bozhd. He flung the panel wide. Anderview stood framed in the opening, the whites of his eyes showing. He held a shatter-gun, his hand was trembling. He saw Omon Bozhd; his shoulders sagged, his jaw slackened.

"Excuse me for not asking you in," said Farr. "We're a little crowded."

Anderview reorganized his passion. "What's going on in here!"

Mrs. Anderview pushed out upon the catwalk. "Nothing," she said in a throaty voice. "Nothing at all." She swept down the corridor.

In a negligent voice Omon Bozhd spoke to Anderview. "There is nothing for you here. Perhaps you had better join your lady."

Anderview slowly turned on his heel, departed.

Farr felt weak in the knees. Here were depths he could not fathom, whorls of motive and purpose... He sank down on the bunk, burning at the thought of how he had been played for a sucker.

"An excellent pretext for expunging a man," remarked the Iszic. "At least in the framework of Earth institutions."

Farr glanced up sharply, detecting a sardonic flavor to the remark. He said grudgingly, "I guess you saved my hide — two or three square feet of it, anyway."

Omon Bozhd moved his hand, gesturing with a non-existent viewer. "A trifle."

"Not to me," Farr growled. "I like my hide."

The Iszic turned to go.

"Just a minute," said Farr. He rose to his feet. "I want to know what's going on."

"The matter is surely self-explanatory?"

"Maybe I'm stupid."

The Iszic examined him thoughtfully. "Perhaps you're too close to the situation to see it in its whole."

"You're of the Szecr?" asked Farr.

"Every foreign agent is of the Szecr."

"Well, what's going on? Why are the Anderviews after me?"

"They've weighed you, balanced your usefulness against the danger you represent."

"This is absolutely fantastic!"

Omon Bozhd focused both fractions of his eyes on Farr. He spoke in a reflective key. "Every second of existence is a new miracle. Consider the countless variations and possibilities that await us every second — avenues into the future. We take only one of these; the others — who knows where they go? This is the eternal marvel, the magnificent uncertainty of the second next to come, with the past a steady unfolding carpet of dénouement —"

"Yes, yes," said Farr.

"Our minds become numbed to the wonder of life, because of its very pressure and magnitude." Omon Bozhd at last took his eyes off Farr. "In such a perspective this affair has intrinsic interest no more or less than taking a single breath."

Farr said in a stiff voice, "I can breathe as many times as I care to; I can die only once, so there does seem a certain practical difference. Apparently you think so too — and I admit to being in your debt. But — why?"

Omon Bozhd swung his absent viewer. "Iszic rationale is of course different to that of the Earther; we nevertheless share certain instincts, such as reverence for vitality and the impulse to aid our acquaintances."

"I see," said Farr. "Your action then was merely a friendly good turn?"

Omon Bozhd bowed. "You may regard it as such. And now I will bid you good night." He left the cabin.

Farr sat numbly upon his bed. In the last few minutes the Anderviews had metamorphosed from a kindly, rather remote, missionary and his attractive wife to a pair of ruthless murderers. But why? *Why?*

Farr shook his head in abject puzzlement. The Szecr sub-commandant had mentioned a poisoned thorn and a poisoned drink: evidently their responsibility as well. Angrily he jumped to his feet, strode to the door, which he slid back and looked along the catwalk. To right and left glimmered the gray glass ribbon. Overhead a similar ribbon gave access to the cabins next above. Farr quietly left the cabin, walked to the end of the catwalk, looked through the arch into the lounge. The two young tourists, the sanitary engineer, a pair of Iszic were playing poker. The Iszic were ahead of the game, with one fraction of their eyes focused on the cards, the other on the faces of their opponents.

Farr turned back. He climbed the ladder to the upper deck. There was silence except for the normal half-heard sounds of the ship — sigh of pumps, murmur of circulating air, subdued mutter from the lounge.

Farr found the door with a placard reading *Merritt and Anthea Anderview*. He hesitated, listening. He heard nothing, no sounds, no voices. He put his hand out to knock, paused. He recollected Omon Bozhd's dissertation on life, the infinity of avenues to the future...He could knock, he could return to his cabin. He knocked.

No one answered. Farr looked up and down the catwalk. He could still return to his cabin. He tried the door. It opened. The room was dark. Farr put his elbow to the molding; light filled the room. Merritt Anderview, sitting stiffly in a chair, looked at him with a wide fearless gaze.

Farr saw he was dead. Anthea Anderview lay in the lower bunk, relaxed and quite composed.

Farr made no close inspection, but she was dead too. A shatter-gun vibrating at low intensity had homogenized their brains; their thoughts and memories were brown melange; their chosen avenues into the future had come to a break. Farr stood still. He tried to hold his breath, but he knew the damage had already been done. He backed out, closed the door. The stewards would presently find the bodies... In the meantime — Farr stood thinking with growing uneasiness. He might have been observed. His stupid flirtation with Anthea Anderview might be common knowledge; perhaps even the argument with Merritt Anderview. His presence in the cabin could be easily established; there would be a film of his exhalations on every object in the room. This constituted positive identification in the courtrooms, if it could be shown that no other person aboard the ship fell into his exhalation group.

Farr turned. He left the cabin, crossed the lounge. No one appeared to observe him. He climbed the ladder to the bridge, knocked at the door of the Captain's cabin.

Captain Dorristy slid the panel back—a stocky taciturn man with squinting black eyes. Behind Dorristy stood Omon Bozhd. Farr thought that his cheek muscles tightened; that his hand gave a jerk as if he were twirling his viewer.

Farr felt suddenly at ease. He had rolled with whatever punch Omon Bozhd was trying to deliver. "Two passengers are dead—the Anderviews."

Omon Bozhd turned both eye-fractions on him: cold animosity.

"That's interesting," said Dorristy. "Come in."

Farr stepped through the door. Omon Bozhd looked away.

Dorristy said in a soft voice, "Bozhd here tells me that you killed the Anderviews."

Farr turned to look at the Iszic. "He's probably the most plausible liar on the ship. He did it himself."

Dorristy grinned, looking from one to the other. "He says you were after the woman."

"I was politely attentive. This is a dull trip. Up to now."

Dorristy looked at the Iszic. "What do you say, Omon Bozhd?"

The Iszic swung his non-existent viewer. "Something more than politeness brought Mrs. Anderview to Farr's cabin."

Farr said, "Something other than altruism brought Omon Bozhd to my cabin to prevent Anderview from shooting me."

Omon Bozhd feigned surprise. "I know nothing whatever of your liaisons."

Farr checked his anger, turned to the Captain. "Do you believe him?"

Dorristy grinned sourly. "I don't believe anyone."

"This is what happened. It's hard to believe but it's true." Farr told his story. "—after Bozhd left, I got thinking. I was going to get to the bottom of it, one way or the other. I went to the Anderviews' cabin. I opened the door, saw they were dead; I came here at once."

Dorristy said nothing, but now he was examining Omon Bozhd rather than Farr. At last he shrugged. "I'll seal the room; you can sweat it out when we get to Earth."

Omon Bozhd obscured the lower half of his eyes. He swung the absent viewer nonchalantly. "I have heard Farr's story," he said in a thoughtful voice. "He impresses me with his frankness. I believe I am mistaken; it is not likely that he performed the crime. I retract my accusation." He stalked from the cabin. Farr gazed after him in angry triumph.

Dorristy looked at Farr. "You didn't kill them, eh?"

Farr snorted. "Of course not."

"Who did?"

"My guess would be one or another of the Iszics. Why I have no idea."

Dorristy nodded, spoke gruffly from the side of his mouth, "Well — we'll see when we put down at Barstow." He glanced sidewise at Farr. "I'll take it as a favor if you keep this matter quiet. Don't discuss it with anyone."

"I didn't intend to," said Farr shortly.

Chapter VIII

THE BODIES WERE PHOTOGRAPHED and removed to cold storage; the cabin was sealed. The ship buzzed with rumor; Farr found the Anderviews a difficult topic to avoid.

Earth grew closer. Farr felt no great apprehension, but the uncertainty, the underlying mystery remained: why had the Anderviews waylaid him in the first place? Would he run into further danger on Earth? Farr became angry. These intrigues were no concern of his; he wanted no part of them. But an uncomfortable conviction kept pushing up from his subconscious: he was involved, however bitterly he rejected the idea. He had other things to do — his job, his thesis, the compilation of a stereo which he hoped to sell to one of the broadcast networks.

And there was something else, a curious urgency, a pressure, something to be done. It came at odd moments to trouble Farr — a dissatisfaction, like an unresolved chord in some deep chamber of his mind. It had no direct connection with the Anderviews and their murderer, no link with anything. It was something to be done, something he had forgotten... or never known...

Omon Bozhd spoke to him only once, approaching him in the lounge. He said in an offhand voice, "You are now aware of the threat you face. On Earth I may be unable to help you."

Farr's resentment had not diminished. He said, "On Earth you'll probably be executed for murder."

"No, Aile Farr Sainh, it will not be proved against me."

Farr examined the pale narrow face. Iszic and Earther — evolved from different stock to the same humanoid approximation: simian, amphibian — there would never be a rapport or sympathy between the races. Farr asked curiously, "You didn't kill them?"

"Certainly it is unnecessary to iterate the obvious to a man of Aile Farr's intelligence."

"Go ahead, iterate it. Reiterate it. I'm stupid. Did you kill them?"

"It is unkind of you to require an answer to this question."

"Very well, don't answer. But why did you try to pin it on me? You know I didn't do it. What have you got against me?"

Omon Bozhd smiled thinly. "Nothing whatever. The crime, if crime it was, could never be proved against you. The investigation would delay you two or three days, and allow other matters to mature."

"Why did you retract your accusation?"

"I saw I had made a mistake. I am hominid — far from infallible."

Sudden anger threatened to choke Farr. "Why don't you stop talking in hints and implications? If you've got something to say — say it."

"Farr Sainh is himself pressing the matter. I have nothing to say. The message I had for him I delivered; he would not expect me to lay bare my soul."

Farr nodded, grinned. "One thing you can be sure of — if I see a chance to spike the game you're playing — I'll take it."

"I am a businessman," said the Iszic. "I play no games."

Every hour the star that was Home Sun brightened; every hour Earth was closer. Farr found himself unable to sleep. A sour lump formed in his stomach. Resentment, perplexity, impatience compounded into a malaise whose effects were physical. In addition, his scalp had never healed properly; it itched and smarted; he suspected that he had contracted an Iszic infection. The prospect alarmed him; he pictured the infection spreading, his hair falling out, his scalp bleaching to the watered-milk color of the Iszic skin. Nor did the mysterious inner urgency diminish. He sought through his mind; he reviewed the days and months, he made notes and outlines, synthesized and checked without satisfaction; he bundled the whole problem, all the notes and papers, into an angry ball and cast it aside.

And at last, after the longest, most exasperating voyage Farr had ever made the SS *Andrei Simic* drifted into the Solar System...

Chapter IX

SUN, EARTH, THE MOON: an archipelago of bright round islands, after a long passage through a dark sea. Sun drifted off to one side, Moon slipped away to the other. Earth expanded ahead: gray, green, tan, white, blue; full of clouds and winds, sunburn, frosts, draughts, chills and dusts; the navel of the universe, the depot, terminal, clearing-house, which the outer races visited as provincials.

It was at midnight when the hull of the *Andrei Simic* touched Earth. The generators sang down out of inaudibility, down through shrillness, through treble, tenor, baritone, bass, and once more out of hearing.

The passengers waited in the saloon, with the Anderviews like holes in a jaw from which teeth had been pulled. Everyone was taut and apprehensive, sitting forward in their seats, standing stiffly.

The pumps hissed, adjusting to the outer atmosphere; lights glared in through the ports. The entrance clanged open; there was a murmur of voices; Captain Dorristy ushered in a tall man with blunt intelligent features, cropped hair, dark-brown skin.

"This is Detective-Inspector Kirdy of the Special Squad," said Dorristy. "He will investigate the deaths of Mr. and Mrs. Anderview. Please give him your cooperation; we'll all be at liberty the sooner."

No one spoke. The Iszic stood like statues of ice to one side. In deference to Earth convention they wore trousers and capes; their attitude conveyed suspicion, distrust, as if even on Earth they felt impelled to protect their secrets.

Three subordinate detectives entered the room, stared around curiously, and the tautness in the room increased.

Inspector Kirdy spoke in a pleasant voice, "I'll delay you as little as possible. I'd like to speak to Mr. Omon Bozhd."

Omon Bozhd inspected Kirdy through the viewer, which he now carried, but Detective-Inspector Kirdy's right shoulder blazed into no banner of various lights; he had never visited Iszm; he had never ventured past Moon.

Omon Bozhd stepped forward. "I am Omon Bozhd."

Kirdy took him to the Captain's cabin. Ten minutes passed. An assistant appeared in the door. "Mr. Aile Farr."

Farr rose to his feet, followed the assistant from the saloon.

Kirdy and Omon Bozhd faced each other, a study in contrasts: the one pale, austere, aquiline; the other dark, warm, blunt.

Kirdy said to Farr, "I'd like you to listen to Mr. Bozhd's story, tell me what you think of it." He turned to the Iszic. "Would you be kind enough to repeat your statement?"

"In essence," said Omon Bozhd, "the situation is this. Even before leaving Jhespiano I had reason to suspect that the Anderviews were planning harm to Farr Sainh. I communicated my suspicions to my friends —"

"The other Iszic gentlemen?" asked Kirdy.

"Exactly. With their help I installed an inspection-cell in the Anderviews' cabin. My fears were justified. They returned to their cabin, and here they themselves were killed. In my cabin I witnessed the occurrence. Farr Sainh of course had no part in the matter. He was — and is — completely innocent."

They scrutinized Farr. Farr scowled. Was he so obviously ingenuous, so undiscerning?

Omon Bozhd turned a fraction of his eyes back to Kirdy. "Farr, as I say, was innocent. But I considered it wise to have him confined away from further danger, so I falsely accused him. Farr Sainh, understandably, refused to cooperate, and forestalled me. My accusation was arousing no conviction in Captain Dorristy, so I withdrew it."

Kirdy turned to Farr. "What do you say to all this, Mr. Farr? Do you still believe Mr. Bozhd to be the murderer?"

Farr struggled with his anger. "No," he said between his teeth. "His story is so — so utterly fantastic that I suppose it's the truth." He looked at Omon Bozhd. "Why don't you talk? You say you saw the whole thing. Who did the killing?"

Omon Bozhd swung his viewer. "I have glanced over your laws of criminal procedure. My accusation would carry no great weight; the authorities would need corroborative evidence. That evidence exists. If and when you find it, my statement becomes unnecessary, or at best supplementary."

Kirdy turned to his assistant. "Take skin-scrapings, breath and perspiration samples of all the passengers."

After the samples were collected, Kirdy stepped into the saloon and made a statement. "I will question you separately. Those who so desire will be allowed to give their evidence with the cephaloscope as an adjunct, and these responses will naturally take on more weight. I remind you that cephaloscope evidence can not be introduced in court to prove guilt — only to prove innocence. The cephaloscope at worst can only fail to eliminate you from the suspects. I remind you further that refusal to use the cephaloscope is not only a privilege and a right, but considered by many a moral duty; hence those who prefer to give evidence without cephaloscope verification incur no prejudice. Use of the instrument is optional with you."

The interrogations lasted three hours. First to be queried were the Iszic. They left the saloon one at a time, returning with identical expressions of bored patience. The Codain were interviewed next, then the Monagi, then the various other non-Earthers, and then Farr. Kirdy indicated the cephaloscope. "Use of the instrument is at your option."

Farr was in a bad humor. "No," he said. "I despise the contraption; you can take my evidence as I give it or not at all."

Kirdy nodded politely. "Very well, Mr. Farr." He consulted his notes. "You first met the Anderviews at Jhespiano, on Iszm?"

"Yes." Farr described the circumstances.

"You had never seen them before?"

"Never."

"I understand that during your visit to Iszm you witnessed a tree-raid."

Farr described the event and his subsequent adventures. Kirdy asked one or two questions, then allowed Farr to return to the saloon.

One at a time the remaining Earthers were interrogated: Ralf and Willeran, the Wlewskas, the young students, until only Paul Bengston the gray-haired sanitary engineer remained. Kirdy accompanied the students back to the saloon. "So far," he said, "either the cephaloscope or other evidence has cleared everyone I have interviewed — the other evidence consisting principally of the fact that the breath components of no one I have interviewed match the film detected on the wrist-band worn by Mrs. Anderview."

Everyone in the room stirred. Eyes wandered to Paul Bengston, who went white and red by turns.

"Will you come with me, sir?"

He rose, took short steps forward, looked left and right, then preceded Kirdy into the Captain's cabin.

Five minutes passed. Kirdy's assistant appeared in the lounge. "We are sorry to have kept you waiting. You are all at liberty to debark."

There was talk around the lounge — a sputter and hum. Farr sat silent. A pressure began to build up inside him: anger, frustration, humiliation. The pressure grew, and finally burst up, to flood his mind with fury. He jumped to his feet, strode across the lounge, climbed the steps to the Captain's cabin.

Kirdy's assistant stopped him. "Excuse me, Mr. Farr. I don't think you'd better interrupt."

"I don't care what you think," snapped Farr. He yanked at the door. It was locked. He rapped. Captain Dorristy slid it open a foot, pushed his square face out. "Well? What's the trouble?"

Farr put his hand on Dorristy's chest, pushed him back, thrust open the door, stepped inside. Dorristy started a punch for Farr's face. Farr would have welcomed it as an excuse to strike back, to smash, to hurt. But one of the assistants stepped between.

Kirdy stood facing Paul Bengston. He turned his head. "Yes, Mr. Farr?"

Dorristy, seething, muttering, red in the face, stood back.

Farr said, "This man — he's guilty?"

Kirdy nodded. "The evidence is conclusive."

Farr looked at Bengston. His face blurred and swam and seemed to alter, as if by trick photography, with the candor and mild good humor becoming deceit and cruelty and callousness. Farr wondered how he could have been deceived. He bent a little forward; Paul Bengston met his eyes with defiance and dislike.

"Why?" he asked. "Why did all this happen?"

Bengston made no answer.

"I've got a right to know," said Farr. "Why?"

Still no answer.

Farr swallowed his pride. "Why?" he asked humbly, "Won't you please tell me?"

Paul Bengston shrugged, laughed foolishly.

Farr pled with him. "Is it something I know? Something I've seen? Something I own?"

An emotion close to hysteria seemed to grip Bengston. He said, "I just don't like the way your hair is parted." And he laughed till the tears came.

Kirdy said grimly, "I haven't got any better from him."

"What could be his motive?" asked Farr plaintively. "His reason? Why would the Anderviews want to kill me?"

"If I find out I'll let you know," said Kirdy. "Meanwhile — where can I get in touch with you?"

Farr considered. There was something he had to do... It would come to him, but in the meantime: "I'm going to Los Angeles. I'll be at the Imperador Hotel."

"Chump," said Bengston under his breath.

Farr took a half-step forward. "Easy, Mr. Farr," said Kirdy.

Farr turned away.

"I'll let you know," said Kirdy.

Farr looked at Dorristy. Dorristy said, "Never mind. Don't bother to apologize."

Chapter X

WHEN FARR RETURNED to the lounge, the other passengers had debarked and were passing through the immigration office. Farr hurriedly followed them out, almost in claustrophobic panic. The SS *Andrei Simic*, the magnificent bird of space, enclosed him like a clamp, a coffin; he could wait no longer to leave, to stand on the soil of Earth.

It was almost morning. The wind off the Mojave blew in his face, aromatic with sage and desert dust; the stars glinted, paling in the east. At the top of the ramp, Farr automatically looked up, searched out Auriga. There: Capella, there — the faintest of glitters — Xi Aurigae beside which swung Iszm. Farr walked down the ramp, planted his foot on the ground. He was back on Earth. The impact seemed to jar an idea into his head. Of course, he thought, with a feeling of relief: the natural thing to do, the obvious man to see: K. Penche.

Tomorrow. First to the Hotel Imperador. A bath in a hundred gallons of hot water. A hundred gallons of Scotch for a nightcap. Then bed.

Omon Bozhd approached. "It has been a pleasure knowing you, Farr Sainh. A word of advice: use vast caution. I suspect that you are still in great danger." He bowed, walked away. Farr stood looking after him. He felt no disposition to scoff off the warning.

He passed immigration quickly, dispatched his luggage to the Imperador. By-passing the line of helicabs, he stepped down the shaft to the public tube. The disk appeared under his feet (always a thrill in the shaft, always the thought: suppose the disk doesn't come? Just this once?).

The disk slowed to a stop. Farr paid his fare, summoned a one-man car to the dock, jumped in, dialed his destination, relaxed into the seat. He could not marshal his thoughts. Visions seeped through his mind:

the regions of space, Iszm, Jhespiano, the many-podded houses. He sailed in the *Lhaiz* to Tjiere Atoll; he felt the terror of the raid on the fields of Zhde Patasz, the fall down the root into the dungeon, the confinement with the Thord — and later, the terrible experience on Zhde Patasz's experimental islet...The visions passed; they were a memory, far away, farther than the light years to Iszm.

The hum of the car soothed him; his eyes grew heavy; he started to doze.

He pulled himself awake, blinking. Shadowy, phantasmagorical, this whole affair. But it was real. Farr forced himself into a sober frame of mind. But his mind refused to reason, to plan. The stimuli had lost their sting. Here in the tube, the sane normal underground tube, murder seemed impossible...

One man on Earth could help him: K. Penche, Earth agent for the Iszic houses, the man to whom Omon Bozhd brought bad news.

The car vibrated, jerked, shunted off the main tube toward the ocean. It twisted twice more, threading the maze of local tubes, and coasted finally to a stop.

The door snapped open, a uniformed attendant assisted him to the deck. He registered at a stereoscreen booth; an elevator lofted him two hundred feet to the surface, another five hundred feet to his room level. He was shown into a long chamber, finished in pleasant tones of olive green, straw, russet and white. One wall was sheer glass looking over Santa Monica, Beverly Hills and the ocean. Farr sighed in contentment. Iszic houses in many ways were remarkable, but never would they supersede the Hotel Imperador.

Farr took his bath, floating in hot water faintly scented with lime. Rhythmical fingers of cooler water jetted and surged, massaging his legs, back, ribs, shoulders...He almost fell asleep. The bottom of the tub elevated, angled gently to vertical, set him on his feet. Blasts of air removed his wetness; sunlamp radiation gave him a quick pleasant scorch.

He came out of the bath to find a tall Scotch-and-soda waiting for him; not a hundred gallons, but enough. He stood at the window, sipping, enjoying the sense of utter fatigue.

The sun came up; golden light washed in like a tide across the vast reaches of the world-city. Somewhere out there, in the luxury district that had once been Signal Hill, dwelt K. Penche. Farr felt an instant of puzzlement. Strange, he thought, how Penche represented the solution to everything. Well, he'd know whether that was right or not when he saw the man.

Farr polarized the window, light died from the room. He set the wall clock to call him at noon, sank into bed, and fell asleep.

The window depolarized; daylight entered the room. Farr awoke, sat up in bed, reached for a menu. He ticked off coffee, grapefruit, bacon, eggs, jumped out of bed, went to the window. The world's largest city spread as far as he could see, white spires melting into the tawny haze, everywhere a trembling and vibration of commerce and life.

The wall extruded a table set with his breakfast; Farr turned away from the window, seated himself, ate and watched news on the stereo-screen. For a minute he forgot his troubles; after his long absence, he had lost the continuity of the news. Events which he might have over-looked a year ago suddenly seemed interesting. He felt a cheerful flush; it was good to be home on Earth.

The news-screen voice said, "Now for some flashes from outer space. It has just been learned that aboard the Red Ball Packet *Andrei Simic* two passengers, ostensibly missionaries returning from service in the Mottram Group —"

Farr watched, his breakfast forgotten, the cheerful glow fading.

The voice recounted the affair; the screen modeled the *Andrei Simic*: first the exterior, then a cutaway, with an arrow directing attention to 'the death cabin'. How pleasant and unconcerned was this commenta-tor! How remote and incidental he made the affair seem!

"—the two victims and the murderer have all been identified as members of the notorious Heavy Weather crime-syndicate. Appar-ently they had visited Iszm, third planet of Xi Aurigae, in an attempt to smuggle out a female house."

The voice spoke on. Simulacra of the Anderviews and Paul Bengston appeared.

Farr clicked off the screen, pushed the table back into the wall. He rose to his feet, went to look out over the city. It was urgent. He must see Penche.

From the Size 2 cupboard he selected underwear, a suit of pale blue fiber, fresh sandals. As he dressed he planned out his day. First, of course, Penche…Farr frowned, paused in the buckling of his sandals. What should he tell Penche? Come to think of it, why would Penche worry about his troubles? What could Penche do? His monopoly stemmed from the Iszic; he would hardly risk antagonizing them.

Farr took a deep breath, shrugged aside these annoying speculations. It was illogical, but quite definitely the right place to go. He was sure of this; he felt it in his bones.

He finished dressing, went to the stereoscreen, dialed the office of K. Penche. Penche's symbol appeared — a conventionalized Iszic house, with vertical bars of heavy type, reading *K. Penche — Houses*. Farr had not touched the scanning button; and his own image did not cross to Penche's office, an act of instinctive caution.

A female voice said, "K. Penche Enterprises."

"This is —" Farr hesitated and withheld his name. "Connect me to Mr. Penche."

"Who is speaking?"

"My name is confidential."

"What is your business, please?"

"Confidential."

"I'll connect you to Mr. Penche's secretary."

The secretary's image appeared — a young woman of languid charm. Farr repeated his request. The secretary looked at the screen. "Send over your image, please."

"No," said Farr. "Connect me with Mr. Penche — I'll talk directly to him."

"I'm afraid that's impossible," said the secretary. "Quite contrary to our office procedure."

"Tell Mr. Penche that I have just arrived from Iszm on the *Andrei Simic*."

The secretary turned, spoke into a mesh. After a second her face melted, the screen filled with the face of K. Penche. It was a massive powerful face, like a piece of heavy machinery. The eyes burnt from deep rectangular sockets, bars of muscles clamped his mouth. The eyebrows rose in a sardonic arch; the expression was neither pleasant nor unpleasant.

"Who's speaking?" asked K. Penche.

Words rose up through Farr's brain like bubbles from the bottom of a dark vat. They were words he had never intended to say. "I've come from Iszm; I've got it." Farr heard himself in amazement. The words came again. "I've come from Iszm..." He clamped his teeth, refused to vocalize; the syllables bounced back from the barrier.

"Who is this? Where are you?"

Farr reached over, turned off the screen, sank weakly back into his chair. What was going on? He had nothing for Penche. 'Nothing' meant a female house, naturally. Farr might be naive but not to that degree. He had no house — seed, seedling or sapling.

Why did he want to see Penche? Pent-up common-sense broke through to the top of his mind. Penche couldn't help him... A voice from another part of his brain said, Penche knows the ropes; he'll give you good advice... Well, yes, thought Farr weakly. This might be true enough.

Farr relaxed. Yes, of course — that was his motive. But, on the other hand, Penche was a businessman, dependent on the Iszic. If Farr were to go to anyone it should be to the police, to the Special Squad.

He sat back rubbing his chin. Of course, it wouldn't hurt to see the man; maybe get it off his chest.

Farr jumped to his feet in disgust. It was unreasonable. Why should he see Penche? Give him just one good reason...There was no reason whatever. He came to a definite decision: he would have nothing to do with Penche.

He left the room, descended to the main lobby of the Imperador, crossed to the desk to cash a bank coupon. The coupon was screened to the bank; there would be a wait of a few seconds. Farr tapped his fingers on the counter impatiently. Beside him a burly frog-faced man argued with the clerk. He wanted to deliver a message to a guest, but the clerk was skeptical. The burly man began to bite off his words in anger; the clerk stood behind his glass bulwark, prim, fastidious, shaking his head. Serene in the strength given him by rules and regulations, he took pleasure in thwarting the large man.

"If you don't know his name, how do you know he's at the Imperador?"

"I know he's here," said the man. "It's important that he get this message."

"It sounds very odd," mused the clerk. "You don't know what he looks like, you don't know his name…You might easily deliver your message to the wrong party."

"That's my look-out!"

The clerk smilingly shook his head. "Apparently all you know is that he arrived at five this morning. We have several guests who came in at that time."

Farr was counting his money; the conversation impinged on his consciousness. He loitered, adjusting the bills in his wallet.

"This man came in from space. He was just off the *Andrei Simic*. Now do you know who I mean?"

Farr moved away quietly. He knew quite clearly what had happened. Penche had been expecting the call; it was important to him. He had traced the connection to the Imperador, and had sent a man over to contact him. In a far corner of the room he watched the large man lurch away from the desk in rage. Farr knew he would try elsewhere. One of the bell-boys or a steward would get him his information for a fee.

Farr started out the door, turned to look back. A nondescript middle-aged woman was walking toward him; he happened to meet her eyes, she looked aside, faltered the smallest trifle in her step. Farr had already been keyed to suspicion, or he might not have noticed. The woman walked quickly past him, stepped on the exit-band, was carried through the Imperador orchid garden and out upon Sunset Boulevard.

Farr followed, watched her melt into the crowds. He crossed to a traffic umbrella, took the lift to the helicab deck. A cab stood empty beside the shelter. Farr jumped in, picked a destination at random. "Laguna Beach."

The cab rose into the southbound level. Farr watched from the rear port. A cab bobbed up a hundred yards astern, followed.

Farr called to the driver, "Turn off to Riverside."

The cab behind turned.

Farr told his driver, "Put me down right here."

"South Gate?" asked the driver, as if Farr were not in his right mind.

"South Gate." Not too far from Penche's office and display yard on Signal Hill, thought Farr. Coincidence.

The cab dropped him to the surface. Farr watched the pursuing cab descend. He felt no great concern. Evading a pursuer was a matter of utmost simplicity, a technique known to every child who watched the stereos.

Farr followed the white arrow to the underground shaft, stepped in. The disk caught him, bumped to a gentle halt. Farr called over a car, jumped in. The underground was almost made to order for shaking off a shadow. He dialed a destination, tried to relax into the seat.

The car accelerated, hummed, decelerated, halted. The door snapped open. Farr jumped out, rode the lift to the surface. He froze in his tracks. What was he doing here? This was Signal Hill — once spiked with oil derricks, now lost under billows of exotic greenery: ten million trees, bushes, shrubs, merging around mansions and palaces. There were pools and waterfalls, carefully informal banks of flowers: scarlet hibiscus, blazing yellow banneret, sapphire gardenia. The Hanging Gardens of Babylon were as nothing. Bel-Air was frowzy in contrast; Topanga was for the parvenus.

K. Penche owned twenty acres on the summit of Signal Hill. He had cleared off his land, ignoring protests and court orders, winning lawsuits. Signal Hill now was crowned by Iszic tree houses: sixteen varieties in four basic types; the only models Penche was allowed to sell.

Farr walked slowly along the shaded arcade that once had been Atlantic Avenue. Interesting, he thought, that coincidence should bring him here. Well, he was this close; perhaps it might be a good idea to see Penche…

No! said Farr stubbornly. He had made the decision; no irrational compulsion was going to make him change his mind! An odd matter, that in all the vast reaches of Greater Los Angeles, he should wind up almost at K. Penche's front door. Too odd; it went beyond mere chance. His subconscious must be at work.

He glanced behind him. No one could possibly be following, but he watched for a moment or two as hundreds of people, old and young, of all shapes, sizes and colors passed. By a subtle evaluation he fixed on a slender man in a gray suit; he struck a false note. Farr reversed his direction, threaded the maze of open-air shops and booths under the arcade, ducked into a palm-shaded cafeteria, stepped out of sight behind a wall of leaves.

A minute passed. The man in the gray suit came briskly past. Farr stepped out, stared hard into the well-groomed, well-pomaded countenance. "Are you looking for me, mister?"

"Why no," said the man in the gray suit. "I've never seen you before in my life."

"I hope I don't see you again," said Farr. He left the cafeteria, stalked to the nearest underground station, dropped down the shaft, jumped into a car. After a minute's thought he dialed Altadena. The car hummed off. No easy relaxation now; Farr sat on the edge of his seat. How had they located him? Through the tube? Incredible.

To make doubly sure, he canceled Altadena, dialed Pomona.

Five minutes later he wandered with apparent casualness along Valley Boulevard. In another five minutes he located the shadow, a young workman with a vacant face. Am I crazy? Farr asked himself; am I developing a persecution complex? He put the shadow to a rigorous test, strolling around blocks as if looking for a particular house. The young workman ambled along behind him.

Farr went into a restaurant, called the Special Squad on the stereoscreen. He asked for and was connected with Detective-Inspector Kirdy.

Kirdy greeted him politely, and positively denied that he had assigned men to follow Farr. He appeared keenly interested. "Wait just a shake," he said. "I'll check the other departments."

Three or four minutes passed. Farr saw the blank young man enter the restaurant, take an unobtrusive seat, order coffee.

Kirdy returned. "We're innocent around here. Perhaps it's a private agency."

Farr looked annoyed. "Isn't there anything I can do about it?"

"Are you being molested in any way?"

"No."

"We really can't do anything. Drop into a tube, shake 'em off."

"I've taken the tube twice — they're still after me."

Kirdy looked puzzled. "I wish they'd tell me how. We don't try to follow suspects anymore; they brush us off too easily."

"I'll try once more," said Farr. "Then there'll be fireworks."

He marched out of the restaurant. The young workman downed his coffee, came quickly after.

Farr dropped down a tube. He waited, but the young workman did not follow. So much for that. He called over a car, looked around. The young workman was nowhere near. No one was near. Farr jumped in, dialed for Ventura. The car sped off. There was no conceivable way it could be traced or followed through the tubes.

In Ventura his shadow was an attractive young housewife who seemed out for an afternoon's shopping.

Farr jumped into a shaft, took a car for Long Beach. The man who followed him in Long Beach was the slender man in the gray suit who had first attracted his attention at Signal Hill. He seemed unperturbed when Farr recognized him, shrugging rather insolently, as if to say, "What do you expect?"

Signal Hill. Back again; only a mile or two away. Maybe it might be a good idea after all to drop in on Penche.

No!

Farr sat down at an arcade cafe in full view of the shadow and ordered a sandwich. The man in the natty gray suit took a table nearby and provided himself with iced tea. Farr wished he could beat the truth out of the well-groomed face. Inadvisable; he would end up in jail. Was Penche responsible for this persecution? Farr reluctantly rejected the idea. Penche's man had arrived at the Imperador desk while Farr was leaving. The evasion had been decisive there.

Who then? Omon Bozhd?

Farr sat stock-still; then laughed — a loud clear sharp bark of a laugh. People looked at him in surprise. The gray man gave him a glance of cautious appraisal. Farr continued to chuckle, a nervous release. Once he thought about it, it was so clear, so simple.

He looked up at the ceiling of the arcade, imagining the sky beyond. Somewhere, five or ten miles overhead, hung an air-boat. In the air-boat sat an Iszic, with a sensitive viewer and a radio. Everywhere that Farr went, the radiant in his right shoulder sent up a signal. On the viewer-screen Farr was as surreptitious as a lighthouse.

He went to the stereo-screen, called Kirdy.

Kirdy was vastly interested. "I've heard of that stuff. Apparently it works."

"Yes," said Farr, "it works. How can I shield it?"

"Just a minute." Five minutes passed. Kirdy came back to the screen. "Stay where you are; I'll send a man down with a shield."

The messenger presently arrived. Farr went into the men's room and wrapped a pad of woven metal around his shoulder and chest.

"Now," said Farr grimly. "Now we'll see."

The slim man in the gray suit followed him nonchalantly to the tube shaft. Farr dialed to Santa Monica.

He rose to the surface at the Ocean Avenue station, walked northeast along Wilshire Boulevard, back toward Beverly Hills. He was alone. He made all the tests he could think of. No one followed him. Farr grinned in satisfaction, picturing the annoyed Iszic at the viewer-screen.

He came to the Capricorn Club—a large, rather disreputable-looking saloon, with a pleasant old-fashioned odor of sawdust, wax and beer. He turned in, went directly to the stereo-screen, called the Hotel Imperador. Yes, there was a message for him. The clerk played back the tape, and for the second time Farr looked into Penche's massive sardonic face. The harsh deep voice was conciliatory; the words had been carefully chosen and rehearsed. "I'd like to see you at your earliest convenience, Mr. Farr. We both realize the need for discretion. I'm sure your visit will result in profit for both of us. I will be waiting for your call."

The stereo faded; the clerk appeared. "Shall I cancel or file, Mr. Farr?"

"Cancel," said Farr. He left the booth, went to the far end of the bar. The bartender made the traditional inquiry: "What's yours, brother?"

Farr ordered. "Vienna Stadtbrau."

The bartender turned, spun a tall oak wheel twined with hop vines, gay with labels. A hundred and twenty positions controlled a hundred and twenty storage-tubes. He pushed the bumper; a dark flask slipped out of the dispenser. The bartender squeezed the flask into a stein, set it before Farr. Farr took a deep swallow, relaxed, rubbed his forehead.

He was puzzled. Something very odd was going on; no question about it. Penche seemed reasonable enough. Perhaps, after all, it might be a good idea—wearily Farr put the thought away. Amazing how many guises the compulsion found to clothe itself. It was difficult to guard against all of them. Unless he vetoed out of hand any course of action that included a visit to Penche. A measure of uncompromising rigor, a counter-compulsion that set shackles on his freedom of action. It was a mess. How could a man think clearly when he could not distinguish between an idiotic subconscious urge and common sense?

Farr ordered more beer; the bartender, a sturdy apple-cheeked little man with pop-eyes and a fine mustache, obliged. Farr returned to his thinking. It was an interesting psychological problem, one that Farr might have relished in different circumstances. Right now it was too close to home. He tried to reason with the compulsion. What do I gain by seeing Penche? Penche had hinted of profit. He clearly thought that Farr had something he wanted.

It could only be a female house.

Farr had no female house; therefore — it was as simple as that — he gained nothing by going to Penche.

But Farr was dissatisfied. The syllogism was too pat; he suspected that he had oversimplified. The Iszic were also involved. They must also believe that he had a female house. Since they had attempted to follow him, they were ignorant of where he would deliver this hypothetical house.

Penche naturally would not want them to know. If the Iszic learned of Penche's involvement, breaking his franchise was the least they would do. They might well kill him.

K. Penche was playing for high stakes. On the one hand he could grow his own houses. They would cost him twenty or thirty dollars apiece. He could sell as many as he liked at two thousand. He would become the richest man in the universe, the richest man in the history of Earth. The moguls of ancient India, the Victorian tycoons, the oil-barons, the Pan-Eurasian syndics: they would dwindle to paupers in comparison.

That was on the one hand. On the other — Penche at the very least would lose his monopoly. Recalling Penche's face, the cartilaginous bar of his mouth, the prow of his nose, the eyes like smoked glass in front of a furnace — Farr instinctively knew Penche's position.

It would be an interesting struggle. Penche probably discounted the subtle Iszic brain, the fanatic zeal with which they defended their property. The Iszic possibly underestimated Penche's massive wealth and

Earth's technical genius. It was the situation of the ancient paradox: the irresistible force and the immovable object. And I, thought Farr, am in the middle. Unless I extricate myself, I will very likely be crushed... He took a thoughtful pull at his beer. If I knew more accurately what was happening, how I happened to become involved, why they picked on me, I'd know which way to jump. Yet — what power I wield! Or so it seems.

Farr ordered another beer. On sudden thought he looked up sharply, glanced around the bar. No one appeared to be watching him. Farr took the container, went to a table in a dark corner.

The affair — at least his personal participation in it — had stemmed from the Thord raid on Tjiere. Farr had aroused Iszic suspicion; they had imprisoned him. He had been alone with a surviving Thord. The Iszic had released hypnotic gas through a root-tubule. The Thord and Farr had been stupefied.

The Iszic had certainly searched him unit by unit, inside and out, mind and body. If he were guilty of complicity, they would know it. If he had seed or seedling on his person, they would know it.

What had they actually done?

They had released him; they had facilitated, in fact they had prompted, his return to Earth. He was a decoy, a bait.

Aboard the *Andrei Simic* — what of all that? Suppose the Anderviews were Penche's agents. Suppose they had apprehended the danger that Farr represented and sought to kill him? What about Paul Bengston? His function might have been to spy on the first two. He had killed the Anderviews either to protect Penche's interests, or cut himself a larger slice of the profits. He had failed. He was now in custody of the Special Squad.

The whole thing added up to a tentative, speculative, but apparently logical conclusion: K. Penche had organized the raid on Tjiere. It was Penche's metal mole that the wasp-ship had destroyed eleven hundred feet underground. The raid had nearly been successful. The Iszic must have writhed in terror. They would trace the source, the organization of the raid, without qualm or restraint. A few deaths meant nothing. Money meant nothing. Aile Farr meant nothing.

And small cold chills played up Farr's back.

A pretty blonde girl in gray sheen-skin paused beside his table. "Hi, Cholly." She tossed her hair roguishly over her shoulder. "You look lonesome." And she dropped into a seat beside him.

Farr's thoughts had taken him into nervous territory; the girl startled him. He stared at her without moving a muscle, five seconds—ten seconds.

She forced an uneasy laugh, moved in her chair. "You look like you got the cares of the world on your head."

Farr put his beer gently to the table. "I'm trying to pick a horse."

"Out of the air?" She pushed a cigarette in her mouth, archly pushed it toward him. "Give me a light."

Farr lit the cigarette, studying her from behind his eyelids, weighing her, probing for the false note, the non-typical reaction. He had not noticed her come in, nor had he seen her promoting drinks anywhere else around the bar.

"I could be talked into taking a drink," she said carelessly.

"After I buy you a drink—then what?"

She looked away, refusing to meet his eyes. "I guess—I guess that's up to you."

Farr asked her how much, in rather blunt terms. She blushed, still looking across the bar, suddenly flustered. "I guess you made a mistake...I guess I made a mistake...I thought you'd be good for a drink."

Farr asked in an easy voice, "You work for the bar, on commission?"

"Sure," she said, half-defiantly. "What about it? It's a nice way to pass the evening. Sometimes you meet a nice guy. Whatcha do to your head?" She leaned forward, looked. "Somebody hit you?"

"If I told you how I got that scab," said Farr, "you'd call me a liar."

"Go ahead, try me."

"Some people were mad at me. They took me to a tree, pushed me inside. I fell down into a root, two or three hundred feet. On the way down I hit my head."

The girl looked at him sidelong. Her mouth twisted into a wry grimace. "And at the bottom you saw little pink men carrying green lanterns. And a big white fluffy rabbit."

"I told you," said Farr.

She reached up toward his temple. "You've got a funny long gray hair."

Farr moved his head back. "I'm going to keep it."

"Suit yourself." She eyed him coldly. "Are you gonna spring, or do I gotta tell you the story of my life?"

"Just a minute," said Farr. He rose to his feet, crossed the room, to the bar. He motioned to the bartender. "That blonde at my table, see her?"

The bartender looked. "What about her?"

"She usually hang out here?"

"Never saw her before in my life."

"She doesn't work for you on commission?"

"Brother, I just told you. I never seen her before in my life."

"Thanks."

Farr returned to the table. The girl was sullenly rapping her fingers on the table. Farr looked at her a long moment.

"Well?" she growled.

"Who are you working for?"

"I told you."

"Who sent you in here after me?"

"Don't be silly." She started to rise. Farr caught her wrist.

"Let go! I'll yell."

"That's what I'm hoping," said Farr. "I'd like to see some police. Sit down — or I'll call them myself."

She sank slowly back into the chair, then turned, flung herself against him, put her face up, her arms around his neck. "I'm so lonesome. Really, I mean it. I got in from Seattle yesterday. I don't know a soul — now don't be so hard to get along with. We can be nice to each other... can't we?"

Farr grinned. "First we talk, then we can be nice."

Something was hurting him, something at the back of his neck, where her hand touched. He blinked, grabbed her arm. She jumped up, tore herself loose, eyes shining with glee. "Now what, now what'll you do?"

Farr made a lurch for her; she danced back, face mischievous. Farr's eyes were watering, his joints felt weak. He tottered to his feet, the table fell over. The bartender roared, vaulted the bar. Farr took two staggering steps for the girl, who was composedly walking away. The bartender confronted her.

"Just a minute."

Farr's ears were roaring. He heard the girl say primly, "You get out of my way. He's a drunk. He insulted me — said all kinds of nasty things."

The bartender glared indecisively. "There's something fishy going on here."

"Well — don't mix me up in it."

Farr's knees unhinged; a dreadful lump came up his throat, into his mouth. He sank to the floor. He could sense motion, he felt rough hands, and heard the bartender's voice very loud, "What's the trouble, Jack? Cantcha hold it?"

Farr's mind was off somewhere, tangled in a hedge of glass branches. A voice gurgled up his throat. "Call Penche...Call K. Penche!"

"K. Penche," someone voiced softly. "The guy's nuts."

"K. Penche," Farr mumbled. "He'll pay you...Call him, tell him — Farr..."

Chapter XI

AILE FARR WAS DYING. He was sinking into a red and yellow chaos of shapes that reeled and pounded. When the movement stilled, when the shapes straightened and drew back, when the scarlets and golds blurred, deepened to black — Aile Farr would be dead.

He saw death coming, drifting like twilight across the sundown of his dying... He felt a sudden sharpness, a discord. A bright green blot exploded across the sad reds and roses and golds...

Aile Farr was alive once more.

The doctor leaned back, put aside his hypodermic. "Pretty close shave," he told the patrolman.

Farr's convulsions quieted; mercifully he lost consciousness.

"Who is the guy?" asked the patrolman.

The bartender looked skeptically down at Farr. "He said to call Penche."

"Penche! K. Penche?"

"That's what he said."

"Well — call him. All he can do is swear at you."

The bartender went to the screen. The patrolman looked down at the doctor, still kneeling beside Farr.

"What went wrong with the guy?"

The doctor shrugged. "Hard to say. Some kind of female trouble. So many things you can slip into a man nowadays."

"That raw place on his head..."

The doctor glanced at Farr's scalp. "No. That's an old wound. He got it in the neck. This mark here."

"Looks like she hit him with a slap-sack."

The bartender returned. "Penche says he's on his way out."

They all looked down at Farr with new respect.

Two orderlies came into the bar. The doctor rose to his feet. "Here's the ambulance."

The orderlies placed stretcher poles one on each side of Farr; metal ribbons thrust beneath him, clamping over the opposing pole. They lifted him, carried him across the floor. The bartender trotted alongside. "Where you guys taking him? I got to tell Penche something."

"He'll be at the Long Beach Emergency Hospital."

Penche arrived three minutes after the ambulance had gone. He strode in, looked right and left. "Where is he?"

"Are you Mr. Penche?" the bartender asked respectfully.

"Sure he's Penche," said the patrolman.

"Well, your friend was took to the Long Beach Emergency Hospital."

Penche turned to one of the men who had marched in behind him. "Find out what happened here," he said and left the bar.

The orderlies arranged Farr on a table, cut off his shoes. In puzzlement they examined the band of metal wrapped around his right shoulder.

"What's this thing?"

"Whatever it is — it's got to come off."

They unwound the woven metal, washed Farr with antiseptic gas, gave him several different injections, moved him into a quiet room.

Penche called the main office. "When can Mr. Farr be moved?"

"Just a minute, Mr. Penche."

Penche waited; the clerk made inquiries. "Well, he's out of danger now."

"Can he be moved?"

"He's still unconscious, but the doctor says he's okay."

"Have the ambulance bring him to my house, please."

"Very well, Mr. Penche. Er — are you assuming responsibility for Mr. Farr's care?"

"Yes," said Penche. "Bill me."

Penche's house on Signal Hill was a Class AA Type 4 luxury model, a dwelling equivalent to an average custom-built Earth house of 30,000 dollars value. Penche sold Class AA houses in four varieties for 10,000 dollars — as many as he could obtain — as well as Class A, Class BB and Class B houses. The Iszic, of course, grew houses infinitely more elaborate for their own use — rich ancient growths with complex banks of interconnecting pods, walls shining with fluorescent colors, tubules emitting nectar and oil and brine, atmospheres charged with oxygen and complex beneficiants, phototropic and photophobic pods, pods holding carefully filtered and circulated bathing pools, pods exuding nuts and sugar crystals and succulent wafers. The Iszic exported none of these, and none of the three- and four-pod laborer's houses. They required as much handling and shipping space, but brought only a small fraction of the return.

A billion Earthers still lived in sub-standard conditions. North Chinese still cut caves into the loess, Dravidians built mud huts, Americans and Europeans occupied decaying apartment-tenements. Penche thought the situation deplorable; a massive market lay untapped. Penche wanted to tap it.

A practical difficulty intervened. These people could pay no thousands of dollars for Class AA, A, BB and B houses, even if Penche had them to sell. He needed three-, four-, and five-pod laborer's houses — which the Iszic refused to export.

The problem had a classical solution: a raid on Iszm for a female tree. Properly fertilized, the female tree would yield a million seeds a year. About half these seeds would grow into female trees. In a few years Penche's income would expand from ten million a year to a hundred million, a thousand million, five thousand million.

To most people the difference between ten million a year and a thousand million seems inconsequential. Penche, however, thought in units of a million. Money represented not that which could be bought, but energy, dynamic thrust, the stuff of persuasion and efficacy. He spent little money on himself, his personal life was rather austere. He lived in his Class AA demonstrator on Signal Hill when he might have owned a sky-island, drifting in orbit around Earth. He might have loaded his table with rare meats and fowl, precious conserves, the valued wines, curious liquors and fruits from the outer worlds. He could have staffed a harem with the houris of a Sultan's dream. But Penche ate steak; he drank coffee and beer. He remained a bachelor, indulging himself socially only when the press of business allowed. Like certain gifted men who have no ear for music, Penche had only small taste for the accoutrements of civilization.

He recognized his own lack, and sometimes he felt a fleeting melancholy, like the brush of a dark feather; sometimes he sat slumped, savage as a boar, the furnaces glaring behind the smoked glass of his eyes, but for the most part K. Penche was sour and sardonic. Other men could be softened, distracted, controlled by easy words, pretty things, pleasure; Penche knew this well and used the knowledge as a carpenter uses a hammer, incurious about the intrinsic nature of the tool. Without illusion or prejudice he watched and acted; here perhaps was Penche's greatest strength, the inner brooding eye that gauged himself and the world in the same frame of callous objectivity.

He was waiting in his study when the ambulance sank to the lawn. He went out on the balcony, watched as the orderlies floated out the stretcher. He spoke in the heavy harsh voice that penetrated like another man's shout. "Is he conscious?"

"He's coming around, sir."

"Bring him up here."

Chapter XII

AILE FARR AWOKE in a pod with dust-yellow walls, a dark brown ceiling vaulted with slender ribs. He raised his head and blinked around the pod. He saw square dark heavy furniture: chairs, a settee, a table scattered with papers and a model house or two, an antique Spanish buffet.

A wispy man with a large head and earnest eyes bent over him. He wore a white cloth jacket, he smelled of antiseptic: a doctor.

Behind the doctor stood Penche. He was a large man but not as large as Farr had pictured him. He crossed the room slowly, looked down at Farr.

Something stirred in Farr's brain. Air rose in his throat, his vocal chords vibrated; his mouth, tongue, teeth, palate shaped words; Farr heard them in amazement.

"I have the tree."

Penche nodded. "Where?"

Farr looked at him stupidly.

Penche asked, "How did you get the tree off Iszm?"

"I don't know," said Farr. He rose up on his elbow, rubbed his chin, blinked. "I don't know what I'm saying. I don't have any tree."

Penche frowned. "Either you have it or you don't."

"I don't have any tree." Farr struggled to sit up. The doctor put an arm under his shoulders, helped him up. Farr felt very weak. "What am I doing here? Somebody poisoned me. A girl. A blonde girl in the tavern." He looked at Penche with growing anger. "She was working for you."

Penche nodded. "That's true."

Farr rubbed his face. "How did you find me?"

"You called the Imperador on the stereo. I had a man in the exchange waiting for the call."

"Well," said Farr wearily. "It's all a mistake. How or why or what — I don't know. Except that I'm taking a beating. And I don't like it."

Penche looked at the doctor. "How is he?"

"He's all right now. He'll get his strength back pretty soon."

"Good. You can go."

The doctor left the pod. Penche signaled a chair up behind him, sat down. "Anna worked too hard," said Penche. "She never should have used her sticker." He hitched his chair closer. "Tell me about yourself."

"First," said Farr, "where am I?"

"You're in my house. I've been looking for you."

"Why?"

Penche rocked his head back and forth, a sign of inward amusement. "You were asked to deliver a tree to me. Or a seed. Or a seedling. Whatever it is, I want it."

Farr spoke in a level voice. "I don't have it. I don't know anything about it. I was on Tjiere Atoll during the raid — that's the closest I came to your tree."

Penche asked in a quiet voice that seemed to hold no suspicion, "You called me when you arrived in town. Why?"

Farr shook his head. "I don't know. It was something I had to do. I did it. I told you just now I had a tree. I don't know why..."

Penche nodded. "I believe you. We've got to find out where this tree is. It may take a while, but —"

"I don't have your tree. I'm not interested." He rose to his feet. He looked around, started for the door. "Now — I'm going home."

Penche looked after him in quiet amusement. "The doors are cinched, Farr."

Farr paused, looking at the hard rosette of the door. Cinched — twisted shut. The relax-nerve would be somewhere in the wall. He pressed at the dusty yellow surface, almost like parchment.

"Not that way," said Penche. "Come back here, Farr..."

The door unwrapped itself. Omon Bozhd stood in the gap. He wore a skin-tight garment striped blue and white, a white cloche flaring rakishly back on itself, up over his ears. His face was austere, placid, full of the strength that was human but not Earth-human.

He came into the room. Behind came two more Iszic, these in yellow and green stripes: Szecr. Farr backed away to let them enter.

"Hello," said Penche. "I thought I had the door cinched. You fellows probably know all the tricks."

Omon Bozhd nodded politely to Farr. "We lost you for a certain period today; I am glad to see you." He looked at Penche, then back at Farr. "Your destination seems to have been K. Penche's house."

"That's the way it looks," said Farr.

Omon Bozhd explained politely. "When you were in the cell on Tjiere, we anesthetized you with a hypnotic gas. The Thord heard it. His race holds their breath for six minutes. When you became dazed he leapt on you, to effect a mind transfer and fixed his will on yours. A suggestion, a compulsion." He looked at Penche. "To the last moment he served his master well."

Penche said nothing; Omon Bozhd returned to Farr. "He buried the instructions deep in your brain; then he gave you the trees he had stolen. Six minutes had elapsed. He took a breath and became unconscious. Later we took you to him, hoping this would dislodge the injunction. We met failure; the Thord astounded us with his psychic capabilities."

Farr looked at Penche, who was leaning negligently against the table. There was tension here, like a trick jack-in-the-box ready to explode at the slightest shock.

Omon Bozhd dismissed Farr from his attention. Farr had served his purpose. "I came to Earth," he told Penche, "on two missions. I must inform you that your consignment of Class AA houses cannot be delivered, because of the raid on Tjiere Atoll."

"Well, well," said Penche mildly. "Not so good."

"My second mission is to find the man Aile Farr brings his message to."

Penche spoke in an interested voice. "You probed Farr's mind? Why weren't you able to find out then?"

Iszic courtesy was automatic, a reflex. Omon Bozhd bowed his head. "The Thord ordered Farr to forget; to remember only when his foot touched the soil of Earth. He had enormous power; Farr Sainh has a brain of considerable tenacity. We could only follow him. His destination is here, the house of K. Penche. I am able therefore to fulfill my second mission."

Penche said, "Well? Spit it out!"

Omon Bozhd bowed. His own voice was calm and formal. "My original message to you is voided, Penche Sainh. You are receiving no more Class AA houses. You are receiving none at all. If ever you set foot on Iszm or in Iszic suzerainty, you will be punished for your crime against us."

Penche nodded his head, his sign of inner sardonic mirth. "You discharge me, then. I'm no longer your agent."

"Correct."

Penche turned to Farr, spoke in a startling sharp voice. "The trees — where are they?"

Involuntarily Farr put his hand to the sore spot on his scalp.

Penche said, "Come over here, Farr, sit down. Let me take a look."

Farr growled, "Keep away from me; I'm not cat's-paw for anybody."

Omon Bozhd said, "The Thord anchored six seeds under the skin of Farr Sainh's scalp. It was an ingenious hiding place. The seeds are small. We searched for thirty minutes before we found them."

Farr pressed his scalp with distaste.

Penche said in his hoarse harsh voice, "Sit down, Farr. Let's find out where we stand."

Farr backed against the wall. "I know where I stand. It's not with you."

Penche laughed. "You're not throwing in with the Iszic?"

"I'm throwing in with nobody. If I've got seeds in my head, it's nobody's business but my own!"

Penche took a step forward, his face a little ugly.

Omon Bozhd said, "The seeds were removed, Penche Sainh. The bumps which Farr Sainh perhaps can feel are pellets of tantalum."

Farr fingered his scalp. Indeed — there they were: hard lumps he had thought part of the scab. One, two, three, four, five, six... His hand wandered through his hair, stopped. Involuntarily he looked at Penche, at the Iszic. They did not seem to be watching him. He pressed the small object he found in his hair. It felt like a small bladder, a sac, the size of a grain of wheat; and it was connected to his scalp by a fiber. Anna, the blonde girl, had seen a long gray hair...

Farr said in a shaky voice, "I've had enough of this...I'm going."

"No you're not," said Penche, without heat or passion. "You'll stay here."

Omon Bozhd said politely, "I believe that Earth law prohibits holding a man against his will. If we acquiesced, we become equally guilty. Is this not correct?"

Penche smiled. "In a certain restricted sense."

"To protect ourselves, we insist that you perform no illegalities."

Penche leaned forward truculently. "You've delivered your message. Now get the hell out!"

Farr pushed past Penche. Penche raised his arm, put his palm flat on Farr's chest. "You'd better stay, Farr. You're safer."

Farr stared deep into Penche's smouldering eyes. With so much anger and frustration and contempt to express, he found it hard to speak. "I'll go where I please," he said finally. "I'm sick of playing sucker."

"Better a live sucker than a dead chump."

Farr pushed aside Penche's arm. "I'll take my chances."

Omon Bozhd muttered to the two Iszic behind him. They separated, went to each side of the sphincter.

"You may leave," Omon Bozhd told Farr. "K. Penche cannot stop you."

Farr stopped short. "I'm not kicking in with you either." He looked around the pod, went to the stereo-screen.

Penche approved; he grinned at the Iszic.

Omon Bozhd said sharply, "Farr Sainh!"

"It's legal," Penche crowed. "Leave him alone."

Farr touched the buttons. The screen glowed, focused into shape. "Get me Kirdy," said Farr.

Omon Bozhd made a small signal. The Iszic on the right sliced at the wall, cut the communication tubule; the screen went dead.

Penche's eyebrows rose. "Talk about crime," he roared. "You cut up my house!"

Omon Bozhd's lips drew back to show his pale gums, his teeth. "Before I am through —"

Penche raised his left hand; the forefinger spat a thread of orange fire. Omon Bozhd reeled aside; the fire-needle clipped his ear. The other two Iszic moved like moths; each jabbed the pod wall with meticulous speed and precision.

Penche pointed his finger once more. Farr blundered forward, seized Penche's shoulder, swung him around; Penche's mouth tightened. He brought up his right fist in a short uppercut; it caught Farr where ribs met belly; Farr missed with a roundhouse right, staggered back. Penche wheeled to face the three Iszic. They were ducking behind the sphincter, which cinched in after them. Farr and Penche were alone in the pod. Farr came lurching out from the wall and Penche backed away.

"Save it, you fool," said Penche.

The pod quivered, jerked. Farr, half-crazy in the release of his pent rage, waded forward. The floor of the pod rippled; Farr fell to his knees.

Penche snapped, "Save it, I said! Who are you working for, Earth or Iszm?"

"You're not Earth," gasped Farr. "You're K. Penche! I'm fighting because I'm sick of being used." He struggled to gain his feet; weakness overcame him. He leaned back, breathless.

"Let's see that thing in your head," said Penche.

"Keep away from me. I'll break your face!"

The floor of the pod flipped like a trampoline. Farr and Penche were jolted, jarred. Penche looked worried. "What are they doing?"

"They've done it," said Farr. "They're Iszic, these are Iszic houses! They play these things like violins."

The pod halted — rigid, trembling. "There," said Penche. "It's over... Now — that thing in your head."

"Keep away from me...Whatever it is, it's mine!"

"It's mine," said Penche softly. "I paid to have it planted there."

"You don't even know what it is."

"Yes I do. I can see it. It's a sprout. The first pod just broke out."

"You're crazy. A seed wouldn't germinate in my head!"

The pod seemed to be stiffening, arching like a cat's back. The roof began to creak.

"We've got to get out of here," muttered Penche. The floor was groaning, trembling. Penche ran to the sphincter, touched the open-nerve.

The sphincter stayed shut.

"They've cut the nerve," said Farr.

The pod reared slowly up, like the bed of a dump-truck. The floor sloped. The vaulted roof creaked. *Twang!* A rib snapped, fragments sprang down. A sharp stick missed Farr by a foot.

Penche pointed his finger at the sphincter; the cartridge lanced fire into the sphincter iris. The iris retaliated with a cloud of vile steam.

Penche staggered back choking.

Two more roof ribs snapped.

"They'll kill if they hit," cried Penche, surveying the arched ceiling. "Get back, out of the way!"

"Aile Farr, the walking greenhouse...You'll rot before you harvest me, Penche..."

"Don't get hysterical," said Penche. "Come over here!"

The pod tilted, the furniture began sliding down into the mouth; Penche fended it away desperately. Farr slipped on the floor. The whole pod buckled. Fragments of ribs sprang, snapped, clattered. The furniture tumbled over and over, piled upon Farr and Penche, bruising, wrenching, scraping.

The pod began to shake, the tables, chairs began to rise, fall. Farr and Penche struggled to win free, before the heavy furniture broke their bones.

"They're working it from the outside," panted Farr. "Pulling on the nerves..."

"If we could get out on the balcony —"

"We'd be thrown to the ground."

The shaking grew stronger — a slow rise, a quick drop. The fragments of rib, the furniture began to rise, shake and pound like peas in a box. Penche stood braced, his hands against the table, controlling the motion, holding it away from their two soft bodies. Farr grabbed a splinter, began stabbing the wall.

"What are you doing?"

"The Iszic stabbed in here — hit some nerves. I'm trying to hit some other ones."

"You'll probably kill us!" Penche looked at Farr's head. "Don't forget that plant —"

"You're more afraid for the plant than you are for yourself." Farr stabbed here, there, up and down.

He hit a nerve. The pod suddenly froze into a tense, rather horrible, rigidity. The wall began to secrete great drops of a sour ichor. The pod gave a violent shake, and the contents rattled.

"That's the wrong nerve!" yelled Penche. He picked up a splinter, began stabbing. A sound like a low moan vibrated through the pod. The floor humped up, writhed in vegetable agony; the ceiling began to collapse.

"We'll be crushed," said Penche huskily. Farr saw a shimmer of metal — the doctor's hypodermic. He picked it up, jabbed it into the chalky green bulge of a vein, pulled the trigger.

The pod quivered, shook, pulsed. The walls blistered, burst. Ichor welled out, trickled into the entrance channel. The pod convulsed, shivered, fell down limp.

The shattered fragments of ribs, the broken furniture, Farr and Penche tumbled the length of the pod, out upon the balcony, through the dark.

Farr grabbed on the tendrils of the balustrade, broke his fall. The tendril parted; Farr dropped. The lawn was only ten feet below. He crashed into the pile of debris. Below him was something rubbery. It seized his legs, pulled with great strength: Penche.

They rolled out on the lawn. Farr's strength was almost spent. Penche squeezed his ribs, reached up, grasped his throat. Farr saw the sardonic face only inches from his. He drew up his knees — hard. Penche winced, gasped, but held fast. Farr shoved his thumb up Penche's nose, twisted. Penche rolled his head back, his grip relaxed.

Farr croaked, "I'll tear that thing out — I'll crush it —"

"No!" gasped Penche. "No." He yelled, "Frope! Carlyle!"

Figures appeared. Penche rose to his feet. "There's three Iszic in the house. Don't let 'em out. Stand by the trunk — shoot to kill."

A cool voice said, "There won't be any shooting tonight."

Two beams of light converged on Penche. He stood quivering with anger. "Who are you?"

"Special Squad. I'm Detective-Inspector Kirdy."

Penche exhaled his breath. "Get the Iszic. They're in my house —"

The Iszic came into the light.

Omon Bozhd said, "We are here to reclaim our property."

Kirdy inspected them without friendliness. "What property?"

"It is in Farr's head. A house-seedling."

"Is it Farr you're accusing?"

"They'd better not," said Farr angrily. "They watched me every minute, they searched me, hypnotized me —"

"Penche is the guilty man," said Omon Bozhd bitterly. "Penche's agent deceived us. It is clear now. He put the six seeds where he knew we'd find them. He also had a root tendril; he anchored it in Farr's scalp, among the hairs. We never noticed it."

"Tough luck," said Penche.

Kirdy looked dubiously at Farr. "The thing actually stayed alive?"

Farr suppressed the urge to laugh. "Stayed alive? It sent out roots — it put out leaves, a pod. It's growing. I've got a house on my head!"

"It's Iszic property," declared Omon Bozhd sharply. "I demand its return."

"It's my property," said Penche. "I bought it — paid for it."

"It's my property," said Farr. "Whose head is it growing in?"

Kirdy shook his head. "You better all come with me."

"I'll go nowhere unless I'm under arrest," said Penche with great dignity. He pointed. "I told you — arrest the Iszic. They wrecked my house."

"Come along, all of you," said Kirdy. He turned. "Bring down the wagon."

Omon Bozhd made his decision. He rose proudly to his full height, the white bands glowing in the darkness. He looked at Farr, reached under his cloak, brought out a shatter-gun.

Farr ducked, fell flat.

The shatter-bolt sighed over his head. Blue fire came from Kirdy's gun. Omon Bozhd glowed in a blue aureole. He was dead, but he fired again and again. Farr rolled over the dark ground. The other Iszic fired at him, ignoring the police guns: flaming blue figures, dead, acting under command-patterns that outlasted their lives. Bolts struck Farr's leg. He groaned, lay still.

The three Iszic collapsed.

"Now," said Penche, with satisfaction, "I will take care of Farr."

Farr said, "Keep away from me."

"Easy, Penche," said Kirdy.

Penche halted. "I'll give you ten million for what you've got growing in your hair."

"No," said Farr wildly. "I'll grow it myself. I'll give seeds away free…"

"It's a gamble," said Penche. "If it's male, it's worth nothing."

"If it's female," said Farr, "it's worth —" he paused as a police doctor bent over his leg.

"— a great deal," said Penche dryly. "But you'll have opposition."

"From who?" gasped Farr.

Orderlies brought a stretcher.

"From the Iszic. I offer you ten million. I take the chance."

The fatigue, the pain, the mental exhaustion overcame Farr. "Okay… I'm sick of the whole mess."

"That constitutes a contract," cried Penche in triumph. "These officers are witnesses."

They lifted Farr onto the stretcher. The doctor looked down at him, noticed a sprig of vegetation in Farr's hair. He reached down, plucked it out.

"Ouch!" said Farr.

Penche cried out. "What did he do?"

Farr said weakly, "You'd better take care of your property, Penche."

"Where is it?" yelled Penche in anguish, collaring the doctor.

"What?" asked the doctor.

"Bring lights!" cried Penche.

Farr saw Penche and his men seeking among the debris for the pale shoot which had grown in his head, then he drifted off into unconsciousness.

Penche came to see Farr in the hospital. "Here," he said shortly. "Your money." He tossed a coupon to the table. Farr looked at it. Ten million dollars.

"That's a lot of money," said Farr.

"Yes," said Penche.

"You must have found the sprout."

Penche nodded. "It was still alive. It's growing now… It's male." He picked up the coupon, looked at it, put it back down. "A poor bet."

"You had good odds," Farr told him.

"I don't care for the money," said Penche. He looked off through the window, across Los Angeles, and Farr wondered what he was thinking.

"Easy come, easy go," said Penche. He half-turned, as if to leave.

"Now what?" asked Farr. "You don't have a female house; you don't deal in houses."

K. Penche said, "There's female houses on Iszm. Lots of them. I'm going after a few."

"Another raid?"

"Call it anything you like."

"What do you call it?"

"An expedition."

"I'm glad I won't be involved."

"A man never knows," Penche remarked. "You might change your mind."

"Don't count on it," said Farr.

Jack Vance was born in 1916 to a well-off California family that, as his childhood ended, fell upon hard times. As a young man he worked at a series of unsatisfying jobs before studying mining engineering, physics, journalism and English at the University of California Berkeley. Leaving school as America was going to war, he found a place as an ordinary seaman in the merchant marine. Later he worked as a rigger, surveyor, ceramicist, and carpenter before his steady production of sf, mystery novels, and short stories established him as a full-time writer.

His output over more than sixty years was prodigious and won him three Hugo Awards, a Nebula Award, a World Fantasy Award for lifetime achievement, as well as an Edgar from the Mystery Writers of America. The Science Fiction and Fantasy Writers of America named him a grandmaster and he was inducted into the Science Fiction Hall of Fame.

His works crossed genre boundaries, from dark fantasies (including the highly influential *Dying Earth* cycle of novels) to interstellar space operas, from heroic fantasy (the *Lyonesse* trilogy) to murder mysteries featuring a sheriff (the Joe Bain novels) in a rural California county. A Vance story often centered on a competent male protagonist thrust into a dangerous, evolving situation on a planet where adventure was his daily fare, or featured a young person setting out on a perilous odyssey over difficult terrain populated by entrenched, scheming enemies.

Late in his life, a world-spanning assemblage of Vance aficionados came together to return his works to their original form, restoring material cut by editors whose chief preoccupation was the page count of a pulp magazine. The result was the complete and authoritative *Vance Integral Edition* in 44 hardcover volumes. Spatterlight Press is now publishing the VIE texts as ebooks, and as print-on-demand paperbacks.

Colophon

This book was printed using Adobe Arno Pro as the primary text font, with NeutraFace used on the cover.

This title was created from the digital archive of the Vance Integral Edition, a series of 44 books produced under the aegis of the author by a worldwide group of his readers. The VIE project gratefully acknowledges the editorial guidance of Norma Vance, as well as the cooperation of the Department of Special Collections at Boston University, whose John Holbrook Vance collection has been an important source of textual evidence.

Special thanks to R.C. Lacovara, Patrick Dusoulier, Koen Vyverman, Paul Rhoads, Chuck King, Gregory Hansen, Suan Yong, and Josh Geller for their invaluable assistance preparing final versions of the source files.

Source: John Rick; Digitize: Donna Adams, Denis Bekaert, Richard Chandler, Jon Hunt, Charles King, John Rick, Hans van der Veeke; Diff: Charles King, Hans van der Veeke; Diff-Merge: Rob Friefeld; Tech Proof: Rob Friefeld, Fred Zoetemeyer; Text Integrity: Rob Friefeld, Steve Sherman, Tim Stretton, Suan Hsi Yong; Implement: Donna Adams, Mark Adams, Derek W. Benson, Joel Hedlund; Security: Paul Rhoads; Compose: Andreas Irle, John A. Schwab; Comp Review: Marcel van Genderen, Karl Kellar, Charles King, Bob Luckin, Billy Webb; Update Verify: Bob Luckin, Paul Rhoads; RTF-Diff: Mark Bradford, Patrick Dusoulier, Charles King, Bill Schaub; Textport: Patrick Dusoulier; Proofread: Kristine Anstrats, Mike Barrett, John H. Chalmers, Christian J. Corley, Michael Duncan, Patrick Dusoulier, Damien G. Jones, Jody Kelly, Charles King, Per Kjellberg, Roderick MacBeath, S.A. Manning, John McDonough, Michael Mitchell, Till Noever, Glenn Raye, David Reitsema, Jeffrey Ruszczyk, Lyall Simmons, Mark J. Straka, Anthony Thompson, Fred Zoetemeyer

Artwork (maps based on original drawings by Jack and Norma Vance): Paul Rhoads, Christopher Wood

Book Composition and Typesetting: Joel Anderson
Art Direction and Cover Design: Howard Kistler
Proofing: Steve Sherman, Dave Worden
Jacket Blurb: Rob Friefeld, Koen Vyverman
Management: John Vance, Koen Vyverman